The Insiders

by

C. S. Poulsen

The Insiders

Cover Art by *The Wild Rose Press, Inc.*

The Wild Rose Press, Inc.
PO Box 708
Adams Basin, NY 14410-0708
Visit us at www.thewildrosepress.com

Publishing History
First Edition, 2025
Trade Paperback ISBN 978-1-5092-6010-2
Digital ISBN 978-1-5092-6011-9

Published in the United States of America

Dedication

For my hero, my son, Luke.
And for the best grandkids ever: Grant, Brooke, Josie,
and Kate Poulsen who brought so much joy to my life.

PREFACE

Before Earth somersaulted, changing the world's weather, topography, and electromagnetic fields, a fantastical time existed when an awesome entity bestowed superpowers to street kids all over the world. The following chronicles tell why the formidable Face chose my gang and trained us for a humanitarian job that turned out to be one great battle after the other.

Chapter 1

I learned that safety came in numbers when surviving on the street. But finding kids who approved of my aversion to drugs and alcohol proved to be challenging. I detested mind-altering stuff that made parents and guardians act stupidly, turned them mean, or made them slaves to addictions.

A lot of homeless kids forgot the situations that made them choose street life. Like robots programmed genetically, they inherited the addiction gene from their parents, trying drugs for fun just once. But they ended up like their folks, while I refused to become like mine. I figured the only way to stay free from that poison was to avoid them and the people who used them.

Straight kids like me didn't exist near my hangout. So, I gave up, determined to become comfortable alone. I knew where I stood on the streets and liked it. No one was supposed to love me there; how could I be disappointed? It was weird, though—after I stopped looking, kids began to find me. One by one, they showed up by my hideout until I became the leader of a small gang of six: Picker, Motor, Bat, Lookout, Ears, and Baby.

Each member brought a different talent that was useful for survival, like picking locks or having great hearing, eyesight, or mechanical and computer skills. You get the picture. Like pieces of a puzzle, each person fit into my gang.

I'm not saying we were angels. Sure, we avoided drugs and booze, but we shoplifted clothes, food, and any general needs. As we got older, gangsters wanted our well-honed skills. They insisted we become their drug runners. We refused. Still, they wouldn't let up on us. Their threats turned into action when they trashed our hideout as a warning to cooperate… or else.

That didn't sit right with me. It was important to react strongly, to let those criminals know without a doubt that we would never work for them. My gang did just that when I planned our first act of revenge against the biggest hoods in town.

When payback's success depends on a town's routine, mistakes can happen. You better hope for good luck to be on your side. At age twelve, I didn't think about chance as my gang huddled like football jocks in the shadows behind the pizza parlor. We lived in the moment, inhaling the mild winter. Our hearts raced from excitement.

****

Businesses closed on Sundays as shoppers preferred the indoor malls that surrounded Landstown, a brick-and-mortar whistlestop on the rim of Philadelphia. Even Petrona's Pizza locked its doors on bleak, barren Centre Street. Downtown was the logical place to spring my stinky trap.

Earlier that day, we had stoked our enemy's temper, knowing he would seek revenge if he wanted to hold onto what little respect he had. My plan counted on it and, just as we predicted, the gangster hunted us. He was out there, but I couldn't pinpoint where. I signaled Ears to help. He slinked into the lead position, shut his eyes, and cupped his hand behind his ear, listening.

"They're three blocks away and checking every alley," Ears whispered. "We better hurry, Chief."

Silently, I held up my hand and signaled. Ears, Bat, and Motor sprang into position and acted as a ladder for Lookout to climb over them and pull himself up to the fire escape landing. Once there, Picker passed a snow shovel to him, careful not to bang it against the iron railings.

Next, my boys tossed up a loaded Hefty trash bag. Lookout caught it and took a covert position on the roof before dumping the dog poop that we had shoveled, mashed, and pureed… before mixing the foul mess with industrial-strength glue.

Lookout watched as our pursuers disappeared into the next alleyway. He gestured for us to run, and we sprinted down Centre Street like Olympians before we ducked behind the next building. Our nemesis, a hulk covered in bling, had more brawn than brains. He turned his back toward our position as he strutted onto another side street searching for us. Bus, a nickname he'd earned from his massive size, stepped back out into the road and just missed us.

We pushed ourselves to work even faster, using the remaining daylight to spread the second bag of modified poop. In that bag, we replaced the glue with oil; the mixture smelled worse than the first. Baby, the youngest of the gang, held her nose, letting us know she was standing too close to our putrid revenge.

As planned, Bat lifted her pint-sized frame high into the only tree in the block. The bushy pine concealed her like a hidden ornament and kept her safe from Bus's temper.

"All right, Itty-bitty, mum's the word." Bat, our oversized, musclebound member, turned around once more and put his fingers to his lips, reminding Baby to be quiet. She smiled, pleased to be chosen for the critical job of recording the event. But there were other hidden cameras; Motor, our resident genius, had taped a few to rain spouts that would film at different angles. We would add that footage to Baby's recording.

Everything was quiet in the firehouse that sat only a few feet away from us. The firefighters lived upstairs, where they rested after fighting the flames for hours at Bus's favorite dealing spot, a crack house. We guessed that the exhausted crew would focus on food, cards, or television while they waited for the next call—a call my gang hoped would never come because it would destroy our entire plan.

I nodded to Picker, my gutsy best friend. He had greased the station's old window the day before, and it lifted smoothly for our plan. Once inside, Picker sneaked to the pump truck with Ears trailing behind when his allergies acted up. Ears caught himself in the middle of a sneeze that he muffled with the crook of his arm.

"Hichee."

"Sh," Picker said. "Not now, man."

"You know I can't help it," Ears whispered.

"I heard that, Ears," I said in a harsh whisper. "We better hope the firemen didn't hear it."

We listened for a few seconds. When no sounds drifted down from above, I nodded for them to continue.

The hose challenged their kid-sized arms, but Picker and Ears wrestled it to the window and stuck the nozzle out. Bat and I eased it through, stringing it to the far end of the alley. I gave Bat a thumb-up.

"Tally ho!" Bat said in his thick British accent, excited at what was about to happen. He banged his club on the concrete, the noise echoing down the alleyway.

"Yo! Down this way," Bus yelled. He and his boyz sprinted toward our alley.

Lookout shouted, "Looking for someone, Boyz?"

The four came to a dead stop, confused and not knowing where to focus.

"Up here, dawgs," Lookout teased before he began to hiccup. For a moment I thought the plan might fall through, but Lookout kept going, ignoring the hiccups best he could.

The hapless trio made a crucial mistake—when you look up, shut your mouth. Lookout let the poop fly, and it landed on target. In shock, the gangsters stood their ground as Lookout let the second, third, and fourth loads fly from his arms, working them like an automatic weapon. Sticky poop clung to their clothes and hair. The gangbangers uttered inhuman noises, wretched, gargled, spitting sounds coming from them like zombies in a horror movie.

We heard laughter from above as Lookout's hiccups competed with his joy. Picker stepped out onto the sidewalk hooting as he mocked them. "Booyah, Skunk Man! Hey, you stink."

I joined him ribbing the gangsters. "Word up, yo. You crap up our home, we give *you* crap, man. Stay away from us and our hideout, Dawgs."

We teased threateningly before dashing around the corner through the narrow, cleared path to the far end of the alley. As expected, the trio took off after us. When their feet hit the greased filth, they fell like dominoes, one on top of the other. They tried to regain their footing repeatedly, but when one managed to stand, Bat turned on the fire hose nozzle, aiming it at their gut. This flipped them to their backs, again leaving them writhing in muck.

The gang hooted over that. Picker taunted the hoodlums: "Oops. My bad, boys. I shoulda picked up after my dogs, because you *reek*. You need a good shower."

Our treacherous concoction and the pounding water trapped the turds—they couldn't come closer. Bat handed the hose to Ears and Lookout so he could gently lower Baby from the tree. She enjoyed filming the three stooges who tried expressing their displeasure, only to find their tongues glued to their teeth.

Suddenly, the firehouse lights switched on below. As the firefighters slid down the pole, we dropped the hose and ducked from sight. We dashed to the next building that gave us easy-roof access. Picker silently pulled up the ladder behind us, as he had greased the rusty structure too. Flat on our bellies, we watched the show from the third-floor roof as the sun set behind us.

Firemen recognized Bus as a problem in the neighborhood. "Holy crap. That is some stink!"

Their chief stepped outside. "Police are on the way," he growled. "You finally stepped in it big time, you three. Stay where you are, boys—or you'll get more of that hose."

They happily guarded the human stench until the first police car arrived with sirens blaring. They used their spotlight on our victims; Baby continued her video from above while the trio tried to explain their innocence, but only incoherent gibberish spilled out. Gesturing, the hoods begged for something to wash the glue mixture from their mouths. The more they mumbled, the more everyone laughed.

The unexpected show received police radio coverage. Within minutes, squad cars appeared from all directions with an audience that appreciated the break from their boring Sunday routines. Bus seethed at their amusement, peeling off the poop-covered hoodie—but he forgot the unregistered weapon tucked in his pants.

"Gun!" an officer shouted. Everyone drew their revolvers. "Put your hands behind your head! Face down on the ground."

Bus wasn't happy—he muttered about being face down in the muck and was grimacing as if he had a mouthful of the stuff. One officer removed Bus's pistol while another searched his pants and sweatshirt, visibly annoyed with the filth. They discovered enough crack in each of their pockets to arrest Bus and his boyz for dealing. We wanted to cheer as we laid above, peeking from the twilight. But I reminded the team to hold our pleasure to muffled giggles.

Since no one in law enforcement wanted the stench in the backseats of their vehicles, firefighters hosed down the dealer and his crew. But the glue-poop mixture was too potent for removal by water and stuck everywhere. The police ultimately ordered our targets to strip down to their skivvies in forty-degree temperatures. There were loud catcalls when Bus revealed his Sponge Bob Tighty-Whities. One police officer broke out singing a version of the cartoon's theme:

"Who lives in the alley… is stupid and stinks?"

A chorus of cops answered, "Sponge Bus Tighty Pants."

Our payback was a riot—better than expected. My

gang kept their mouths covered, but our bodies vibrated with happiness.

"Brennan, we don't want dem idiots to get off on a technicality," the captain squeezed out between guffaws. "Take dem fools to Emergency before we book 'em." Still howling over the song, he continued. "In fact, I'll meet you over there. I'm not going to miss the reaction from the doctors and nurses to this case."

Ears and Lookout turned to me. "Yeah, go on," I said. "Get it on film, but *don't* get caught. The rest of us will be waiting on ya."

While Ears and Lookout played the hospital video they made over and over, my friends took covert positions in the crowded emergency room while filming Bus's gang enjoying the relief of warm blankets. But as doctors and nurses tried to invent a concoction capable of dissolving the filthy glue in their mouths without poisoning them, their short rest turned to humiliation.

"Oh, honey, that's some bad breath," a seasoned nurse managed while trying to stifle a giggle. "It's a bad condition to be stuck with."

Personnel, gawking at the weird case, laughed uncontrollably as the cops guarding them even let out a hoot.

"I've been here all day," the head nurse said. "I am too *pooped* to figure out what to do about these bad boyz and their potty mouths. I'm just dog-gone tired."

A specialist rounded the corner and looked at the chart in disbelief. "Crap, you got to be kidding! Sometimes this job stinks."

Motor added the hospital scene and uploaded it to a new website called YouTube. Its title was "Stinkin' Gangstas." It went viral within days, adding a deep satisfaction to a job well done. At twelve years old, give or take a year, my gang had taught our older adversaries a lesson. That day was right and just.

Not like the first part of our lives.

Each of my gang wrestled with memories they wanted to forget, just as I did with mine. My recollections attacked me like a ninja when I slept. My dream began with a drunken mom who wanted nothing to do with Dad or me. I dove out of that nightmare into another: the smell of my meth-addicted dad, an unshaven lug who created a cyclone of noise by slamming doors, overturning chairs, and breaking bottles after he grappled them away from Mom. Being a toddler was no defense against either of them. My bony mother threw me across the room, shouting, "You messed up my life! Get lost!"

That's when I woke up, sweaty and ashamed for no good reason. Amazing how my gang found each other, broken and damaged as we were. Coming from our un-peaceful worlds, we all searched for the same thing—safety, security. We arrived on the streets unloved, unwanted, and defective. Bound by the same pain, we untied each other's hearts until we fused to each other instead.

We survived the streets together on our own terms. We continued to steal what we needed to live while keeping away from people like Bus. My team, my tribe, kept secluded… although I promised to create something fun, something happy. I called my members of survival the clan; a group of people all from the same bloodline. Okay, so we didn't have the same blood, but we came from the same line—the line of trouble. My clan loved me because I created something original for a bunch of damaged misfits whose broken souls needed mending.

Chapter 2

One morning, as Picker and I scavenged for food behind a local grocery store, a voice came out of the shadows. "Yo, you Chief?"

"Who's asking?"

"A YouTube fan, Chief Poop. I heard some talk and wanted *yuse* guys to know. It's about Bus. He plans to take you down when he gets out of jail."

"Yeah, I figured, but he's behind bars for a long time, man."

"Six months ain't long, Chief."

I couldn't believe the news. *"That's all Bus got?"*

"Yeah, he hired a slick lawyer and copped a plea. His boyz are out sooner. Word is they're going to shadow your every move for Bus. Anyway, a bunch of us is betting you'll take care of Bus before he takes care of you. Good luck."

The stranger sank back into the alley and disappeared.

"Bus. What a stupid name," Picker said. "I'll call him Greyhound. No... better yet, *Hound.* We sure had him whimpering like a dang hound dog. "'*Ahwoo.* They made us eat poop. *Ahwoo.*'" Picker's antics always tickled me.

"You call him anything you want, bro, but we better take defensive action before his creepy sidekicks are let out."

The goon wanted revenge, and I understood. Thanks to us, everyone considered him and his boyz the town fools. Prison would give him time to plan how to regain status within the hood—time to devise a way to take us down. The bothersome trio would insist on allowing us precious little time to enjoy life without them.

****

We kept a low profile that spring while constructing our new camouflaged home. It seemed nothing more than a tumbling-down building, but Motor showed us how to shore up the walls to keep us safe. To an outsider, it was an old industrial firetrap. To us, it was a haven, a castle, and a beauty. More importantly, Bus and his idiots would never find it.

By summer, we yearned for outdoor exploration. We ventured past the town boundaries, a safe place to have fun. That's how we found Point Park, a mini-amusement park with a rollercoaster, carousel, elongated mirrors, and cotton candy. It called to us—we couldn't resist.

Lookout cased the outside fences. "Yo, Chief, over here."

"Good work, man," I said.

Lookout had found just the right spot where no cameras would see us as we scaled the chain link. We kept flashlights low as we scanned the area while enjoying an aroma we didn't get downtown—freshly cut grass. A snack booth stood in front of us, a good luck sign for the night.

"Brilliant! I'm starving," Bat said with his English accent thicker than ever. Baby agreed.

"You guys are like sharks, eating twenty-four/seven," I said. Picker worked his magic, opening the padlock in seconds. Once inside, I plugged in the roaster. We feasted on hotdogs, corndogs, and soft pretzels until our stomachs begged us to stop.

Ears and Lookout seemed to like the same foods. Without asking, they passed back and forth things like mustard, ketchup, salt, and pepper. And the connection wasn't just with food; they shared similar features too. Sure, Lookout was taller, and their taste in clothes made them look stylishly different. Ears was preppy while Lookout was more of a jock. Yet something seemed the same about both. Each one suffered peculiar ailments, too. Lookout hiccupped after eating and sometimes for no reason. Ears sneezed after meals for no clear cause I could determine (I filed it away in my brain to solve one day).

But only fun was on our agenda for that night.

"Chief, *hic*. Sorry. Chief, *hic*. I'll begin—*hic*—to put things—*hic*—away."

"Hichee. Hichee."

"Yo, Ears, it's *achoo*, not hichee," Picker teased.

"I know—*hichee*. It just—*hichee*—comes out that way."

"Well, at least you've managed to turn the volume down on your hiccups and sneezes, guys," I said as they cleaned up our mess. When I first met them, their hiccups and sneezes projected a block away. My gang relished a perverse sense of enjoyment, leaving everything as we found it with no evidence of entry. Until the vendor checked his stock, nothing would appear violated.

We were smart, unlike the hoodlums who left their mark bragging about how they trashed one thing or another then wondering why the law caught up with them. That was so stupid, I told my guys. We never left evidence behind.

Our code made us unique and, away from the hood, we were invincible.

After our feeding frenzy, we set out to find fun.

"Whatever we do, let's do it where it's cooler. I'm melting," Bat complained. He was right; the day's abnormal heat seemed trapped in the breezeless park.

"Hey, there's water up ahead," Lookout said excitedly.

The gang took off running to a man-made stream that flowed through the park. We followed a path against the current that disappeared under an overpass with a Tunnel of Terror sign at the entrance. That intrigued us more. Past the tunnel, we found a dock with fantasy boats tied to it and chose to commandeer the biggest, a Viking rowboat.

When Motor explained a power surge would alert the night guard, we piled in, cast off the line, and bobbed with the natural current. Flashlights lit our way as we held them low, pointing down. We splashed each other with cold water while trying not to rock the boat for Captain Lookout who kneeled on the bow while dipping an oar, keeping us in the middle of the current.

As we entered the Tunnel of Terror, the temperature dropped. We breathed a collective sigh of relief in the bone-chilling darkness. Ears' flashlight illuminated grotesque animatronics too cheap and fake, to spook us. While he provided the spotlight, we spoke for each monster.

Bat's voice boomed: "I want to suck your blood."

Ears added a melodic ghost: "Boo. *Boo-oo*."

Picker joined with a joke to ease Baby's indecision between fear and laughter: "Hi, Baby, I'm Barbie. I seem to be missing my head. Ken, oh Ken, do you have my head?" Baby laughed until she cried.

We owned the moment, enjoying the sweet abandonment of our troubles when, in an instant, all hell broke loose. Not one of us expected that one beast would be real.

In a flash, a nightmarish face appeared before us. Its voice bellowed with threatening commands that echoed over and over. Lookout let out a girlish yelp, reacting physically with a frightened hop that tipped over the boat.

We spilled out, dropping our flashlights as we sank into darkness. Kicking my legs, I grabbed for the boat, but it had disappeared from reach. Meanwhile, the terrible-looking monster threatened to drown us with blood curdling sounds. I treaded water, wanting to help my friends—none of us swam well. "Hold on to something!" I hollered.

Suddenly, I heard Bat's voice and Baby's screams. I turned toward the sound and saw Bat treading water while lifting Babe above it with one arm. With his free hand, he swung the club at the monster towering over him. A hazy light emanated directly from that being.

"Bollocks!" Bat hollered. "Be gone fiend!"

The beast's configurations changed each second, from fire to wind to stone to starlike brightness, and sometimes a combination of them while maintaining that face. Its voice thundered, insisting we surrender, but in the echo of the tunnel, everything mixed up in my ears and thoughts.

I dove under the water to escape the sound, and to help Bat with Baby. As I surfaced, Bat's weapon came down on top of my head. A sickening crack sounded. The horrid blare of that face stopped ringing in my ears as I sank into darkness.

One by one, members of the clan appeared as in a documentary. I relived the stories that brought them to me from a unique vantage point hovering somewhere back in time.

Suddenly, my first encounter with Picker appeared before me like a hologram. A patch of his brilliant red afro caught my attention—a new kid hanging too close to my hideout. He looked awkward, dressed in clothes a size-or-three too small. And he lacked street smarts. I stood by as he approached a bum with all the money he owned.

"Hey, mister, do you have change for a five?" he asked. "I'm thirsty and need ones for the soda machine."

"Yeah, I got change for ya." The bum laughed. He stole the five with one hand and grabbed Picker's shirt with the other. "Now get out of my face, kid."

I kicked the bum in the shins and grabbed the money. "Come on. Run!"

"Wait for me, bro!" Picker hollered.

The new kid lacked the muscles and lung power of a runner back then, but that would change. We ran around the block to the back end of the laundromat.

"You saved my life," Picker rasped, out of breath. "That old man could have killed me."

"Man, never trust a wino. Come on, which soda do you want?" I knew the old machine and could play it like a pinball. Grinning, I whacked the sweet spot with the heel of my hand and knee. When it dropped two soft drinks, I handed the kid a bottle of Coke—and his five dollars.

"No, man, keep it," he said humbly. "You saved my

life."

"Thanks, bro. I'll hold it… in case you need it, ya know." Something about the kid made me smile, as if he were a clown. We started hanging out every day. When I trusted him enough to reveal my hideout, I swore him to secrecy with a spit and a handshake.

"Whoa, this is cool!" Picker exclaimed. He acted like my home was the empire state building, as if he'd just landed on the planet. The last thing I saw of that scene was Picker changing into the name-brand clothes that I pilfered from Goodwill.

Abruptly my view changed. Instead of reliving our meeting, I hovered within a tattered apartment watching Picker's sad experience as a foster kid. His substitute parents fed him canned ravioli when they fed him at all, while they ate steak and drank beer.

"Okay, kid, you clean up this dump. We got places to go."

"Yes, ma'am."

Picker sneaked the last bits of meat from their plates and shoved them into his mouth, savoring each morsel. He scrubbed the burnt pan and dried the dishes, putting them away with good nature—he didn't complain or seem to mind the work. He spoke to his guardians before they left.

"Uh, by the way, I need new clothes. I'm popping out of these."

"Money don't grow on trees, kid. Loosen your belt, okay? You got another month of wear in them."

His jailers locked Picker in the apartment while they hit the streets, doing whatever they did to feed their habits. Picker spent his days and nights watching cartoons and learning antics from Tool Time reruns, like how to pick a lock. He tried out the new knowledge on his front door and never again spent a sunny day in the house.

Locks populated the outside world, and eleven-year-old Picker figured out how to open each one. He didn't do it for profit; he did it because he could. By summer's end, Picker had become a part of my life and stopped going home.

We watched as the postman delivered the government checks that continued despite his disappearance; his charges never notified the authorities of a missing child. Picker, the stocky, freckle-faced, toothy-grinned imp, kept me smiling with his eternal optimism. I enjoyed the review of our meeting still, my heart broke for Picker's lonely life.

Woosh! Another energy yanked my weightless body toward it. I saw an infant's crib rocking in an automotive repair shop, and I heard a baby chortle and adult voices. An older woman argued with a mechanic.

"An infant doesn't belong in this greasy, grimy atmosphere, and I'm too old to raise a child. My sister would understand if you put him up for adoption, Rick."

"None of that is true. Stella wanted this baby—she'll watch over him."

"Rick, babies require love. They need to be touched and held often. Ghosts cannot do that. Stella is dead and buried. She cannot help you." She pointed to the dingy surroundings. "The little one deserves better than being raised here."

"Listen, Eva, I ain't givin' up the baby. Stella didn't mind me bein' a motorhead, and she won't mind the baby bein' one neither. The little man is all I have left of her. I'll do the best I can—he won't go hungry. Not many buses headed to Arizona. You don't want to miss yours."

Suddenly, the movie flashed forward in time to Motor as a toddler playing with hammers, wrenches, any tool he could get his hands on. Like a film running too fast, I saw his growth as he worked on an engine with his dad. The sight surprised me because his dad wasn't half-bad, and neither was Motor's life. His father enjoyed teaching his son everything he knew about cars and about how things worked in general. He recognized that Motor understood matters far beyond his age.

Rick's frustrated energy filled my heart. Somehow, I understood his wish to send his boy to a fancy school that could train him for a better future than their garage allowed. But this brave dad's hopes ended when a stray bullet from a drive-by shooting found the back of his head.

"Dad!" Motor screamed. "No, Dad, no."

Motor held and rocked the lifeless body until a passerby called an ambulance. Instinctively, I floated behind him and reached to comfort him, but my hand went right through his body. I understood then that Motor suffered a more significant loss than any of us— he'd lost a real dad. Motor had lost *love*.

Out west, his elderly aunt awaited Motor's arrival, but he disappeared before family services put him on the bus. He wisely hid from violent street gangs. He was skinny and tan with black hair, dressed in clean jeans with a collared shirt. But garage grease stained his hands and nails. His first words to me were confident and firm.

"I can fix anything if you need me," he said. "I'm good with computers too."

"Sure," I replied enthusiastically. I knew I had done

the right thing by Motor and for us.

Whirled around by an unseen power, I spotted Ears as I knew him in the present. His good looks charmed the moms for a food donation in the grocery store parking lot; he kept his clean-cut, dirty blonde hair short and wore a polo and khaki shorts. In the mall, he looked like a lanky all-American boy who whipped out a harmonica to fill out his pockets.

He had earned his name because of his extraordinary hearing. Ears eavesdropped from long distances, spying for us like a human listening device. His talent alerted us to other gangs, police, and snarling dogs.

Suddenly, young Ears appeared before me inside a nice but small apartment. He sang and danced to the Michael Jackson "Thriller" video and practiced the moonwalk. I sensed that he wanted to surprise his mother, a big Michael Jackson fan. I was most surprised to experience the love he and his parents enjoyed.

But as the clock hands moved forward in a sped-up motion of time, Ears' physical growth and maturity were countered by his parents' decline. The disappointment and loneliness in his heart reached mine as his parents aged before my eyes. Their pleasant attitudes soured, and they became irritable. His parents, professional musicians, were using drugs.

Can't they see what is happening to them?

The doorbell rang. An older Ears checked the clock—his parents were late.

"Mom must have forgotten the key," he muttered. "Coming, Mom."

He undid the deadbolt and flung open the door. Two police officers, shy, hesitant, and almost embarrassed, greeted him with soft voices. The female officer asked, "Are you, Jerome Richter?"

Ears nodded and sighed. The day he'd feared the most had become real.

"Son, I'm sorry to tell you this, but emergency services found your parents in a car this evening. EMS medevac'd them to the hospital."

"Are they going to be okay?" Ears asked. He hung his head, already knowing the answer.

The officers stared at each other, neither anxious to speak. "I'm afraid both died... well, overdosed. It was heroin."

The color drained from Ear's face.

"Son, we don't have anyone else on record living here with you. You need to come downtown with us and wait for family services."

The patrol officer was kind, but Ears understood. He was an orphan with no family. His parents, both orphans, were raised in foster homes—no family claimed them, either.

His brain worked quickly.

"Thank you, ma'am, but my aunt... Auntie Em... lives with us. She's at work now."

"Oh? We don't have her name anywhere. May I call her for you, Jerome?"

"I'm the man of the house now—I'll take care of it," Ears said. "Thank you, Officers."

He shut the door before the officers questioned his lie. His thoughts and feelings ran inside me. He was determined not to end up like his parents, shipped from one foster home to the next. He stuffed clothes into a garbage bag, then he pocketed money from a coffee can on the shelf. He stopped, staring at a photo of his parents during better times. He threw it in the bag along with a small album of family photos, memories of happier times I guessed. He jammed harmonicas into his jacket before he climbed out the back window, fearful the police were checking his story and would return to take him away.

Weeks later, I met him as he curled up in a culvert, playing scales on his instrument. Ears refused to take an aspirin out of principle; like me, he resented drugs. Although I guessed that he missed his parents, Ears never admitted it, hiding his pain behind his music.

"They chose drugs over family," he said about his loss.

I listened from above as Ears entertained with his humming and harmonica. He played to crowd out the neglect, the sorrow.

That same feeling all of us experienced.

When the music faded, another spectacle appeared. Lookout lifted his pillow and placed a large stuffed envelope under it labeled AUNTIE. He eased out of a rotten wood window held open by a stack of rain-soaked books. It seemed to me Lookout had practiced the escape route many times before. This time he climbed out of his bedroom to the fire escape with eyes blackened and a swollen, bloody nose. I heard adults screaming at each other in the background.

"My boy brings home plenty of money. It's not like we are living off food stamps."

"It isn't enough. My son gives his mom plenty— unlike your slacker kid."

"That's because your son steals everything they eat. He'd never get a real job like my boy."

"Your boy? He's not even your real son. He's a

foster kid!"

"Don't you ever hit him again or… or…"

"Or what?"

Lookout slid down the spout rails, hiccupping nonstop. He wore mountain trek boots, odd for a city landscape. His cargo shorts bulged and jingled with every bump. I realized they were full of coins. One final clink sounded as he jumped the last two feet to the ground.

The sight quickly moved to Lookout working odd jobs where he made money through honest means. He washed windows and swept floors, asking anybody for work. I watched him stalk gangs like a Mohawk lurking in shadows until he understood what they were about. He moved on until he found us.

I reviewed the first time I met him, an occasion when he gifted a bag of potato chips and a six-pack of cola, offering to be our lookout. "I'll prove to you that your gang needs me," he said.

His eyes saw in the distance things the rest of us couldn't possibly see, like street change a block away, or cops heading our direction. He whipped sandy blonde hair from his eyes as he recited the tail number of a jet in the sky. He read the hidden engraving on a ten-dollar bill. He was right—his talents came in handy.

Lookout had pronounced features: a prominent nose, blue eyes like a Husky. He stood straight as a telephone pole, his slenderness layered with muscle. His laid-back demeanor matched that of Ears, softening his chiseled appearance. Lookout didn't need to run things and never gave me an ounce of trouble. I appreciated both of my quiet friends, assets to the team.

There was no way anyone's skills could have seen

the trouble waiting for us at Point Park.

I hoped neither one carried that weight on their shoulders.

Again, the location and time altered. I hung above the local tenement slums like a marionette. Little Bat, who lived with his single mom, appeared with an adult-sized afro.

"Momma, I'm Batboy!" He was a cute kid, jumping off the coffee table with his Halloween mask and cape in the middle of the summer. "Batboy needs some sugar, Momma."

His mother laughed. "Oh, I got plenty of sugar to give my Batboy."

She showered him with kisses and tickles before Batboy went back to being his momma's hero.

Again, the scene fast forwarded as his mom, a Whitney Houston lookalike, attracted a never-ending string of suitors but stuck with the worst, a drug dealer. Bat called him, "Uncle," as his momma instructed, until he became old enough to realize Uncle was the source of his momma's sickness.

I watched him the day he confronted the dealer: "You make my momma sick."

Without warning, the man punched Bat and threw him out of the house. When the dealer left, Bat curled up next to his momma. He pulled her lethargic arm around him, crying because he couldn't protect her. As I fought back tears for my friend, the view switched to the Bat I know. He was older and musclebound when he stopped a stranger from breaking into his home.

The trespasser, high from the drugs he sold, attacked him with a long knife. Panicked, Bat swung the baseball bat hard. The man fell to the ground, his eyes wide open. Bat ran, terrified and carried the weapon with him, never putting it down.

I stayed at the scene as Bat's momma ignored the death at her front door. Instead, she frantically searched through his pockets for what she needed to beat back the withdrawal pains. She found the powder, quickly prepared her arm, and jabbed in a needle without much thought. She took a deep breath and smiled as her eyes rolled back.

She died seconds later.

An unidentified caller tipped off the police, who arrived to find the notorious dealer at the apartment door with the knife still in his hand. Inside, they found a dead hooker. Common sense told me Bat protected himself and his mother. But Bat's intense guilt hid under his calm demeanor—he'd forgotten to empty the dealer's pockets before he ran. He blamed himself for his mother's death. I hoped I could ease Bat's conscience of that burden one day.

Meanwhile, I agreed with the police: solving one drug dealer's death was not worth police effort. Good thing, too, as Bat was hard to hide. Big and black, his muscular frame looked almost adult instead of twelve. That was about the time Bat adopted an English accent and changed his colossal afro to waves. He morphed into a muscled gentleman who carried a bat for protection.

I squinted, anticipating the appearance of the most damaged member of my clan. Sure enough, I relived the day Baby wandered up to us while we hung out on the corner. She wore a new party-style dress that contrasted the poverty of her tattered flip-flops. Her hair, pulled from her face, exposed an angel with big blue eyes that stood out from her ebony skin. She clutched a dirty, naked doll as though it were a real baby.

Baby planted herself at my feet. We figured she was about seven, but she acted strangely—she baby-talked and avoided eye contact. Day by day, we earned her trust by feeding her while encouraging her to talk. It took a year before we learned her story.

Until I found myself floating in her house witnessing the molestation, I hadn't really understood the severity of her situation. To protect her, I tried to propel mentally into action, but my predicament made me useless. I hated feeling her pain.

The abuse included a mother who openly smoked joints in the living room, a woman too high or evil, apparently, to rescue her child. A sigh of relief escaped me when the scene changed to our hideout with Baby spending more time there. I had championed her, but it was Bat who adopted the role of protector—he noticed that she reverted into a make-believe world when he walked her home.

I relived the night we staked out her building, watching as Baby's mother left the apartment dressed for a night of street business. As soon as she was gone, a stranger arrived with a key to the brownstone. Bat went berserk knowing Baby was alone with the pervert, sprinting toward the front door and kicking it down. He ripped Baby out of the scum's hands, slamming him against the wall and knocking him unconscious. For good measure, Bat reached into the man's pockets and removed the key to Baby's house.

My heart palpitated as Bat spoke, because the same feeling about Baby lived in me.

"Don't worry, love," he said. "I will protect you, princess."

All of us became the protective big brothers she never had, but Baby gravitated towards me and the gentleness of Bat—he never let our newest member out of his sight.

No one spotted missing handbills for Baby or any of us; nobody noticed we dropped off the face of the earth. Our families of origin disappeared from our memories as we formed bonds with each other forged by understanding and respect. We dropped our birth names, using our talents as labels instead. I was proud of all of us until the spectacle changed for the last time.

Helplessly, I gawked in horror to see each of us floating face down in the murky current at Point Park.

Chapter 3

It seemed a lifetime later when I opened my eyes. Death didn't feel bad but warm, comfy warm. I lifted my hands, touched my hair, my face, my neck. I wiggled my toes and bent my legs. I was alive but maybe a dream captured me. The ceiling, high above, looked like rock. I reached out and touched the walls, finding stone there, too. Panic gripped me. Was I in a tomb?

I tried sitting up, managing to swing my feet over the side of the cot despite the dizziness. The stone floor radiated warmth. I stared at my feet peeking from under unfamiliar pants—I was wearing a dark blue jumpsuit. Thoughts ran through my head: Where did it come from? Who put it on me? Where was I? Where was the clan?

"Hey!" I shouted.

The cave-like structure was too small for an echo, but it added a familiar reverb quality to my voice, the same sound I heard in the Tunnel of Terror. My body shook when I remembered the booming voice. I visualized the menacing creature that scared me to the depths of my being.

At a tender age, I learned fear was my enemy; it made me a defenseless victim. Only action and control made me the king of my destiny, even if I was the king of skipping school, the king of thievery, and the king of revenge. Action gave me life on my terms. But after the Tunnel of Terror, I was lost. What choices needed attention? What direction should I turn? Would an utterance call the horrible beast to kill me? Should I shut up and never speak again?

Did that thing capture the rest of my team?

Sneaking into the park had been my suggestion. It was up to me to escape, and if my friends were there, help them, too. Like Picker, I watched TV and spy films. My first move was to locate any hidden cameras or microphones. The dim light made it difficult to baby-step around the cubical as I searched for a door.

Panic grabbed me again. Was I buried alive?

I stopped, closed my eyes, and slowed my breathing. I was determined to search for an outside access. First, I reached high, then made my way straight down to the floor. My fingers discovered no cracks or handles, nothing to indicate an opening. I took a small sidestep and tried again. I repeated the process until I heard the grind of stone against stone.

The terrible face flashed before me.

This time the creature took the form of a massive, muscular body before it morphed from second to second into an angry flame, fog, or smoke, all terrifying me. Finally, when I saw a facial feature, a boyish eye was replaced by a lion's eye... turned into a girl's eye while the nose and mouth altered. The whole time, which seemed like an eternity, that face whirled before me with a gleaming sword hovering by its side.

My knees shook and weakness overtook me. I was horrified. Sweat rolled off my forehead as I cowered against the wall. I tried to speak, but nothing came out. When the creature spoke, I heard it with every shaking ounce of my being.

"If you want to live, do as I say; do whatever I

command you. You are mine to deal with as I wish. Do you choose life, or shall I take your head?" The blade flew slowly to my cheek.

I panicked again but did not want to die. I collected myself and bravely stammered, "Sure, sure… yeah, okay… whatever you want me to be… your slave? Okay, yeah."

The monster became furious. As he did, the sword swung back at an angle. If it came down, my life would be over.

"You think you appease me with words from a lying heart? Do you think I, Face of all things, am a fool?"

As the sword sliced towards my neck, I lost all composure. The creature wasn't bluffing.

"No, don't kill me. I'll do anything. *Anything*." The words came out of my mouth and continued nonstop. "Please don't kill me." The dread shook me down to the pee in my pants.

The sword stopped and hung in midair. The being's voice deepened, and the face spoke quietly into my every fiber.

"If you fear me, if you remain obedient to me, the sword will not strike. Forget the fear and the sword will seek you out to remind you of your fate."

The sword flew in slow motion. Its sharp edge left a small nick in my chin and drew a trickle of blood with its sting. I became faint, nauseated, feeble, and overwhelmed with my weakness. I instantly realized how small I was; I was a kid, a boy, at the feet of something much bigger and petrifying. There was nowhere to turn, no one to protect me. When I raised my head, it—that *face*—was gone.

I knew I would never be the same.

Once I roamed the streets in freedom. Now, I belonged to a creature who would scrutinize my every move. Maybe that face read my thoughts and understood I had hit bottom. I crawled back onto the cot in a fetal position and fell asleep in the stench of my urine.

****

Hours passed before I woke up, or maybe days—there was no way to tell. But a comforting smell of freshly baked bread filled my room. Refreshed, I took clear-headed notes of my small surroundings. A uniform lay on the bottom of my cot, clean and folded. Steamy water ran down the wall. I got the message—that monster didn't need to tell me in person. An aromatic bar of soap sat on a stool next to the natural shower.

The hot water soaked my hair and trickled down my neck as I soaped the sore muscles that had fought to keep me afloat. The soreness vanished. I gargled away the nasty coating on my tongue with the same water when the flow stopped on its own.

Drying off, I reached for the new jumpsuit that appeared on the cot. As I zipped my uniform, the rumble of my empty stomach made me wish for food. When I raised my head, a small table stood in front of my bed. It held a crude, wooden plate of warm bread and cheese. I wolfed down the meal in seconds. I finished with a piece of strange-looking fruit. Its juiciness and creaminess reminded me of an orange creamsicle.

My captor wanted me alive, but for *what*? I pushed back the black thoughts as I thought of Baby and shivered to think I might share the same fate. What did the creature want from me? Did the others get away from him, or did they lose their heads? I spent days, maybe weeks alone with my thoughts, beaten down. No one would rescue me. Mom and Dad were relieved that I had disappeared from their lives. Why would anyone want to save me?

Authorities had called me "trouble." Why? It wasn't like I robbed banks, mugged strangers, dealt drugs, or worse. But for the first time, a twinge of guilt hit me. The neighborhood prankster disappeared; the residents had the right to cheer my fate. I never did anything for them. I blew off schoolwork and eventually stopped showing up for classes.

Maybe if I had become a part of something—some club, some team—someone would be missing me. Knowing the truth and the reality of my situation, I hung my head in defeat until the grating sound of stone on stone surprised me.

I braced my emotions as I fell to my knees. It won— Face won. It let me live; it fed and clothed me. Bowing my head until the wall finished opening, I avoided eyeballing him. But only silence greeted me, not the terrible entity. No one threatened me, so I dared a peek and spotted an opening to a hallway. I had given up, but now I wondered if this was a chance to escape after all.

Sprinting into the corridor, I stopped when I saw that it was lit by the unseen, too. That strange being was there, nearby. I shook my head at the stupidity of my thoughts. *There is no escape, you idiot.* The hallway led to a cavernous rock chamber, twenty times the size of my cell. Stone benches and tables filled the space. Other captives must have come before me. In the walls, rough-hewn hollows contained picks, axes, and shovels.

"Crap, is this how that face creature is going to use me for the rest of my life?" I muttered.

A heavy shovel leaned against the wall. While

turning the worn-raw handle in my hand, I heard a faint noise somewhere in the distance.

Great. Now I'm beginning to crack.

But the sounds continued. And when I recognized the voices coming toward me, my heart jumped! I shouted, "Thank you, thank you!" to the captor who granted my deepest wish as the gang appeared before me.

Bat, Baby, Lookout, Motor, Ears, Picker, and I ran to the middle of the room, colliding with hugs and high fives. We laughed and, for the first time in our lives, we experienced the joy of family lost but found. We shared our stories of rescue and capture—the changing face, the sword, the stone cubicles. Only Baby's story was different. She never saw the sword of death. Comforted by a beautiful white dove, she was never threatened. Instead, it shared its message of love and peace with her. The god-like entity spared Baby from the fear that had brought the rest of us to our knees. We basked in the satisfaction that we were together. But why did Face want us?

Our reunion stayed joyful until the dim light evaporated in a brilliant flash. We fell to the floor in terror, all except Baby who continued to stand. She looked at us with amusement—no fear captured her as she turned toward the light and kneeled reverently. Out of the corner of my eye, I saw her glow with a peacefulness she never bared before. She kneeled alone, not clinging to Bat or me. My thoughts of pulling her head down to the floor dissipated.

Suddenly, a voice boomed as the sword flew into the room. "Does everyone here fear me?"

The glimmering blade hovered from person to person. Our foreheads on the ground did not seem good enough. I prostrated myself before the terror.

"We fear you," echoed from each of our terrified mouths.

The sword moved to the center of the room, suspended by the unseen as an unrecognizable face spoke to us directly.

"Your work begins today. Follow my instructions. Rest when I tell you to rest. Drink when I allow you to drink. I expect your best work. Those who disobey earn punishment or removal. Do you understand my words?"

I became the leader again, this time for a bunch of kids who survived the crushing power of a black hole, yet re-emerged as a small tribe of scared servants.

"Yes, we understand," I said.

The face and sword vanished.

Unsolicited images formed in my mind with pictures of captured kids who carved out the prison with picks and axes, kids like us. When the vision ended, I explained our work to the clan.

"We choose a wall of solid rock, chipping away until it becomes cubical," I said.

Ears shook his head and said, "We can't do this. We're too young."

Immediately the sword hovered at his neck.

"Ears, you can do this. Say it," I coaxed. "Say you can do this."

Ears understood. "Okay. I can… I can do this."

The clan joined in: "We can. Yes, we can."

The sword vanished.

I spoke to my friends with urgency. "If we want to live, not one of us says *no* or *can't.* Only listening and obeying will keep us safe. Most of all, we fear *Face.* No matter how well or how badly that thing treats us, remember it is bigger and more powerful than us."

As I spoke, I glared into their eyes because they needed to internalize the truth as I had. We remained captives, rodents in a trap, but at least we were together. Each friend nodded as they hung their heads, resigned to our fate.

I handed the pail to Baby. "You're the youngest and smallest. This bucket is little enough for you to carry away the rock chips."

"Where do I put them?"

She had a point. Our eyes followed the dim light that began to shine brighter on the other side of the room. Baby and I followed the beam as the ground shuddered. I grabbed Baby's elbow to steady her.

Before our eyes, a hole appeared in the floor. Baby laughed at the sheer magic of it. We knew where the loose rock would go—but I had an idea. I grabbed a pickaxe and hit the wall hard. Slivers of stone flew everywhere.

"Ears, I need you to listen." I commanded everyone to be quiet as I dropped a chunk into the hole.

"I don't hear the bottom," Ears said. "It must be miles deep."

If Ears couldn't hear it hit bottom, I believed a bottom didn't exist. Baby peered over and lost her balance. I caught her and moved her back.

"Baby, be careful, please. I don't want you falling into that pit." I used a shard of stone to scratch lines around the hole. "Don't step past the boundary, okay, Baby?"

"I'll be careful, Chief."

It was good to see her sweet grin, but I worried about what other dangers existed in the strange network of caves.

I took charge of our new, strange existence. "Okay, time to work," I said. "Don't overdo it. Get to know your tools and what they can do."

We all chipped away, first at a snail's pace as the heavy tools challenged us. We grunted and groaned from the labor and were soon tired. The pads on my palms bled raw—heavy work required more skill than our bodies had.

One by one, we wore down. When one of us thought about quitting, the sword appeared.

"Do you value your lives? Do you fear me?" Face's voice emanated from the sword.

"Yes, yes, we fear you," we hollered, turning back to the wall, ignoring the open blisters that would harden into calluses.

It seemed hours later that a light shined on a table. Dropping our tools, we seated ourselves and drank what had appeared, eating something that looked like mashed potatoes but tasted like chocolate. That was a nice surprise. Immediately our blisters began to heal.

"Yo, check it out," Lookout said, holding up hands that were blistered moments before. When we finished eating and healing, the light moved back to the wall. We resumed our work when I noticed something unusual.

"Yo, Lookout! Ears! I haven't heard a single hiccup or sneeze," I said.

"Dude, they stopped after eating Face's food," Ears replied.

"Wow, my hiccups *are* gone too," Lookout added.

"Amazing, guys," I said while concentrating every muscle to swing one more time when I was ready to drop.

"Chief," Bat said, "I'll take the pick. It won't be hard

for me to use."

"Thanks, Bat. We need to rotate the tools so we will all build muscle to handle the heaviest ones. Hey, Bat?"

"Yo, Chief."

"Where did your English accent go?"

"Holy Toledo—it's gone," he said. "I'm Philadelphian again, I guess."

"Prove it, Bat. Say w-a-t-e-r," Picker instructed.

"Wooder."

"Yep. Guess you aren't a Beatle after all," Picker laughed as he swung the sledgehammer.

I wondered what else would change as captives.

"Chief, how much longer?" Picker asked. "The wall we're working on is turning dark."

My friend had a point; the light in the passageway had brightened. "Must be quitting time," I said.

We left the work area with sore muscles and legs heavy as lead. We stumbled to our cubicles, looking like the walking dead. I assumed everyone had drinks and food waiting there like me. After I ate, the shower started magically, and a new uniform appeared before I fell into bed. My friends said they experienced the same as me, day after day.

Chapter 4

Each morning, we greeted one another. As the workdays progressed, I cheered the clan on. "We have food and shelter. Our fate could have been much worse on the outside." I turned to Motor. "You, Motor, you're way too smart, too skilled for street life. Someone would have found you, using your engine skills for stealing whether you wanted to cooperate or not. Those guys always do time. Rotting in jail would be a waste of your brain.

"Picker," I continued, "breaking-and-entering requires someone slow and careful. Your love for fun compromised cautiousness. Ending up in juvie was a sure thing for you. That place is no joke from what I hear.

"Ears, man, you're better off here. Remember the time you didn't know you had an ear infection but swore a building was empty? Picker got us through the door. The next thing you know, we're sprinting down the street with Dobermans on our tails."

Ears smiled at the memory as I moved down the line.

"Bat, you know why the gangs wanted you. Your future pointed to the rest of your life in prison or worse. Now, you're free from the club.

"Lookout, you kept us out of sticky situations by keeping watch—but you don't have eyes in the back of your head. In a severe attack on us, you would have gone down first.

"Baby, you're safer here with a family who loves you. Besides, work never hurt anyone, right, gang?"

I was the luckiest. Instead of being behind bars for lifting—or killed by a drug dealer whose crack house I burned down—I was with friends. They chafed at slavery as I did, but we had to make the best of it.

Although time eluded us, we learned to trust our captor. As we worked, we listened to the sounds around us. Above the noise of our tools against stone, a gentle voice spoke—motherly, silky smooth. As we listened, we came to understand it was Earth, our planet. It was communicating and teaching us, sharing mysteries we city kids never knew existed.

Earth was not a ball of rock spinning in space, but was every bit alive like the plants and animals upon her. She cringed with every bomb that exploded above and below her surface. She ached from each oil well that drained her blood. She mourned for the waters contaminated by factories and trash from all around the world.

When we understood what humankind had done to her, we were ashamed for the greed and insensitivities that caused her harm. As our minds and bodies grew in strength, we loved Earth even more. Motivated by her truths, we became eager to begin our work in the mornings and learn more from her.

We fell into a rhythm of duty. Then, one evening, pleased at a day's work, I patted Baby on the head when I realized she had changed. She had grown taller and, well, fuller. Like *wow*, fuller. When I studied how much my family had matured, I realized years must have passed.

Shoulders had broadened, spines lengthened,

strengthened, and our muscles bulged. Hair grew where there was none before. Everyone looked older but relaxed and focused on the job at hand. Work changed our minds for the better. Bitterness and self-pity evaporated. We no longer felt entitled to steal or seek revenge, even if we were free to do so. The anger we nurtured before capture melted away; we loved our work and loved each other. We had become even closer.

Also, we had a purpose—we lived to serve Face, not because we were too scared not to, but out of love and awe. Sometimes, though, my human pride surfaced before his declaration resounded in my head.

"Do you still fear me?"

Yes, I will always fear you.

We finished one room of cubicles after the other, becoming stronger than teenagers I remembered on the outside and powerful in ways that counted. Working the caves gave us character, but sometimes we were prone to reminiscing.

"Chief, you have to admit our last act of revenge was brilliant and funny, too," Picker said. "We didn't hurt anyone by it, did we?"

"I'm sure the glue wore off, but we shot them with a big humiliation bullet," I replied. "That can last forever, man. Seemed like a good idea at the time, but I wonder if the retribution was more for me. You know, making the hoods feel small so that I could feel big." I hit a rock too hard and needed to catch my breath.

"Yeah, you guys were twisted when I joined— always trying to prove something, especially Chief," Motor said. "I figured I better stick around to keep you guys out of big trouble." He smiled. "The best part was Picker's lame jokes."

"True that," Ears laughed. "That's why I joined up—it took my mind off my troubles. Chief was full of it, too, wasn't he?"

"Who's next?" I asked, smiling as they enjoyed roasting me. "Lookout?"

"I checked you guys out," he said, "and thought you were all nuts, always looking for a good time, stealing what you needed to survive, living in rundown dives with no electricity or water. I couldn't let you act like a bunch of fools without watching out for you."

"Who was looking out for whom?" Bat said as he hammered away.

Baby giggled. "We looked out for each other because we loved each other."

"Out of the mouths of babes, my momma used to say," Bat replied.

I finished the cubicle and helped Picker with his. "Yeah, Ears is right," I said. "We were messed up, but Face scared all that crap out of us, which left us clean and new. It's good not to have all the crazy, dark thoughts."

"Yeah, the hate, man, hate's a bad thing." Bat put down his sledgehammer. "That's what Face scared out of us. Then he filled us with love—it's all about love."

We stopped working for a moment. The quiet Bat had said a mouthful of truth and we drank in its beauty. It was strange how becoming less negative allowed wisdom to grow inside us. We no longer needed labels, status, or false layers to feel like somebody.

Talents surfaced that we didn't know were inside us. Baby sang while shoveling stone into holes, and she took turns at the pickaxe as she got older. Ears joined her with harmonies while Bat added bass notes; Lookout vocally drummed or moonwalked as he worked.

Picker emceed and provided comedy, usually about me. I caught all the good-natured jokes but knew that I had grown, adding physical fortitude to my body and mind.

I had become a real leader.

Yet, sometimes, confusion wormed its way deep inside of me. I avoided a talk with Face about his plans for us. How long did he plan to keep us in the caves? Was his sentence something that would last a lifetime? We weren't homesick because none of us longed for the past, but we wanted to accomplish more for Face than just digging out walls.

The questions nagged me like bothersome gnats that I kept swatting away. Finally, the courage manifested within me; I must talk with Face. A river of perspiration ran down my forehead as I thought about a one-to-one meeting.

I would choose my words with care.

****

The next evening, I finished my meal, cleaned up, and dressed. I kneeled by my cot to make a concerted effort to connect with Face from my cubicle.

"You are all. You are powerful—the creator of everyone and everything." I followed the praise with a plea. "Face, please hear me. I fear you. I will never go against you. I fear you and revere you now and always."

The sword appeared by my side. "Do you fear me enough, my son?"

I choked out the words, "May I do more for you, my Face? Although I will be happy to serve in these caves for eternity, I want to do more for you. We all do."

An eerie silence filled the room before the Face

appeared and spoke softly with the sword nowhere in sight.

"Most humans no longer fear me. They scoff at my existence, living for themselves—which chains them to ignorance and sadness. Since my creation disrespects life, they have no respect for each other. How can they revere an unseen creator?

"I rescued you from the world," Face continued. "I rebuilt your spirit to withstand the temptations of their perpetual eclipse. Do you remember your old ways? Do you remember the pain of it? Are you strong enough now to come against it?"

"My Face, you made me what I am in these caves. I would not choose a direction away from you. Neither will the others. We love you."

Face whirled around me as I knelt. "I trained many to share the knowledge of how Earth sustains herself. But I task you with a specific goal, utilizing your skills. Go into the world. Save the lost and stolen children. Bring them to me for healing. Are you strong enough for this directive, young Chief?"

"Yes, Face," I said firmly. "We are indebted to you, glad to do your bidding before all else. We will save the children and return them to you."

"Earth is my first living planet. She manages her system, but man's interference tires her. I allow Earth to save herself at all costs… for without her stability, all life upon her will perish. You must complete your task before my planet changes according to her needs."

"Changes?" I asked reverently. "Changes *how*?"

"Earth must cleanse. She must change the position of her axis to do so."

I thought about the devastation of all life that

flipping of the axis could cause. But I understood Earth's survival was most important.

"I am ready," I said. "*We* are ready to begin our work saving innocent children."

Face softened; features changed as he stopped spinning. I saw what I could not see before but lately sensed—a compassionate expression of love.

"Rise, young Chief. I have chosen well. You have learned well."

For the first time, a dove glided around my cubicle, stopping to rest on my shoulder. "He reveres us now, as we do him. It is good."

"Sleep, my son. Tomorrow you shall return."

The dove and Face disappeared. Exhausted, I fell onto my cot, pulling a blanket around my neck. As I closed my eyes, I experienced a sensation that I never had before my capture–a mysterious love that permeated my body, my mind, my spirit—like floating in a sea of love.

Our time in the caves was almost over.

Chapter 5

As usual, we gathered in the workroom the next morning. This time, a pronounced air of excitement filled the space, though no words were spoken between us other than quick greetings—everyone already knew.

The chamber suddenly blasted with the brightest, purest light, much too brilliant for our eyes. We fell to our knees from the overpowering luminesce. That day, Face's many features moved through us, in us, and around us. Gently, Face spoke.

"You grew within my light learning truth, purpose, justice, and love. Earth educated you. Your minds, your souls, flourish because of her revelations.

"Now I reward you with the tools needed to continue your work as Insiders." The sword floated to Lookout's head. "My son, from this moment forth, you shall see far and beyond without obstacles blocking your vision." The sword graced Lookout's brow. He fell back with a glimmer before he vanished from the room.

Again, the sword hovered. "Motor, to you, I give knowledge and power over physics. Be warned, no matter what the price, use your gift to benefit humanity and for nothing else. As you think, you will be able to *do*."

As the sword touched his head, he, too, illuminated before vanishing.

"Ears, you earned the power to hear, comprehending

beyond walls, beyond distance, beyond language." As the sword touched each ear, my friend reacted with surprise before he evaporated.

"Picker, you will walk through obstacles, creating pathways for yourself and others." After the sword encircled his body, Picker left us like a puff of smoke vanishing into the air.

"Bat, corruption abounds in the outside world. Some who realize their errors and want my redemption need protection, for evil hates dissenters. Your power protects all Insiders. Use the authority with wisdom, Bat." The sword flew towards him with cyclonic energy that encircled his frame before he disappeared in a breeze.

Baby kneeled. "May I stay? May I stay with you forever, Face?"

The dove landed on the crown of Baby's head. "Child, in these walls you discovered love, security, and peace. Share these attributes to influence others and save the devastated children. Will you do this for me, my child?" Baby nodded as tears graced her cheeks. The dove lifted off and, for the first time, the sword circled Baby's head before she melted from my site.

The sword rested in the air near my head. "Chief, your strength, intellect, and wisdom join your new spirit. I increase each attribute, adding the gift of second sight—you will sense those in need of your help."

"I promise not to let you down, my Face," I said solemnly. I understood Baby's emotions; I would miss Face, too. But as the blade pressed down on my head, a surge of power ran through my body and catapulted me from the room.

I awoke to a blurry vision of white, but not the light I had grown accustomed to in the caves. Instead, my eyes flinched from a cold, piercing illumination along with noise—beeping and hollered words.

"Doctor, he tried to open his eyes," a shrill voice said.

"Son, can you hear me? Luke, wake up."

No one spoke that name in eons. Luke was the name my parents gave me, the name I left behind. My friends—where were they? *Where was I?* I struggled to think and to keep my eyes open. I tried to talk, but a lump in my throat obstructed my voice.

"He's conscious," another woman said. "Luke, do you remember how you got here? Shake your head yes or no."

I shook my head no.

"We'll remove the tube from your throat in a few minutes."

A different approach for talking was needed. I motioned for a pen and paper and scrawled WHERE ARE MY PEOPLE?

"Your family?" A doctor asked in surprise. He told a nurse to notify my family immediately before softening as he checked my vitals. "Son, they are in for a big surprise. You were unconscious for a long time. Take it easy—you'll be groggy for a while."

I thought about his words as they bounced around in my head, not quite connecting them. What did he mean? I didn't see my family anywhere, but I could feel them. Waking up hooked to wires and tubes outside the caves reminded me that our freedom would not be a smooth adventure. The original clan no longer existed because we had graduated to Insiders and would soon begin our work.

We were free.

****

I regained full consciousness disconnected from the tubes and machines. A beautiful nurse leaned in and asked, "How are you?"

"Okay. I'm okay," I whispered with a weak voice and a foggy brain. Even though my throat hurt from the tube, it was good to communicate with someone new. "How long have I been here?"

The nurse sat on the side of my bed, stroking my hand. "Luke, you were twelve when they found you floating in the water. You're seventeen now."

"It can't be. Yesterday, he permitted us to—" I stopped, remembering not to mention Face.

"Five years of dreams add to your muddle about what is real and what isn't real," the nurse said sympathetically. "Do not rush it. Your brain will clear."

"Where are the others?" I asked again.

The nurse touched me. "Luke, I have sad news. Both of your parents passed on while you were in a comatose state. May we call anyone for you?"

"Not them," I said, absorbing the deaths of my parents with no emotion. "Where are my *friends*? They fell in the water, too."

"Oh, those others. You and your friends piqued the interests of several scientists. We have been caring for you for years. It really is amazing…"

I tried a different angle. "Did they wake up yet?"

"Well, I don't know. Did you think all of you would wake at the same time? Various locations contain them." I could see the proverbial light bulb flash on in her brain. "I'll call and—" The nurse dashed out of the room in excitement.

I wanted to jump up and reassure my friends, but not in the flimsy hospital gown I wore. Where were my clothes? I thought of my uniform, the waiting showers, food on the table. I never needed to ask… everything was always there. That time was over. I would have to pay for my keep.

And I would *never* go back to the old way of life before I met Face.

A buzz existed outside my room. People lingered before they walked past my door, pointing, whispering, smiling, and waving. A uniformed photographer ducked in with a camera and took a few pictures before a security guard yanked him out.

The nurse came back with a gaggle of physicians. The lead doctor approached me.

"Son, your friends—well, they awakened, too," he said. "Each one of them is asking for Chief. Is that you?"

I smiled and nodded. "Yes, sir. Are they okay?"

"That is the thing, Luke. Your friends are *more* than okay. You must understand that after finding you floating face down in the water for hours, and after five years on breathing machines, no brain damage occurred—no wasting muscle mass.

"You look like powerlifters," the doctor continued. "We never understood why you showed brain activity in the first place, as you had no other vitals when they pulled you from the water. That made you unique survivors. We're hoping you and your friends will tell us what you know, what you remember of that day."

The nurse placed a tray with broth and water by my bed. "Sure, doc, I'll tell you if I remember something, but right now, I'm starving. Okay if I eat first? And doc…?"

"Yes, Luke?"

"My name isn't Luke. It's *Chief*. That's what my friends call me."

A military man who stood in the back stepped forward. He wore a chest full of brass, but his red bulbous nose gave away his weakness for alcohol. Although he held himself with an air of importance, the nose and a protruding belly suggested an officer with a self-discipline problem, and I guessed, a hater of all oddities just like the dad I barely remembered.

"Son, you'll see your friends soon," he said brusquely. "We are in the middle of coordinating their transportation from their individual hospitals to this location. We thought it would be easier to find the underlying cause of this mystery if we put you together in one facility."

"Mystery?" I asked as I sipped mediocre broth. It was inferior to the soup on the inside.

"Son, we need to understand how all of you trained and the source of your excellent health. We must see how you and your friends relate, testing if there is secondary damage. We'll observe for a while to determine if breached security is a possibility."

Big Brass's voice faded at the end, and he lowered his eyes. I was older now, a long way from the streets, but I could still smell a rat. I studied the inquisitive faces around me. Soldiers, a few with lots of brass in multiple senses of the word, gathered to size me up. Understanding that we Insiders were trapped again (but not for our benefit this time), I kept my cool.

"Training? Security? What?" I asked calmly. "The nurse said I've been unconscious here for years. I'm confused; I want to know what happened, too, sir. I remember playing with my friends one day and woke up here the next. You say five years have passed, but in here—" I pointed to my head. "—it has been a day. Oh, and if it's not too much trouble, I'd like some real clothes. This hospital gown looks like a dress."

An officer spoke with a legal pad and pen in his hand. "We requisitioned some uniforms. We want you to be comfortable."

"When do my friends arrive?"

Big Brass answered a little too kindly, "We thought you might require a few days to adjust, but you are doing great. I'll have them here first thing in the morning. Meanwhile, relax and rest."

Big Brass didn't realize how stupid he sounded to me. How much rest did I need? Five years was plenty. I endured more photos until I pretended to tire. Left alone, I swung my hairy, muscled legs over the side of the bed and my feet touched the cold tile floor. I stood on my own and walked to the bathroom. I washed my hands, looking up to study my reflection in the mirror.

A young man with a shaved head stared back at me. My head still had the electrode glue marks while my face showed a shadow of stubble.

I resolved to look neat and clean for my family. Since I never shaved before, I called down the hallway for help. A nurse rushed in, frightened I had fallen—or worse. She found me staring in the mirror, and her fear turned to amusement. I didn't appreciate being a spectacle.

"I want to shave," I said.

The nurse smiled and returned with shaving cream and a razor. "Here, Chief. Take this first." She gave me a cup of water and a blue pill.

Seeing my reluctance, she said, "It's something that will help your brain sort out things. Completely harmless."

After I shaved my beard, I sat back down on my bed, suddenly exhausted. *That pill*, I thought. *That drug*.

Chapter 6

Excitement woke me before dawn. I was eager to see my family.

Our separation seemed much longer than it was. Pacing the floor and trying to acclimate to the concept of time that had eluded us for years, I decided to be patient, but it didn't come easily.

When doctors insisted I eat a mushy breakfast, to "allow my shrunken stomach time to adapt to solid food," I wanted to argue. My muscles hadn't shrunk; why would my stomach? Instead, I scarfed down the repulsive mush as I watched the door. The clock's second hand echoed. I wanted to explore the hallway outside my door, but a guard shooed me back the instant one foot went over the threshold.

I covertly measured the room, checking out the ceiling and the floor. I tapped on walls that had no windows. They were solid—it reminded me of the cubicles. *Dig deeper*, I thought. *Chip away the exterior. Work to find the truth inside.*

"Chief."

I turned to see Baby standing in the doorway. At fourteen she looked radiant, more like a young woman with long sinewy lines and eyes that shined deep and wise through their iridescent blue. Giggling, she ran toward me and jumped into my arms.

I held her tight. "You're safe."

Footsteps ran toward us. Everyone burst in, tackling us in a group hug. We whooped and hollered and jumped on the bed, forgetting we were no longer little kids. Motor played with the buttons of the hospital bed—we rode with him. As our celebration quieted down, we sat in a small circle on the floor. We huddled together gazing at one another in silence, adjusting to the world and the new us. At last, all eyes were on me.

"Be careful of what you say about us," I whispered. "Soldiers discussed observing us. I envision physical and mental tests and don't see anything pleasant happening to us here. We're in danger."

"They were outside my room," Motor said. "According to the learned doctors, I am an *anomaly*. They insisted I shouldn't be in good physical shape after a lengthy coma."

"They're right," Bat smiled, flexing his pectoral muscles. "We sure woke up different."

"I lifted the clipboard on my bed," Picker added. "It said the same thing. They think something's wrong with us 'cause our bodies are in too good shape. Chief is right—we need to be careful of everything and everyone."

"We should work up a getaway plan. I saw the military pull away in limos and Humvees. We've got great transportation if we need it." Motor gave us a wry grin. "Not that I'd steal one. I'd borrow it temporarily."

I thanked my men for thinking ahead. "We know they're up to no good, but let's not panic yet. We don't want anyone to know that we know, so act normal. We won't let anyone, or anything, take away all we earned from Face. And that's where you come in, Ears and Picker. Listen up for any potential problems. Picker, keep reading those reports—find more information. Lookout, search for a way out of here. Motor, do what you do best, then report back to me."

"What about me?" Baby asked.

"You have the hardest job of all, Baby," I replied. "We need you to coordinate this operation by convincing these soldiers to do whatever we need them to do."

Bat looked like a friend in need of a purpose. I smiled at him, knowing we all needed a protector. "Bat, your job is one I hope we won't need: make note of anything in the hospital we can use as a weapon. Who knows how far the military will go to learn our story?"

"Pleased to be needed, my friend," Bat said.

"Most importantly, don't talk about Face," I added, looking at my friends in turn. "We went underwater and woke up here. We don't remember anything beyond that. Agreed?"

Everyone nodded. That made me feel better, but I still worried about our next move.

The bony nurse with the shrill voice popped into the room, interrupting our reunion. "Okay, people, no more tubes and wires, so we are moving to another part of the facility," she announced. "Each of you has a room with a TV and room service, of sorts. Meanwhile, we'll be testing you to make sure… you know… you're healthy. Let's go."

She walked out, clearly waiting for us to follow. Lookout and Ears, whispering, warned us about bugs in our rooms before Lookout assured me that he would find us a secure meeting place. We followed the nurse, taking in the sights around us with opportunistic eyes. Luckily, the same hallway accessed all our rooms.

"Can we visit each other?" I asked the nurse.

"Yes, of course, unless testing in the other wing—" The nurse stopped herself mid-sentence and looked like she knew she'd made a grave mistake. She dashed out of the rooms and must have walked right into someone important.

Ears whispered, "Repeating, Chief."

"Do not talk to them about testing, Nurse Cole. Do not speak to them about anything, not a word. We do not want them running like the last bunch. Keep your mouth shut."

We looked at each other—the military doctor had heard our conversation with the nurse! Ears added that the nurse vowed to be more careful.

****

After we found our quarters (which appeared to be identical), everyone left their rooms and came to mine. Ears whispered, "They plan to listen to our every word."

Lookout turned up the volume of the television. He placed his finger on his lips, signaling us to move around as he used his new vision to examine the room inch by inch with his feet propped up. He soon noticed a tiny lens in the overhead fixture and a listening bug in a lamp. He motioned us to join him in the bathroom. We laughed as we tried to fit into the small space: a couple in the shower, one on the sink, and one on the john. Ears, taking no chances, turned on the faucet.

"This is one place they can't hear us if we whisper when the door is shut," he said.

"Yes, but the sudden quiet will cause suspicion bringing someone to check on us," I replied. "Ears. Go out and create noise. You too, Lookout. Let them hear you having a party. Watch something noisy on TV. I'll bring you up to speed afterward, Lookout."

With them gone, the rest of us continued our meeting. I explained that Ears heard a mention of another Insider group having been here before us—and that some had escaped.

"What did they run from?" Bat asked.

"Picker, search for their records tonight," I said. "Maybe they knew that sinister stuff was going on here. I get the feeling someone here still needs help."

"Maybe, they knew a reason to be scared."

"You might be right, Bat. The shorter our meetings, the better, and Baby, stand by—we may need you to inspire someone."

She went back into the room. I motioned for Lookout to join me so I could update him.

"Picker, wait until tonight when security is the weakest," I said, wrapping up. "Lookout, Bat, Motor, you know your jobs."

Baby spoke up as soon as we were all in my bedroom. "Chief, I'd like to say something."

I pointed to the listening device above. She nodded as if she understood its importance.

"We're all aware I'm not a baby anymore," she said. "It's time I have a new name."

That was a kick in the gut. I wanted Baby to remain the same girl I knew. But while studying the grown her, I knew she was right.

"You've come a long way from the helpless baby we first met," I said.

"You've turned into a, uh, babe," Picker said.

Baby grinned from ear to ear.

"Good thinking, Picker," I said, punching his arm lightly. Then I tapped Baby's shoulders with a plastic spoon. "I pronounce you... *Babe*."

We laughed and bounced her on the bed. But we would never again call her Baby. We spent the afternoon watching TV, catching up on five missed years. I didn't recognize a single entertainer except for Justin Timberlake, and he had become a single act. There was Twitter and Facebook—iPads were everything it seemed. Was it possible to live on Earth without a phone?

****

A guard who monitored video caught Lookout lurking outside his room.

"You'll find lots of sick people and disease around here, son," he said. "Remain in this wing. You may see your friends, but beyond this wing requires a military pass or escort. Is that understood?"

I watched from the doorway as Lookout smiled. "Yes, sir," he said. "Just wondering what kind of hospital this is, sir."

"A military hospital, of course."

Babe stepped forward. "Hi, I'm Babe. What is your name, sir?"

"Call me Serge, little lady," he said, starting off down the hallway.

"Sergeant, I've been gone for a long time. You know, asleep. I'm trying to catch up on what's happened in the world while I was, ah…"

"Making like Sleeping Beauty," Lookout finished for her.

Pausing, the guard turned to face Babe. "The world is a complicated place. How 'bout I bring a current newspaper and magazines to help you catch up with things?"

Babe locked eyes with him. "That would be nice,

Sergeant. You have the same eyes as mine," she said.

I had a great view and saw that he was transfixed, almost enchanted with Babe.

"Sergeant, you won't remember this moment," Babe continued. "You did not see us out of our rooms. You'll erase the surveillance video when you get back to your desk—right, Sergeant?"

"Yes, ma'am," the dazed soldier agreed.

"Sergeant, I want you to be happy but lazy. A couple of hours after dinner, take a nice long nap. You'll wake up in the morning refreshed. Your superior wants you to feel alert, doesn't he, sergeant?"

"Yes, little lady."

"Very good. Go now," Babe instructed.

"Wow," I whispered when Babe returned to us. "You think he'll really erase security tapes and delete paperwork?"

"I'm certain of it," she said.

"I discovered the filing cabinets just outside our rooms," Lookout said after we gathered in his bathroom. "While Babe sweet-talked the sergeant, I peered into them. Insider files are in the third set of cabinets from the left, top drawer, but the locks require Picker's expertise."

Picker said with an air of pseudo-innocence, "What kind of locks are they? Oh, I forgot... I don't need to concern myself with picking locks anymore."

Clowning, Picker reached through the medicine cabinet door and pulled out a can of shaving cream. We roared with laughter. Everyone asked how he did it.

He shrugged, pleased with his magic trick. "It's all thanks to Face."

"Motor, how are your new computer skills?" I asked.

"Can't wait to find out, Chief."

"Bat, have you tried your new gift?"

"Chief, it's hard to practice skills with cameras all around. Face gave me powers—I'll know what to do when the time comes."

That time arrived two hours after dinner. Motor slipped out first, intending to project a mind force that turned off the cameras and mics. As Babe suggested, the sergeant slept through it.

Motor crouched in front of the computer, communicating with the machine. Lookout checked all the hallways on our floor and looked above us. Personnel was sparse that time of night, the few who were on duty busy with paperwork or watching TV.

Motor deployed our protection first. While Bat kept watch, we devised a coordinated defense plan to see and block the enemy before they saw us. Picker and Lookout then approached the old cabinets that were arranged by alphabet.

"Wouldn't we be in the computer instead of old paper files?" I asked.

"For a time, they copied the computer material as a precautionary method," Motor said. "In case the grid went down."

"They wouldn't be stupid enough to file under I for insiders, would they?" Picker asked.

"Ha!" Lookout peered into the drawer over Picker's shoulders. "What's that fat file there? Stop moving your hand, Picker… okay, go back about an inch. There it is."

"Oh, it's a big one." Picker pulled a three-inch thick file labeled PENNSYLVANIA from the drawer. A subfolder was titled POINT PARK. He handed the file to me.

"Chief," Motor whispered. "I've made it through three firewalls. You should see this!"

"Motor, print a copy we can take; make sure they can't track the print job."

"Make it quick, Motor," Ears said. "Elevator's coming down."

"Motor?" I asked nervously.

"No worries, Chief." Motor's fingers flew over the keys. "The elevator is about to get stuck between floors."

I noticed a glowing ripple emanating from the computer.

"You better hurry or we'll have maintenance people to contend with, too," Ears said.

"Motor?"

"Finished, Chief."

We fled into our rooms as the elevator dinged and the doors slid open.

"Sergeant!" the general barked. "Serge, wake up, dammit. That's an order!"

The sergeant let out a loud snore. "Yes, momma…"

"Sergeant, you're asking for time in the brig…"

Babe, embarrassed for the poor man, snapped her fingers in his direction. The sergeant awoke with a start. He jumped to his feet, mortified his superior caught him napping.

"Sir! Sorry, sir! I don't know what came over me."

"Get a move on," the general said. "Check on our charges."

I heard the sergeant hurrying to our wing of rooms. We pretended to be sound asleep. As soon as he closed the doors, we slipped out of our beds, peeking outside. He hurried back to the video room, rewinding it to satisfy the general that the hallways had remained empty during the night.

"Sergeant, if I ever catch you sleeping on duty again…"

"Sir! No, sir. I swear it will never happen again. Check my record, please. It never happened before—I swear it'll never happen again."

"Sergeant, these kids are a mystery," the general replied, a bit calmer. "They're a mystery this military needs to unravel and exploit. They could be the greatest weapon of our arsenal. We don't want to lose them through carelessness, understand?"

"Sir. Yes, sir."

"Tomorrow morning, we start testing. No one is comatose for five years then wakes up with an Olympian build—I mean no typical patriotic American. They may possess the secret to longevity, suspended animation, and soldiers requiring no rest. They may hold the key to life itself, so do *not* screw up again. I'm warning you, Sergeant."

"It won't happen again, sir," Serge said as the general headed toward the front door.

"And call maintenance. The elevator needs work."

"Yes, sir. Will do, sir."

I slipped the files into my bathroom. While speed reading, I learned that the first captured group had let things slip—the military knew our Insider name. They also knew about an entity called Face, but the information ended there.

I also discovered why the others tried to escape. The tests the military wanted to do on us would prove grueling, with needles, scalpels, blood work, and whatnot. The plans for electroshock therapy and exposure to radioactive particles alarmed me. I was not sure vivisection was off the table, but if one of us died, they would have the excuse they needed.

I would not let that happen.

Face had given us extraordinary gifts, and I planned to use them well. That included relying on Ears' talent.

"Tell everyone to get dressed and come to my room," I whispered to him.

Babe put her hand in the hallway, fluttering it toward Serge. His head nodded forward—he was out. Everyone scooted to my room, still pulling on uniforms.

"Motor, are the mics still off?" I asked in a whisper.

"They're off, Chief."

"We need to get out of here now. The military wants to test us like guinea pigs. They want the secret to what makes us special. I am not willing to share these gifts with anyone in this place. How about the rest of you?"

"We must begin the work we were sent to do," Babe said.

Everyone nodded and murmured agreement.

"Good. But I get an odd feeling someone is crying for help," I said, pointing above.

"Yeah, I've heard weird sounds too," Ears said.

"Try the third floor, Lookout."

"Will do." Lookout scanned the floors above.

"What, you're like Superman with x-ray vision?" Motor asked.

"Close enough. And Ears is right: I see something on the third floor—a couple of people in restraints, even chains, strapped to beds... wow, locked in cells. They're Insiders, Chief, or what's left of them."

Everyone agreed to investigate. Face irradiated my bones, filling them with light.

"Can you protect us, Bat? We want to get out of here with as many Insiders as possible."

"Sure, Chief, consider it done."

"Motor, block the elevators. Lock the doors. Nobody goes in or out until we're ready."

"Check, Chief."

"Picker, walk through each patient's door to determine who the captives are and if they are well enough to leave. Clipboards should be on their beds."

"No problem, my chief of chiefs."

"Babe, go along to calm the captured," I said, still in awe of Babe's gifts.

She smirked while shaking her head *no but saying the opposite*. "Cool, I always wanted to go through a door without opening it."

"We need to hustle," I said. "Lookout, tell us when it's clear."

"Standing by, Chief."

I wish I could explain the harmony between us. Everyone knew what to do and when to do it. Years of teamwork for the Face continued to benefit us.

Chapter 7

It was time to rescue others while we escaped from the military hospital. We avoided the elevators and chose to climb the fire escape stairs instead. Lookout went first. He waved for us to follow him into the hallway that led to the first door. Putting his fingertips to his temples, he penetrated the walls before nodding at Picker to go through. Picker held Babe close as they disappeared to the other side like ghosts.

"That's cool," Bat whispered reverently as he and Lookout stood guard. Meanwhile, Ears listened and repeated what he heard Babe saying.

"Young Insider here... he is big. I mean huge, and encased inside a long box made of metal, maybe lead. I see his face through a small window..."

"Okay," Ears continued. "Good, Babe calmed him down. She's speaking to him."

"You don't need to be afraid. We are here to help you to set you free. Have peace."

"An electronic gizmo seals the casing," Picker reported to Ears. He stuck his head and arm out through the wall. "That's Motor's territory."

"I'll fix that," Motor replied. He grasped Picker's hand. They disappeared through the cement block walls.

"Motor's punching numbers into the electronic keypad lock," Lookout said. "It's open, Chief... Picker was right. Man, this kid is big."

"Quiet!" Ears hissed. "Babe and the kid are talking. Repeating…"

"Who are you?"

"We are the same as you."

"An Insider?"

"Yes, we've come to set you free."

"I knew Face would restore our freedom. Today is the day."

I could hear the boy just fine. He sounded alert and eager to get out of where he was. Picker opened the door from the inside, revealing the strapping Insider. Picker was right—the kid was larger and taller than our Bat.

"We'll make introductions later," I said. "Hurry. There are more to rescue."

"Wait," the boy said. "Some can't go, and some *won't* go. They lost faith and gave the military information that endangered more Insiders."

Great, I thought. "Who are you, and what are your gifts?"

"My name is Peter, but everyone calls me Fly." Peter lifted off the floor, flew down the hallway, *and* disappeared. A tap on my shoulder made me turn. I found him hovering behind me.

"You fly and go invisible? Cool," I said. We shook hands. "Pleased to meet you, Fly. My family calls me Chief."

"Chief, I can point out the true Insiders for you, the ones that didn't forget Face. Torture caused their weaknesses, but devout Insiders refused to cooperate even when I heard screams during interrogation. A few live as shadows of their former selves, but maybe Face will restore them one day."

"Show me the loyal insiders, Peter."

Picker and Babe stepped through to another room he pointed out to us. Ears repeated what he heard inside from Babe:

"A young woman in here. I'm guessing early twenties. She looks like Sleeping Beauty."

"She only looks like she's sleeping," Fly said. "Tell them to watch her face."

"Repeating," Ears said.

"Wait, a golden light moves through her and over her."

Fly nodded at me, indicating that this was par for the course. "Some in this dimension commune with the Face, acting as an antenna or an invisible cable hooked into him. They heal, and sometimes they even bring back life. This one's name is Healer."

Picker and Babe brought her to me. "She's unharmed," Babe said.

Up close, my first impression of Healer was that of a southern belle or a flower child I had seen in movies. I had a good feeling about her, but I knew time was short.

"Peter, I trust you know who's whom. Picker and Babe will release those you name."

****

Most of the Insiders stayed loyal to the Face. A few sat in a stupor. Others proved difficult or hateful, showing no forgiveness toward the creator who gave them the gifts that landed them here. Healer backed away, shaking her head.

"I can't heal them to a level of sanity that would change their attitude toward the Face and warrant their release," she said.

"Maybe I can," Bat replied. He approached each one and explained they had one chance to accept healing.

Most ignored him. Some spat and screamed that Bat would end up like them. They cursed Face, showing no fear of his sword.

Others seemed unable to answer. I wondered what kind of torture could corrupt people handpicked by Face, but I didn't plan on sticking around long enough to find out. We left the fallen Insiders behind, hoping Face would forgive them and help them one day.

Meanwhile, we released the loyal captives who, despite their frailties, were happy when they saw Healer. We freed six, including one in critically bad shape and another bent and twisted. They both required help but there was no time for coddling—daybreak was minutes away. Dawn called for a change of shifts with more personnel arriving. We sleuthed our way to the exit with Healer pushing a wheelchair for a man with bolts in his head.

"Peter, do you know the area outside the base?" I asked.

"Sure do. There's a perfect place to meet outside," he replied. "My group stayed there when we planned Thunder and Healer's escape."

"I see it!" I exclaimed as my second sight kicked in. A video-like scene played in my head; the vision would lead us to our next destination. "Bat, are we covered?"

"Chief, I have everyone's back, including yours. Nobody can touch us... literally." He grinned while chomping on an apple. Bat always snacked, but he appeared too relaxed, too confident. Then he read my mind and the smile faded. "Chief, man, the building and outside grounds are covered. No vehicles in or out except for ours."

As he spoke, two vehicles pulled up to the front

entrance with no drivers at the wheel.

"Wow. Thanks, Motor. This will take getting used to."

"It was Bat's idea, Chief."

I nodded approval to Bat who gave me an "I told you so" look as he worked on his apple.

"Ears, raise your antennae for any communications about us. We need to be a step ahead of these clowns."

"On it, Chief."

"Let's go," I said, re-watching the movie in my head. Our temporary hideout would be an old factory building—boarded and condemned. Just what we were used to as kids.

Bat explained that he'd manifested a protective bubble that shielded us. But it occurred to me that one guard with a transmitter could ruin our escape.

We met that one at the bottom of a stairwell.

"Nobody moves!" a soldier shouted. He pointed an M4 carbine at us while speaking into a transmitter on his shoulder. "Security, breach. Security, there's a breach in building seven."

"Roger that," came a voice through the transmitter that we could hear. Reinforcements would be coming.

"Bat?"

"No problem, Chief," he said as he jump-shot the apple core into a trash bin. "He must have been inside the building before I surrounded us with protection."

At the entranceway, soldiers tried force but could not touch the door handles. They used the butts of their rifles hoping to break the glass, but their attempts failed. Three men stood back and ran toward the door—I watched in disbelief as they ricocheted a dozen feet back.

"Cool, Bat! Good job."

"Reverse whatever you did to those doors, you … bloody demons," the soldier with the M4 shouted.

Babe stepped directly in front of him.

"I'll shoot—"

"Excuse me, sir," she said. "We have no desire to hurt you or anyone. You have no desire to wound us, because that would be an unforgivable mistake in the eyes of your superiors. Look at me… I'm small, but my eyes are large like yours, see?"

It took a second, but he locked eyes with Babe.

"You don't want to carry your weapon anymore, soldier," she said calmly. "You don't wish to hurt anyone. Tell your troops this was a test, and that they performed well. Go ahead; use your radio. Tell them— they will listen to you. My words, in your voice."

The officer spoke dazedly into the transmitter. "Okay, men. This was a drill—I repeat, a drill. Good job."

"Tell them it's time for a nap," Babe added. "Everyone is feeling sleepy."

"I think we all deserve a good nap. Sweet dreams."

He fell to the floor.

"Sweet dreams, yourself," Babe whispered.

Picker laughed. "Awesome! Babe got that badass to wish sweet dreams to his troops."

Babe smiled sheepishly. Outside the entranceway, I saw unconscious soldiers littering the ground. It was a funny sight, I thought, as I marveled at the variations of gifts Face had bestowed on us.

"Ears, can you pinpoint normal conversation, say, at headquarters? I want to know what's going on there."

"I can try, Chief." Ears turned until he faced a direction that could fulfill my request.

"I'll see what's going on too," Lookout offered.

"It's quiet there, Chief," Ears said. "Maybe they're all knocked out."

"Wait a minute. I see it," Lookout said. "The communications officer is yawning. I bet he can't figure out what's going on."

"Yep, he's calling the security office without luck." Ears laughed. "Poor guy is talking to himself... wondering if a computer glitch confused him. Oh, hold on—I hear heavy footsteps."

"Yeah, here comes the general," Lookout said.

"Repeating, Chief."

"Sir, we lost our communication link a few minutes ago during the drill."

"What drill was that, soldier?"

"Sir, back-up was requested for building seven, but it signed off a few minutes later as a drill. No response when I tried to confirm. I'm running diagnostics on our system, sir."

"We don't need to check the system; it's those damn freaks of nature, soldier!"

"Sir?"

"Order men to building seven now! I want a perimeter set up around the entire base. No one gets in or out! Move it!"

"Chief, the general knows we escaped," Ears said. "They're on the way."

"Okay. It's showtime. Healthy Insiders help the damaged ones. Let's go."

"Chief, we need to stay together. We four are family." Healer struggled with the outdated wheelchair carrying the weakest Insider, who had difficulty standing. I couldn't understand what the butchers had done to him; his muscles were ripped, but he seemed zapped of all strength. I assumed that was from the things sticking out of his head.

Two young boys helped. Babe convinced Healer to let her manage the boys. Ears took their place, carrying the mutilated soul while Healer kept her hands on him.

Bat and Picker carried the last captive, another young man with muscles atrophied from what I assumed was constant bed restraint. Lookout and Motor commandeered the two getaway vehicles. One was a cumbersome military truck that held most of us; the other was a Humvee.

After Fly loaded injured Insiders into the transport, I called him to me.

"We need your skills," I said. "Check out the forward perimeter, every inch of it. Soar ahead, let us know what's coming."

"On it, Chief." He disappeared.

"Bat?" I wasn't at all sure he could cover all of us.

"I materialized a protective envelope, Chief, an energy shield like a big soap bubble. You can't see it, but it protects us."

"Can anything penetrate the bubbles?"

"Nothing I know of, but I'm not sure they can't capture us by surrounding and lifting us in the bags as though we're groceries. But the cloaks will protect our skin, our insides. I figure one lasts maybe twenty-four hours at least. Some time after that, we're vulnerable until I bag everyone again."

As drivers started their engines, I asked Ears to report.

"Repeating, Chief," he replied.

"General, the perimeter is secured. No one gets past

us."

"Good work, soldier. I want those kids alive; they're too valuable to be killed—least not without getting what we need first. Do not make that mistake again! We lost valuable resources when the last trigger-happy platoon turned loose on the first group of freaks. Make sure to use enough tranquilizers to get them down and shackle 'em, you hear!"

"Yes, sir. But what if they attack us, General?"

"They're not soldiers, Lieutenant, and not fighters. They're civilian losers with freakish abilities."

"Yes, sir, General. But that concerns me, sir."

"What concerns you?"

"The lieutenant sounds uneasy." Ears laughed. "Repeating."

"The prisoners we broke in the past possessed skills, tricks, whatever you want to call it, sir. Powers of some sort."

"Powers, pfft. They are circus freaks without a circus. Nothing more."

"Sir, a whole group of them with those skills working together—anything could happen. I suggest a new defense of some kind if they attack us."

"Lieutenant, are you worried? They got you scared, Chicken Little? They are abnormal, oddities and abominations, mutant monstrosities. Hell, two of them are girls. Are you afraid of a girl?"

We all looked at Babe and nodded our heads. "Heck, yeah!"

"Wow, the lieutenant is mighty persistent with the general," Ears said. "Repeating."

"They're dangerous, sir. We don't know what they're capable of yet."

"They are capable of scaring you. Listen, I do not care if our prisoner has his hands around your throat, lieutenant! I do not care if they grab your gun and shoot you—no one kills them! Wound if you must, but do I need to repeat it? Yes, I do, apparently—I want them alive! The Pentagon wants them alive! Is that clear enough, soldier?"

"Sir! Yes, sir."

"The poor lieutenant," Lookout said. "Chewed out in front of his men—they're doing their best to stifle their laughter."

"Repeating Chief," Ears said.

"Sir, supplies are on the way, including tranquilizer guns."

"Attention! Attention! No kills under any circumstances. Repeat: no kills. Use tranquilizers. If any cowboys out there can lasso, do it. Go for the tackle. Capture and return these freaks alive to the cells where they belong as per the general's orders. Do you copy?"

"Roger that, General. No kills."

"See to it, Lieutenant. Your career depends on it."

Chapter 8

Arranging an escape was like playing a game of chess without knowing how the pieces were supposed to move. The skill set of my team was uncertain to me.

"Second defense line is forming as we speak, Chief," Lookout said. "By the time we reach the base perimeter, it will be contained."

"Chief," Ears said, frowning in concentration. "Nice that they don't want to kill us, but can they stop us with tranquilizer guns?"

"Bat?" I asked anxiously.

"We're fine, Chief. They will bounce off."

Babe winked at me and nodded towards the microphone. "I suppose these soldiers need a talking to."

"Do it, Babe."

"General, soldiers, there is no cause for alarm," she said in the same voice that mesmerized the lieutenant. "Look into each other's eyes—you will see me bringing you peace and showering you with love. We wish you well as you clear the path ahead of us. As we pass, you will experience a joyous sleep. You will sleep through the day. Now have peace."

Babe repeated this mantra several times as we sped down the main road to the exit. Racing toward the perimeter, we saw soldiers sleeping with silly smiles on their faces, guns askew on the ground. With those who still stirred, Babe simply waggled her fingers.

Yet many soldiers must have been out of earshot of the radio. Seeing their colleagues collapse, they panicked and pulled on gas masks, not understanding what struck down their compatriots.

"We got problems, Chief!" Lookout shouted. "Troops on the way loaded with nets and gas."

"It's Special Ops," Ears added. "Real trouble."

Bat's protective bubble held as soldiers shot tranquilizers. A few of the darts ricocheted right back to the shooters who toppled into lullaby land. Motor worked his gift on the special ops trucks racing toward us. Although the vehicles screeched to a halt, a fighting division donning gas masks, headphones, and rifles spilled out the back.

Before I issued an order, Fly grabbed the two youngest children. With one on his back and one in his arms, he lifted off.

"Meet you there," he said, disappearing before a cloud of tear gas could envelop him. We whisked past the trucks as gas canisters could not infiltrate our bubbles.

As we neared the exit, the unexpected happened. One soldier, shouting hateful obscenities, pulled his handgun out and shot directly at Babe's head. Her bubble held, but the bullet bounced back, striking his forehead. It shocked all of us. Insiders knew the loss of human life was not a choice, but foolish accidents happened. Had the soldier obeyed his commander, he would have lived.

I looked at Healer questioningly. She shook her head. "My powers work with Insiders or innocents. I cannot bring back the life of a slider filled with hate."

"A slider?" I asked. "What's that?"

"Sliders project their ingrained negativity. They

work to slide everyone down to their level like the general does. They aren't rooted in truth and blow in every negative direction that hate or fear dictates."

I concentrated on reaching our destination, but the death saddened us. Our skills were new; we required time to become familiar with our abilities as well as each other's. I hoped the factory would buy that time for us.

"Bat, what about the helicopters?" I asked. They were sputtering.

"They can't shoot," he said. "Motor is handling the rest."

"Don't worry, Chief, I'll set them down easy," Motor said, predicting my next order.

"Wow, man, how do you do that?" Picker asked.

"Mind if I carry a couple more, Chief?" Fly interrupted.

"Take Healer and the sick one in her group," I said. "Wait there with them."

"Right, Chief. It's a few miles flying, but driving will take you longer." Fly picked up the wounded soul in his arms while Healer piggybacked. We turned the Humvee in Fly's direction with the truck close behind us. I read the map installed in my mind and saw many roads with more turns. "It will take us an hour to meet them there in this traffic."

"Don't worry, Chief," Motor replied. "The base will experience vehicle and electronic problems for most of the day."

He was right—no one followed by road or by air. My team choked the base's operations to a standstill, but other military installations were close by. Time was not on our side.

My brain alerted me to the factory's location; we

had almost arrived.

"Hold up, Motor. Make a left here," I said. "We need to dump these vehicles in the river and hope the military buys the diversion when they start mobilizing again."

We jumped from our rides a couple of miles further on. Motor did his thing, and the empty vehicles picked up speed and plowed into the water, where they sunk into the depths. I took a quick roll call: Babe, Ears, Picker, Motor, Lookout, and the last twisted Insider remained.

The rest were waiting for us, I hoped.

As the sun rose higher, we trekked in the shade of the trees. The injured man held us back as Ears and Lookout linked arms to carry him. I wondered if I had taken too big a chance footing the last quarter of a mile.

"I hear more copters on the way," Ears said. "They're talking about contacting local police, but they hesitate to bring them in on their dirty little secret—that secret being us."

"Thanks, Ears."

"Chief." Again, Fly swooped down in front of me. "Need help with Driller? I can carry Babe, too."

"Fly, I told you to stay with the others," I grumbled, but he was right. "Go on, take them." Fly was young, maybe fifteen, but was proving to be an asset. Maybe I'd asked too much of a stranger to obey my orders without question.

The rest of us forged onward. "Hurry, men," I urged.

"There's a path," Lookout said, jogging ahead. "I'll check it out."

"Choppers are going to buzz us in a minute," Ears said.

Through the trees, I spotted smokestacks from a crumbling factory that must have dated from the nineteenth century.

"This way, over here," Lookout called.

We ran through an empty lot to the sound of his voice. Lookout stared at the ground.

"What am I supposed to be seeing?" I asked.

"There's a tunnel beneath our feet, Chief. It runs straight to the factory. It will hide us from heat-seeking devices that could point out our positions."

"Okay, that's smart. Picker?"

"Party of two," Picker said in maître d' fashion.

"Go on, men. We'll wait here," I said.

Picker put his arms around Motor and Lookout. "You two come here often?" They melted through the ground.

I smiled at Ears. "Almost home." I punched him on the arm as I used to back in the day.

"They've spotted the submerged vehicles," Ears said ignoring my attempt at light-heartedness.

"Let's hope it keeps them busy for a while, my friend."

Picker's head emerged from the ground. "Okay, your turn. The tunnel's dark but dry. Take hold of my hands."

Ears and I looked at each other, shrugged our shoulders, and went for it. It's difficult to explain what turning to mush, going through slush, and arriving solid felt like—other than it was the strangest physical experience I'd ever had. I wondered if it seemed the same to Fly when he became invisible.

Our faint glow illuminated the darkness enough to see. Picker led us through as we traced our fingers against the century-old brick. An animal, maybe a rat, scuttled across my feet; I hated rats. A few feet of the wall was slimy and wet. Something glowed ahead—I laughed at the metaphor.

"Yes, a light at the end of the tunnel," I announced.

Fly was overcome with exhaustion as he sat on the floor, fighting to recoup his energy. He needed a deep rest to recuperate; those he had flown in were recovering, or "regenerating" as we called it.

Bat interrupted my thoughts. "Footprints wiped away, Chief, but I didn't erect a shield around the building since there's no reason to suspect we've been near this place."

"Proud of you, Bat," I said. "Thanks, man."

My first concern was the team. I studied each member and determined more rest was essential. The two youngest Insiders huddled together, already sound asleep.

Not smart to run the team's energy down, I thought. Yet I noted the time, wondering how long regeneration would take—strange that I still worked at one hundred percent. I insisted that those still awake take an hour to get quiet, meditate, and regenerate.

"That means you too, Lookout," I added.

"What about you, Chief?"

"I'm good. I'll stand guard for an hour. I need to think anyway."

Everyone found a spot to settle while I paced the floor and ruminated about the reason why Face sent us here: to help the innocents, to help Insiders, and to battle anyone opposed to us, including a military unit that wasted our precious time.

A vision of stolen children from all over the world played in my mind. Saving them was impossible until we ditched the military.

"Chief," Ears said, getting my attention. "The general is barking. Repeating."

"What the hell do you mean, they disappeared?"

"General, the vehicles are in the river. No recovered bodies. We wasted time with the divers. No sign of them, sir."

"Let's get something straight, Lieutenant: you wasted time. I find it hard to believe they didn't leave a trail in or out of the water."

"Not a scrap of a trail, sir. Maybe they used their, uh, magic to disappear."

"Magic again! They are not Harry Potter. Insiders emit more heat. Use flyovers. Pick up those heat signatures. Use infrared, and they will stand out like bogies on radar. Find them and bring them to me. We're gonna have us a little pow-wow."

"A pow-wow?" I asked, questioning Ears' wording.

"Chief, you got it as I heard it."

Suddenly, a plan flashed in my head. We needed to move in a way that would camouflage our glow. To escape further from the city, we had to secure food supplies without the general's detection. I loved the new capabilities of my mind, but to be a good leader, I needed to understand everyone else's gifts too.

"Bat," I said. "Bat, wake up."

He sprang awake. "What? What's up?"

"You have anything that will bag the light we emit? Make us appear invisible on radar?"

Bat shook his head. "Sorry, Chief. The glow comes from Face. We will shine right through it. I'd be more worried more about the heat our glow produces."

"Chief," Healer whispered, "the youngest ones have weather capabilities. Would that help?"

"Maybe. What can the kids do?" I asked.

"Ice brings snow and freezing temperatures. Thunder brings lightning, thunder, and rain."

Motor stretched. "If I twiddle with the infrared signatures while Ice causes an instant freeze, we could blend with the rest of the town."

"Hmm," I said. "It would make for an easier getaway, but aircraft will be a long way up. Can you manipulate electronics from the ground?"

"I doubt it. That's where our new friend comes in, Chief."

Fly stood rested and eager to help. "Don't worry, Chief. I'm bigger and stronger than the general's ego."

Motor hopped on Fly's back. They flew a few feet to prove his point. I was confident with their abilities but worried about Ice's age. He opened his eyes during the conversation and listened.

"This is serious, Ice," I said. "We can't afford capture. Are you positive you can do this?"

"Chief, I never used a gift with anyone else before. It'll be fun." The boy yawned and rubbed his eyes as little kids do. "Besides, the Face gave us what we need."

"Ears?" I asked. "You in?"

"I'll get Fly and Motor off in plenty of time to intercept the planes. Ice, I'll let you know when, okay?"

"Make sure you tell me early," Ice instructed. "I'll put a chill on the area now, then hit it hard when the copters get closer." Ice sat cross-legged with his back against the wall. He closed his eyes but tilted his head upward toward the ceiling. The plan would work although sitting and waiting for them would be nerve-wracking.

Healer introduced me to the other captives. "Chief,

you met Ice," she said. "This is my older son, Thunder, who provides lightning and deafening thunder."

The boy stood and shook my hand. "Hello, sir. It's a pleasure to meet a living legend, Chief Poop."

"Thanks, Thunder." I guessed the video was still on YouTube. "Stand by, Thunder. If anything goes wrong, we may need some well-placed lightning bolts."

"Yes, sir." Thunder stretched out on the floor with his arms crossed behind his head. Healer took my arm, leading me to the Insider with the swollen and bruised face and thin, bolt-like structures that stuck out of his head.

"This is our leader. His nickname is Top Dog, but most people call him T.D. He can't speak much right now. Although tortured, he never gave in. He revealed nothing to the military, but tried to explain we were peaceful people."

"I guess they didn't believe him," I said.

"It made the general angrier," T.D. whispered. "He always wants something or someone to take his anger out on."

"T.D. could have transported elsewhere, but he wouldn't expose his gift; he refused to abandon us. He didn't want to lose us to insanity like the others."

He raised his head. "Violence is a waste of time."

"It's a privilege to know you, T.D. Don't worry—you will recuperate and have your team back." In my mind's eye I saw the Face's pleasure with T.D.—I knew he was extremely important. "Rest and heal before you do the work Face sent you to do. Getting you well is my main priority."

Healer held T.D.'s hand. "The rods in his head interfere with my healing. They need to come out."

She turned to the remaining victim, who was still lying on an old dusty cot. "Driller, I want you to meet, Chief."

The new guy held out his hand. "Sorry if I don't get up for you," Driller said. "I'm still a bit twisted and uncomfortable."

"Driller's been locked in a fetal position for weeks," Healer said. "An obvious attempt to stifle his gift."

"I presume the gift has something to do with drilling?"

"Straight down or through. I cut my teeth on rock and spit out pebbles," he said.

I chuckled. "How soon before you can work?"

Healer shook her head. "Chief, he's regenerating. He needs more time than us."

"We don't have much time. Remember, Face gives us what we need when we need it."

Healer started to say something, but Driller stopped her with a touch of his hand. "I'm weak, but I'll do what I can. We need to get T.D. out of here."

"Driller, we're trapped like feral cats here," I said. "But I have an idea. After we get some nourishment, we can go due west—straight under the river."

My team gasped, but Driller nodded. "If Healer works with me, I'll be ready."

"You put a lot of faith in me."

"You feel the Face. You can heal me, but I won't be fixed at the expense of Top Dog."

She smiled. "T.D. can spare a few minutes, I think."

Top Dog nodded in a daze.

Healer knelt and placed her hands on Driller, one on his back and one on his thigh. She hummed a low tone, mesmerizing the rest of us as Driller slipped into a deep trance. The two of them glowed; not like the light we Insiders emitted, but a radiant bloom of white light.

I glanced at Ears. "Well?"

"It's all right," he said. "Healer doesn't affect our abilities. I can still listen for aircraft, and extra heat from the healing can be covered by Ice."

Ice, confirming this, gave me a thumb-up.

"What a team," I said in amazement.

It took several minutes of Healer's intensive therapy, but Driller stretched and filled out like a long balloon. He became twice the size of the hunched ball we had rescued. In a few moments he stood. Then he walked, shaky at first, but soon moved with stronger steps. Healer stopped the hum.

"Ice?" I asked. "What's your report?"

The small boy sat cross-legged on the floor. He had closed his eyes and was rocking back and forth. He was working on something.

"I blanketed the area with snow, Chief," he said. "You might want to bundle up now." The cavernous factory grew cooler than before. Soon, it was downright cold, and my teeth chattered.

Lookout nudged Ears as he glared through the ceiling. "Yep, I hear them. Time for Motor and Fly."

"You know what to do, my friends," I said. "Good luck."

"Let me help you with a short cut." Picker walked them to the top of the stairs. He put his hands on Motor and Fly; they disappeared through the locked door. I worried that they would freeze despite the extra heat they generated.

Picker stayed outside and watched as Motor jumped on Fly's back. "It's freaking cold out here, Ears," he said, "but they've taken off. Tell Chief."

I paced the floor in anticipation while Ears and Lookout elbowed each other in between chuckles and snorts as the minutes played out.

"Whoa, that was too close!" Lookout hollered.

"Well, tell me about it," I said. "I can't see any of that—I can only hear you."

Lookout burst into laughter, pointing past the ceiling. It was out of view for the rest of us.

Ears guffawed, elbowing Lookout. "They're on the way back. Mission accomplished, Chief. Ha! I didn't know Motor could scream that loud."

I smiled to myself. *Let's hope no military picked up on that*.

No sooner had Picker returned than I ordered him into the cold again.

"Picker, use the shortcut to retrieve your eagles. And what's so funny?"

Picker saluted and went outside in time to see Motor and Fly land. He would parody their touchdown many times in the years to come, thoroughly enjoying messing with them.

"Motor, let go now. Um, Motor, get off me." Fly said gently at first before becoming more insistent. "Motor!"

"Chief, Motor looked around half-dazed, terror all over his face. He couldn't understand they were back on solid ground. I had to pry Motor's hands and fingers out of Fly's back."

"Cut it out, Picker. I couldn't help it. My fingers wouldn't unclamp. Besides, I would love to see your reaction when Fly hollered, 'Dive!' Man, it was cold up there, too. Froze my gonads."

"Hey, be fair," Fly said. "Motor's snoozing back there when this badass helicopter drops out of the clouds close enough to give us a haircut, well, give *me* a haircut."

"And Fly said, 'Hold on!', and next thing I know my stomach's somewhere over Atlanta while the rest of me—"

"Motor's clutching me so tight he had trouble using his hands to work his magic."

"I could have pissed my pants," Motor said.

"You could have?" Fly rubbed his back. "It feels damp back there to me."

Chapter 9

After Picker repeated the scene's antics for the third time, I waited for the laughter to settle down before I introduced Driller.

"If Driller's up to it," I said, "the plan is for him to slip us out of here under the general's nose."

"I'm almost there, Chief, but I need some fuel to get a big job done."

I nodded, mesmerized by Picker's story. But hunger pangs took hold of me as I realized Fly and Driller must have burned tremendous amounts of energy. Since we had no cash or credit, lifting was the only solution.

Although Fly and Motor disabled the heat-seeking devices in the air, I couldn't swear that there weren't vehicles on the street using the same technology. If we made one mistake, the police—or worse—would catch us. But without enough energy, my plan of tunneling under the Schukyll River would fail; the tunnel could claim us midway. I didn't relish the idea of being stuck underneath a river without the energy to continue.

"Fly, have any power left for a shopping trip?" I asked.

"Sure, that hour of regeneration gave me tons of energy. Shopping is easy, but money is a problem."

I gave him a bland look that I knew my family understood. "We'll borrow groceries. Picker and I will go with you. We need food and drinks for everyone—

nutritious, not junk. We stay invisible the moment we step out the door until we're back inside the factory. Ice, can you keep the snowstorm going?"

"For a while, Chief. It starts snowballing on itself and…"

When we laughed, the child in him showed through.

"Ha! I made a joke," he said. "I'll put out a colder freeze in our area until you get back from the store."

"Okay, gang. Peanut butter is high energy. Don't let me forget it, Fly. Get chocolate and jerky and bananas. Milk and juices—no soda. We're looking for energy food, not a party mix."

Minutes later we left, but I suggested the rest of the team rest again while we were gone. I envisioned a grueling jaunt under the river.

"Ready?" Fly asked.

Picker and I touched Fly's shoulders, disappearing into the snow. Invisibility did not feel any different from usual, except it was cool doing it.

"There's a quick store ahead," Picker said. "Chief, I smell hot dogs."

"Shh. Just because people can't see us, it doesn't mean they can't hear us," Fly whispered.

We peered through the glass door of an old 7-Eleven—now Omar's Quick Stop. A lone cashier sat behind the counter.

"I hope this door doesn't beep when we open it," I said. "Let's get through fast."

"Uh, Chief, we don't need to open it," Picker said.

Fly laughed. "I forgot, too. Double duty."

Fly kept us invisible as Picker led us through the door. While the cashier waited on a gas-purchase customer, Picker reached through the counter and took a package of plastic bags. We loaded up with essentials plus a few goodies; every time I put a necessity in the bag, Fly grabbed two more of it. And that was fine since he burned through calories like a furnace went through fuel.

We concentrated on sticking together by intertwining one of our arms. It wasn't easy, and I screwed up first—I slid open the cold storage door before Picker stopped me. It slid shut with a thud.

"Who's there?" The startled clerk looked up. He'd looked ready to relax until he heard the door close. He glanced up at the security mirrors, but the aisles appeared empty.

Picker reached through the glass and grabbed a couple of milk jugs. Carrying more was impossible, but he hooked a quart of chocolate milk with his pinky and pulled it through. I held my breath —the container slipped off Picker's finger, smashed to the floor, and splattered everywhere.

"Hey!" the clerk yelled. He knew something sneaky was going on and patrolled the aisle while brandishing a shotgun. He spotted the chocolate mess, complete with footprints that led to the front door. We hovered invisibly outside, our chocolate-colored shoes covered by newly fallen snow. The clerk opened the door but saw our tracks led to nowhere… they simply vanished.

"Damn kids," he muttered. Shivering, he retreated into the warmth of his store while we hurried to the abandoned factory and shared our harrowing story.

"The clerk passed four inches from us and didn't know we were there," Fly said. "That's when Picker grabbed the cookies."

"Poor guy. I hate to see his face when he discovers

the missing stock after he cleans up the mess we left him—the mess I left him, I mean. Sorry, Chief."

"No worries, Picker," I said. "Next time we need to do better—no slip-ups. If the general's soldiers canvass the area looking for anything out of the ordinary, the store clerk will sing like a bird. They'll know we were holed up here while they sent up search aircraft. We don't want any military to know our skills or how we beat their infrared."

Everyone nodded and murmured agreement.

"Chief?" Babe asked. "How do we fix the fact we're stealing again?"

"Yeah," Motor said. "I don't enjoy robbing a guy trying to make a living."

"Hey, Face didn't send us back with pockets full of money," I said somewhat defensively. "Truth is, we are on the run for our lives. Let's hope the good we do for Earth and humanity will be enough amends." I smiled at Driller. "Good peanut butter, huh?"

"Best I've ever tasted," mumbled a full-mouthed Driller, "once I wrestled a jar from Fly."

We ate like starved hyenas until Picker stood.

"Dessert!" he announced. "Anyone remember Oreos?"

Lookout answered with a *hick*. Ears followed with a *hichee*.

"Where did that come from, guys?" I asked.

"Face's food made us healthy… *hic*."

"This food doesn't… *hichee*."

"But it's delicious," Ears and Lookout answered together.

Even I couldn't pass up the sweets that complemented the last of the milk. Although it was against my no-junk-food order, I secretly wished for a second bag to go around. As we enjoyed the wonder that was an Oreo, I explained how Driller would tunnel under the river to provide a direct route—a shortcut—out of the city that the general could never conceive of. We would soon be on our way to freedom.

Punctuated with *hics* and *hichees*.

****

"Finally, Chief. I'm strong enough to tunnel out of the city by way of the river."

"Okay, Driller." I turned to the others. "Are you rested and ready to go?" Everyone nodded except Top Dog, who slept.

"Ice, the cold water should help mask our heat, don't you think?"

"Yes, Chief, but Driller might create a temperature beyond the normal Insider heat. I best intensify the cold until we are safe. They may have more heat-seeking devices by now."

"Good thinking, Ice. Lead the way, Driller."

"I'll start right here." In the far corner of the room, Driller spun with his hands outstretched. It appeared his feet, then his whole body, acted like a sharp drill bit. Within seconds he was gone, leaving a dark hole behind him. We Insiders were covered in dirt (Healer had the foresight to cover T.D. with her body protecting him from the wet muck).

"Yuck," Babe complained as the guys laughed.

On my knees, I inspected the rough-hewn tunnel. It looked too steep to walk.

"What do you think, Lookout?"

Lookout dropped to his stomach to get a better view. "This is going to be a thrill ride. We will travel by sitting

91

and sliding. It's not big enough for anything else."

Motor searched the storage room. "Use these cardboard boxes. We can sit on them as we slide down. There's enough here for a small army."

I nodded approval. "Lookout and Motor, light the way. Fly, can you make the ride easier for T. D. and Healer?"

"I'll hover a bit to make the ride smoother, but it's going to be a tight fit."

"I know you'll do your best.

"Ears, Ice and Thunder go with you. Picker, you are with Babe and me. Bat, go last to cover our backs. Remember, everyone, the ride might feel like a roller coaster, but silence is essential."

"Chief, I estimate a fifteen-second gap between takeoffs will prevent a pileup," Motor said.

"Thanks. Lookout, go on," I said. Everyone grabbed a few pieces of unfolded cardboard, lined up, and took off. The tunnel was cold, dirty, fast, bumpy, and dark. The heat came through despite several thick layers of cardboard under my bottom.

The ride lasted over a mile. Near the end, every single pebble and rock chip acted like pointy needles underneath me—the impulse to scream took concentration and fortitude to contain. Finally, everyone ended up on level ground deep beneath the earth, grateful to be alive. Driller took a bow as we recovered our nerves while wiping muck from each other's faces.

"Chief, we're on the other side of the river," he said. "If you want, I'll drill a few more miles due west to land us further from town."

"Do it. Walking through this muck will be slow going. By the time we emerge, it should be close to sunset. Fly, as Driller continues expanding the tunnel, I want you first in line to carry Healer and T.D. again. Get them through fast and stay with them, understand?"

"Sure, Chief."

"Send Driller back to us, too."

Healer jumped on Fly's back, crossing her legs around his waist. Fly cradled Top Dog in his arms and flew backward, which meant Healer took the brunt of the dirt instead of T.D. *Good thinking.* Top Dog didn't need an infection on top of everything else.

After the downhill slide, the walk was challenging. We trudged our way around, between, and over broken rock mixed with slippery mud. Lookout put his hand on my shoulder and pointed at Driller who was returning with hands on hips and a smile of satisfaction on his face.

"Good job, Driller," I said, "but we don't want the military to find the tunnel. They will know which direction we are headed. Could you protect our rear and collapse the tunnel from beginning to end?"

Driller looked at his masterpiece, looked at me, and back at the tunnel. He let out a big sigh.

"Sure 'nuff, Chief. I'll get on it."

We reached the end of the tunnel and stared at the opening above us. Fly landed in front of me with a huge smile.

"It's dark up top, Chief. I hid Top Dog and Healer in a small tool shed behind a chapel. There's no other way out except for me."

"Good thinking, Fly. Take Bat and Lookout first. We need sentries and protection."

"Okay, Chief."

I had to admit the kid had grown on me. With his cool superpowers, who could blame him for wanting to carry out decisions on his own? When Fly lifted me above, he looked at me expectantly.

"Well," he laughed. "How do you like Driller's joke?"

The top of the shaft emerged into a rectangular opening: an empty grave in an ancient cemetery. Metaphorically, we had risen from the dead.

"Hmm. I don't like it one bit," I said. "It's creepy."

"Yeah, it is—but perfect," Lookout said. "No one will come around here at night."

Fly pointed to Healer and T.D., who huddled inside the tool shed for warmth. Lookout scanned the area: in the opposite direction a trail wound through the trees. The dirt road would provide wooded cover on both sides if we needed to hide.

"Chief, T.D. needs a break from the cold," Healer said.

"The chapel is over there," Lookout said, and led us to the other end of the graveyard. "It should be warmer for all of us."

Picker opened the locked door. We all needed a brief, dry respite.

"This is where we begin our journey as Insiders," I announced. "T.D., you and your team will stay with us until you're recovered. Removing those rods is next on my list." The man looked weaker than ever.

"Chief?" Motor said. "Remember the papers I printed for you?"

I pulled them from inside my uniform. They told me all I needed to know about the prisoners we helped escape. "What's your birth name, T.D.?"

"Harold Doggett," Healer answered for him.

There it was.

Harold Doggett had volunteered to take part in the military's testing in exchange for his family's well-being. Harold's brain alarmed the military; he stored enormous amounts of unique energy not fathomed by scientists. They wanted to harness the power in his gray matter, and the experimental rods in his head served to capture his energy source and to track the workings of his brain. If the experimenters compromised Harold Doggett's health, they planned to move on to his comrades with more rigorous testing. Face had sent us back just in time.

"A skilled doctor will fix you," I said to T.D., believing Face had a physician waiting for us.

"Face lives inside you more than you realize, Chief," Healer replied. "Your faith could bring many to choose light over darkness."

"Thanks, Healer. Motor and Lookout, see what you can scavenge for vehicles." I looked around—Lookout was missing. I asked where he was.

"He's risking his life in a treetop surveying the area," Ice replied.

Fly stepped up again, but I could see how spent he was from his last cargo lift. "No, Fly. We need you rested and ready."

Babe seemed uncomfortable as she clutched her stomach.

"Babe, are you okay?"

"Uh, we ate Face's food for years. These processed foods are doing a number on me—"

She left out an enormous burp that gave everyone else the liberty to let it rip from attic to basement. For a few minutes, we were a bunch of kids again, laughing at how our escaping air had grown with our bodies.

"Yeah, ya better hit the latrines before we head out," I said, trying not to laugh. "Guess we'll always be human when it comes to that."

"Chief." Lookout returned from his treetop post. "Whew! What's that?" His face scrunched up as he waved the air away from his nose. "There's a junkyard a few miles away, not much of one, but with Motor's skills maybe we can scrounge up transportation."

"Awesome. Bat, go with them. But shield the chapel first, okay?"

"No problem, Chief."

"Yo, Bat, shield my nose while you're at it. Hellish gas, you guys," Lookout added as he followed Bat outside. "*Hic… hic.*"

"The rest of you, it's clean-up time," I said. "Get the mud off. See if this chapel has a lost and found for clothes and coats. I suggest we wear hats too. We'll head for warmer weather, but we don't need to look so, uh, bald."

Babe found a box labeled FOR THE NEEDY. Hey, we were needy. We used everything from blue jeans to winter coats, though everyone felt terrible about stealing again. We had been lame characters on a pathetic stage before the Face captured us. His hard work and routine, well, it gave us something, even before we received our gifts. We had become people with character—what everyone who chooses the way of the Face hoped to be. I made a mental note to replenish their stock one day if I ever had the chance.

"While we're waiting for transportation," I said, "let's rest and gather our thoughts."

"Chief," Ears said. "A truck's heading our way… without an engine… I hear only the tires on the roadway.

And another sound… heavier tires?" He nodded to himself. "Yep, I hear Lookout and Motor laughing at one of Picker's lame jokes. They'll be here soon."

"Thanks, Ears. Time to clean up." With no shower facilities, I used a small sink. Paper napkins took off the worst of the dirt. I appreciated Babe's thoughtfulness when she laid out clean clothes for me. Motor, Lookout, and Bat wandered in dirtier than ever.

"What do you have for us, boys?" I peeked outside. A snowplow and an old ambulance greeted me.

"An old stretcher is still inside. Top Dog can use it," Motor said.

"And why did you bring a snowplow?" I asked with skepticism.

"They were the only transport there, Chief," Bat said. "It could make a good weapon. Ever see *The A-Team*, the old TV show?"

"Okay… but won't it hold us back, Motor?"

"Nah, Chief. It's the fastest snowplow on Earth now."

"I liked driving it," Bat said.

"I guess we'll give it a go, then," I replied. "Wash up like the rest of us. Clean up behind you, too. We don't want anyone to know we were here. Stuff the dirty uniforms deep in the dumpster."

We rested for ten more minutes as the boys took care of their hygiene. Then I stood.

"Insiders, it's time for a road trip."

Chapter 10

The next part of our escape included vehicles. That excited me.

"I want to go with Bat, Chief."

"Oh. Go on, Babe, but pull the seatbelt tight." Something yanked at my guts when I saw Babe and Bat walk away together. I couldn't pinpoint what I was feeling at the time and kept my mouth in check. I closed my eyes, allowing faith in Face to ease my anguish.

"I'm driving!" Motor hollered.

"Shotgun!" Lookout yelled.

"Motor, I'll drive," I said. "You can't get these things to move *and* drive, especially if we have trouble."

"Right, Chief. But I get a turn to drive when we're done running."

Driller took me aside. "My team is out there somewhere, and I want to find them. I was caught by being stupid and a showoff, but after I watched you and your family, I realized what I need to do: it begins by finding what's left of my Insider family. You saved my life, Chief. I was close to breaking when you arrived. Thank you."

"You saved us too, so let's call it even." I smiled at Driller as we shook hands. I got behind the wheel and saw Driller in the rear-view mirror for a few seconds as he spun. Chuckling at my pun, I guessed he was going underground.

The driver's seat adjusted for my average height. Remembering how far the pedal was from my foot when I was a little kid, I managed to touch my big toe to the gas pedal and to the brake. Driving a real car couldn't be much different, I was happy that I could reach the pedals.

"Which way, Picker?"

"Well, pardner, that-a-way," he answered in a cowboy dialect. "Let's giddy-up West."

I led the small convoy, getting used to the feel of wheels beneath me. Each minor pothole shook the van which, in turn, jolted Top Dog's head. Healer sat by his side, transferring her healing energy. Motor kneeled while keeping track of vehicles that approached from behind. Thunder and Ice snoozed next to Fly, who dozed behind me. They were still kids; I wondered how old they were when they met the Face. I hoped to question T.D. about it when he was cured.

"We need to free Top Dog of these rods, Chief," Healer said urgently. "We must get them out soon."

"Fly, it's time to scout ahead. Find a map of this area and a southern map, too."

"Wait, Chief," Motor said. "I spent time with the computer while the sergeant slept. I talked to the machines at chip-level—I created my own SSH RSA key—and I can access the internet because I'm part of the grid now. Tell me what you need."

An RSA key was beyond me, but I told him we wanted a specialized neurosurgery hospital.

"Give me a few seconds," he said.

When I glanced at him in the rearview, Motor was half squinting with the whites of his eyes showing, as if he was staring at something inside his skull.

"Harrisburg, Chief," he said a few seconds later.

"The Center for Brain Injuries. The address is 63rd and Broad."

I listened to Motor's street-by-street directions and safely tucked them away in my enhanced brain. We headed to Harrisburg to find a surgeon capable of saving T.D., a trip that would take almost four hours.

Deciding on a less obvious route, I hoped I had chosen well. I checked the rear-view mirror, pleased at how the snowplow kept pace with us. We avoided traffic, staying alert for trouble. The crew did their best to relax and regenerate—everyone except Healer. She ministered to Top Dog the whole time.

With an hour left to drive, I signaled for the snowplow to pull over.

"Motor, turn off that streetlight, please."

"No problem, Chief."

Moments later, we melted into the pre-dawn darkness.

"Ice, we need a temperature drop again. Make it snow as we enter the city; make a lot of it, so the snowplow doesn't look out of place."

"Got you, Chief."

"Ears, listen in on the military and the police bands."

Ears laughed. "I didn't know my talent was this far-reaching. If you need information bouncing off a satellite, I hear it too."

Healer smiled with approval. She knew T.D. was in the right hands.

"Good job, everyone," I said.

Ears cocked his head, looking pleased. "The general didn't get much sleep last night, and the pilots still suffer his wrath for not locating us. Thanks to Ice's blizzard, bloodhounds and humans couldn't track us."

"Awesome. I wondered how my weather gift would come in handy," Ice said.

"You bought us time, Ice. We needed you, and you came through. Good job."

Driving allowed me time to think about our complicated entry to the outside. Insiders bonded fast with other Insiders; our family grew, not by blood, but by something more profound and pure because our love for each other came from the Face.

I would die for my family and, without a doubt, for any Insider.

"Healer, how's T.D. doing?" I asked.

"He's taking in my curative glow, but not enough to heal. I'm afraid if I weren't here—"

"Don't say it. We are in Harrisburg now—keep nursing him. Make sure you stay by his side, even while they operate on him. We'll find a way."

"Thank you."

"Motor, get on that grid," I said. "Find T.D. the best neurosurgeon here."

"Let's see... Dr. Richard Mass is the chief neurosurgeon of the hospital. Wow, he's advertised as the top in the country."

"Can you hack the department computer and set up an appointment, say, within an hour?"

Motor closed his eyes for a moment. "Done."

"Oh, and shouldn't we need fuel by now? The fuel gauge doesn't work. The snowplow has a smaller tank than ours, doesn't it?"

"Chief, they're empty."

Twisting around, I saw Motor glowing like a work light. The electricity came from Motor and turned the wheels, but how did he get power to the plow? Pondering that, I turned off the highway with the hospital in sight.

"Motor, find a secluded spot to park this thing, along with the plow. Keep in mind that we may have to escape in an instant. Healer and I will go inside with T.D. Ice, keep the cold coming, please." I yawned long, hard, and loud, unusual for me. "Everyone else stays with the group. If trouble heads our way, send Fly to tell us."

"Chief, we'll communicate easier if I come with you," Ears said. "I'll hear of any trouble. We can't let hospital personnel see a flying man or you talking to someone invisible. Plus, you need to regenerate like the rest of us."

Ears was right. Face gave me wisdom but not perfection; I'd driven the long trip instead of dozing and was beginning to feel groggy.

"Good thinking, Ears. Babe will influence the personnel. When they see our patient and this ambulance, they will ask questions. We must contain them." I tried to concentrate. "Healer, play Top Dog's wife. I will be his brother. Babe will be… I need to think about that one." Healer smiled and winked at me, but Ears was concerned.

"Babe will be anyone she wants, Chief," he said. "The hospital will let her in, no problem."

The others stared at me, questioning my words. They had never seen me anywhere but at the top of my game.

"You're right. Let's get T.D. taken care of before I rest, okay?"

Everyone approved as we piled back into our vehicles.

I fishtailed the old ambulance up the snowy hill to the emergency room portico. The sight of our dented, aching vehicle raised eyebrows with the hospital staff.

"Long story," I said. "We need help."

As a medic pulled the gurney out of the ambulance, T.D.'s appearance stunned him and the triage team. An intern rubbed the sleep from his eyes, unable to believe what he saw.

"We're here to see Doctor Mass," I added. "We have an appointment."

"Richard Mass? It will take someone like him to untangle this—and he's in the building. Nurse, prep this man for OR-1."

He then spoke into a handheld Motorola device demanding Dr. Mass be found. He'd barely finished when a voice boomed behind us. The man's name tag read MASS.

"What's going on here?"

Babe spoke up. "He's been abused in an experiment, Doctor."

Dr. Mass stood over T.D. inspecting but not touching the rods. "Who did it? This looks like a criminal matter."

"Look at me," Babe said with authority. "This is a military secret you, and your team, will keep forever. You will not discuss it with anyone or with each other. Your priority is to save this man and repair the damage to his brain. It is your primary concern. His wife, standing right there, will always remain with him. Do you understand?"

The doctor blinked. The other personnel nodded dazedly. "Okay, right." The surgeon shook his head, focusing on the job at hand, and moved to action.

"Nurse, start an IV," Mass said. "With these metallic objects in his head, a cat scan is out of the question. We will probe with an ultrasound. I hope it produces a decent view."

"Do not worry about me, Doctor," Healer said. "I'll keep up with you, but I must be close to him every step of the way."

"Scrub up if you think you can stomach brain surgery, ma'am, but stay out of my way."

Healer nodded. All that mattered was Top Dog's health. Babe followed the doctor to influence the operating team—they were all on board with our agenda. I found the waiting room and sat with my feet in another chair, too wound up to sleep until Babe returned.

She put her face right up to mine. "Chief, rest now."

I gazed into her beautiful blue eyes, realizing I wanted to see Babe's face close to mine day after day.

Chapter 11

The general looked terrified as Insiders chased him through a network of caves. Determined to send the stubborn oaf to the Face, I finally cornered him until a coffee aroma hit my nostrils. Why would the general pat my hand?

Babe's gentle voice registered as I opened my eyes. "Chief, wake up."

Daylight streamed through blinds as I struggled to open my eyes.

"There you are. Were you dreaming?"

"Babe, yes—a good dream too. How long was I out?"

"At least eight hours. Good news: Harry came through the operation. The doctor wants to talk to us about him."

The waiting area I had slept in was filled with strangers. People milled up and down the hospital corridors. Babe read my scrunched-up forehead.

"I have it contained," she said. "Don't worry."

I sipped coffee that Babe sweetened with cream and sugar.

"Mr. Healer?"

"Dr. Mass. How's my brother, Doc?" I asked, feeling fully awake.

"He's alive, no thanks to whoever experimented on him. We removed the electrodes and rods from his head.

The rods were more like acupuncture needles—very fine, thank goodness. My colleagues and I surmise that someone wanted to transfer energy to or from his head. If you look at the ultrasound images, you'll see how meticulously placed those probes were."

"Go on."

"Some mad genius implanted the rods. Yet little damage was done, considering how deeply the probes went. I want to MRI his brain before it heals too much, mapping out the target points for a JAMA medical paper. No one will believe me if I don't document it."

Babe stepped forward. "You don't want to share this experience with anyone, doctor. Keep this to yourself. Use the knowledge you learned from the operation to do good for someone else, but you won't publicize it. All right, Doc?"

"Yes, you're right," Mass said. "Humankind could benefit from the knowledge I extracted. Harry will recover, and perhaps the after-effects will be minimal."

"How optimistic are you?" I asked.

"We kept him conscious and talking during surgery. The brain does not feel any pain—none. His wife stuck by his side every second, and he spoke to her after I removed the rods." The doctor looked bemused. "Mrs. Healer is a talented nurse, but she kept repeating, 'Take my light, take my light.' That was her mantra for the eight hours we worked on him. She is still with him in ICU. Check with the nurse's station, but you're welcome to join her for a few minutes."

"How soon before he can leave, Doc?" I asked.

Dr. Mass snapped out of his Babe-induced trance. "Go? Are you *serious*? He had six holes drilled through his skull that remain open. He requires supervision and a sterile environment. Infection is our biggest enemy now. Also, as optimistic as I am, we do not know if all his mental faculties are intact. We'll have to test in a few days."

Babe waved her hands. "Doctor, look at me. We need T.D. ready to go in a matter of *hours*. Mrs. Healer will nurse him. Send antibiotics and supplies with us. Our people will take up where you left off. You did excellent work, Doctor—no one could surpass your skills. But remember, you and no one from your team will recall we were here. Do you agree, Doctor?"

"Uh… I don't recall who was here," Mass said. I watched him wrestle with mental confusion as he ordered supplies at the nurses' desk before detouring to the men's room. Some color in my face had returned. The sleep helped, but I worried that my regeneration left my team vulnerable.

"We'll hope for an easy exit," I said to myself as Babe, Ears, and I rode the elevator to ICU.

Babe convinced the head nurse to allow us inside. As we huddled around him, Top Dog opened his eyes and smiled.

"How ya feelin', T.D.?" I asked.

"I'm going to live," he said under the influence of a sedative. "It's good to be free, Chief. But I hope my gift is still intact."

"Give it time," Healer whispered. "Gift or no gift, you're one of us. I'm not going anywhere without you."

I admired Healer's affection toward T.D., fondness that went beyond loyalty.

"Listen, we're leaving soon," I said. "Ice gave us snow cover, but when the general figures out what we have done, he will follow storms that pop up making

Ice's camouflage useless. He may have figured it out and be on his way."

"I doubt it," T. D. whispered. "I know him. When he craves something, he loses perspective, sniffing down the same rat hole a hundred times. The general repeats the same actions and gets the same results—nothing. He must be related to someone vital in the organization, or he'd be dismissed by now." T.D.'s eyes began to close, but I needed to know more.

"Dogget, how do you know about him?" I asked.

"I was a military man: second battalion, first infantry, lightning brigade. A suicide bomber ran a checkpoint and headed toward our field hospital. I gunned my Humvee to intercept him and forced him off the road just before he hit the building. That's all I remember. When I woke up, Face had taken us. Anyway, the general had made the security decisions, then was awarded Insider duty." T.D.'s eyes closed again.

"Healer?" I asked.

"The boys and I waited for transport outside the hospital; we all suffered severe injuries from the blast. I suppose you guessed that I *am* his wife, Chief." She smiled. "We ran off from our foster parents—married at seventeen. Harry joined the military to put food on the table. I took nurse training. We both ended up in Iraq. Together, at least.

"On our second tour, we rescued Ice, Thunder, and helped half a dozen other children from the streets of Fallujah who were helping inside the hospital that day. Terrorists could have wiped out an entire wing if not for Harry's courage. Face saved us so we could train as Insiders."

"Wow," I said quietly, reverently.

"The army evacuated our family to Germany. Apparently, when it appeared we were in a permanent coma, they flew us to the U.S. We evolved with the Face and woke up here. We trusted the military more than you did, a mistake we will never make again. I had faith that Face would send someone that could release us."

"Wow, what a story. What about Peter? Was he a part of your family?" I asked.

"No. Fly's group tried to rescue us, but the general caught most of them. I know one died; immortality is not one of our gifts. Then, the rest lost faith. Only Fly remained loyal to Face. In their defense, they suffered horrendous torture, but instead of calling on Face for help, they gave information about their experiences with him. Once that happened, their gifts ended, leaving them no means of escape."

"That's sad," I said.

"Even sadder, the general refused to believe they were powerless," Healer said. "He kept torturing them to make them expose powers they no longer had. They turned on each other but also turned away from Face. Anger and hate fill their hearts now."

Face's words resounded in my head: *"Use your power with wisdom, and never stop fearing me."*

I felt sorry for the Insiders who feared punishment from the general more than they feared Face. They made a horrific choice. I hoped Face would help in his own time, uniquely and just for them. One thing for sure, I would never surrender my loyalty to him as they had.

At least I hoped I wouldn't.

"Healer, time to move. This building and the city won't be safe for us much longer. Can you treat him on the road?"

"Yes, but we'll need nourishment, water, clean bandages, sheets, and enough IV's for a good week or two."

"Babe has the doctor ordering supplies. But let's store up on antibiotics while we are here, not merely for Harry, but enough for anyone who ends up in our crossfire."

"Babe can handle that, too. Right, Babe?"

"No problem, Chief."

"Ears, what is it?"

"The general called off the Philadelphia search when a citizen found our dirty jumpsuits at the chapel. The minister called the police, thinking escaped convicts raided their church. Of course, the military picked up their call. Now the general's crew will concentrate an effort in a northwesterly direction from the chapel.

"They're working on the theory that the missing ambulance and snowplow must be headed to where the heavy snows are."

I didn't double-check the church, and we'd left careless clues. But I couldn't keep second-guessing myself and everyone else. The plow had thrown them off course, but its job was done.

"Ears," I whispered, "tell Motor to find roomier transportation after he ditches the plow somewhere undiscoverable. We'll head south, taking a scenic route that won't be congested this time of year. Babe, meet us outside with supplies. Have the desk call Dr. Mass to ICU. We need his help moving our patient." I thought for a moment. "Ears, tell Bat to bring around the ambulance in ten minutes, please."

"Chief," T.D. said through closed eyes. "We have more time than you think. The general will sweep through Alaska before he admits falling for the snowplow bait."

"I believe you, T.D., but having soldiers riding my tail makes me uncomfortable no matter how clueless and far off he is."

Dr. Mass entered the room, chewing a half-eaten sandwich. He still had not slept. "I had to check on my patient once more."

I explained that we needed the hospital's attendants to push the patient outside and into our ambulance to avoid calling attention to civilians pushing a gurney. Babe reinforced my wishes. The surgeon looked at Babe, who smiled at him and nodded her head. He seemed happy to help and sent a nurse to meet us with supplies at the loading bay at the back of the hospital.

Babe reinforced his order by influencing the confused nurse. A cooler full of IV fluids and antibiotics had been loaded in the ambulance that Bat parked, waiting for us. Motor packed additional supplies inside a drab hearse that he had commandeered. I laughed, thinking of an old TV show.

"How gothic, guys. What are we, the Addams family?"

"The Munsters," Motor said, humming the theme song for us. "They drove cooler cars."

Attendants loaded T.D. with the more modern, comfortable gurney Babe requested. Motor jumped in the ambulance after damaging the hospital's security hard drive, making the video of us loading T.D. impossible to view.

Picker waited in the driver's seat. Bat settled behind the wheel of the hearse, waiting for Babe to join him. I got that twisting feeling in my gut again as she slid in next to him until Healer placed her hand on my arm.

"She needs to go with him, Chief."

But I need her with me. I shook off the thought as I climbed in to ride shotgun.

"Okay, Picker, we're headed south," I said.

"I do declare, Chief, I'm in a quandary about direction," Picker said in a smooth southern drawl.

Lookout pointed the way to the nearest southbound state road. The ambulance and hearse, a contradictory pair of vehicles, traveled toward warmer weather and a mystery destination.

Picker stuck to the speed limit, avoiding maneuvers that might call attention to us, as stolen plates would not help the situation if we were caught. Our most significant risks were troopers too willing to assist an ambulance or a hearse. I glanced around to see Healer nodding off while holding her husband's hand. She deserved the rest.

Everyone snoozed except Motor and Picker. They would require downtime as soon as we arrived at our destination, although I had no clue where that was except to head south. I closed my eyes while listening to the tires on the road. A question ran through my mind.

How would we survive in a world that required money?

Chapter 12

"Heads up, everyone. Time to wake up," Healer said sometime later. "Were almost through West Virginia and T.D. needs a break. Even the new gurney can't protect him from the ambulance's bad shocks."

"West Virginia? That's Driller's home state," I said. "I was hoping we'd be further south."

Due to construction, Picker pulled off the state road following a sign that said BLUEFIELD. The country road wound its way around snow-sprinkled hills. As city kids, we never saw the beauty of our country beyond tv or movies. Everyone marveled at majestic mountains and valleys. Cows, goats, horses, and a few silly donkeys entertained us, too.

"Yo, Picker, there's a store up ahead," Lookout said.

"I'm hungry, too, Chief," Picker said.

"Yeah, everybody could use food. Pull in there, but only for a short visit."

Picker pulled up to an old-time general store that looked like a log cabin on the outside. A sign read TRUCKER FACILITIES.

"Better park in the back," I suggested. The rear of the store opened into an expanse that contained at least ten eighteen-wheelers. We parked by the woodsy area, and everyone stretched their legs except for T.D. Surprisingly, he sat up on the gurney. Color had returned to his cheeks. He glanced at me and grinned.

"By the next stop I'll be strong enough to walk, Chief. For now, I'll breathe this sweet mountain air."

The general store seemed to be a favorite stop for truckers to rest and freshen up. Motor perked up after a shower, but he required even more time to regenerate. Nobody else had Motor's skill set—our transportation relied on him. I went inside and searched for the restroom but got caught up staring at aisles of nonsense gifts with trucker themes. Repair items for trucks and cars were plentiful, too. Above the cash register, a sign said LOTTERY.

"We need money, Motor," I said. "Can you manipulate the machine to make us win a few hundred dollars? We need something small enough to pay out here, but big enough to help us buy meals."

"No problem—if we find the money to buy a ticket. All we need is one buck."

I remembered how I found money as a kid. "Where's the vending machine?"

"By the entrance, Chief."

Four machines stood there. We checked the coin return for quarters. On the fourth machine, a handwritten note on it read OUT OF ORDER. Penciled under it, someone had written STEALS YOUR MONEY.

In *Star Trek* shows, Vulcans splayed their fingers against a person's skull for a "mind meld." Motor mimicked Spock as he leaned forward, eyes closed, his hand trembling against the side of the machine.

"It's jammed," he whispered. "I can fix it. It could be loaded with coins from those who lost their money, too." He frowned before his face began to glow. A moment later, the machine clunked and rattled. Cans of Coke and orange soda dropped into the dispenser as money clinked into the coin-return faster than I could scoop it out. Bingo!

"What's your biggest scratch-off payout?" I asked the cashier.

"Scratch-the-itch pays a few hundred, and others pay much more."

I exchanged four quarters for a small-payout ticket that Motor placed between his palms. It began to glow minimally.

"Oh, Chief! May I scratch off the squares?" Babe sounded like a kid at Christmas with the same wide-eyed wonder.

I smiled and nodded. From the end of the counter, we watched her reveal our numbers.

"We just won three hundred seventy-five dollars," Babe whispered. Suddenly she looked worried, but Motor intervened.

"I figure it's okay, Babe. The state cons poor people into turning over their hard-earned money to the stupid lottery. Knowing the odds, that is dishonest. This evens the score a little."

"Let's cash it in with as little fanfare as possible," I said.

Babe convinced the excited clerk to keep the news to herself. That afternoon, we celebrated with a tailgate party, imbibing juice, and colas, and munching hotdogs, nachos, and Twinkies. We soon heard the familiar *hic* and *hichee*.

"Motor, when you're finished eating, get some sleep in the hearse."

"Yeah, and rest in peace," Picker joked. "I don't want to hear any coughin'. Get it?"

All of us moaned.

"Okay, gang, from now on, we travel at night. We buy our food and drink then." I paused. "It's been my job to pull us together and guide us. Other than head in a southern direction, Face hasn't given me AAA directions to our destination."

Healer sighed. "We're in a difficult position, Chief. Face will fix any of our inadvertent wrongs until we get better at what we do."

"You'll know when you know. Give yourself a break," T.D. said, his voice much stronger. "The life of an Insider is not easy unless Face told you otherwise."

"You're right—he didn't."

Healer smiled. "I know what it's like to miss him. Practice feeling the Face yourself; it will come in time."

I nodded, hoping she was correct. I wanted to do much more than just escape.

Ice and Thunder seemed suddenly frustrated with adult conversation and jumped out of the ambulance.

"Whoa!" Healer said. "Where do you think you're going?"

"We're kids, Mom," Thunder said. "We want to play."

Healer checked with me first—I nodded my approval. She pointed at the woods behind our vehicles where no strangers could notice them.

"Go and explore, but don't go too far—we'll be leaving soon," she said. "Besides, critters live there. Be careful."

Thunder laughed. "If anyone comes after me, I'll hit them with a bolt."

"Yeah, I'll ice them for fun," Ice said as he sprinted away.

"Promise me you'll be careful, boys," Healer

hollered after them.

"We promise," the boys yelled before disappearing into a grove of pines.

Healer gazed at Bat beseechingly. He probably thought she acted overly protective, but he ambled toward the woods to keep an eye on them. The worried mom sighed with relief, knowing her boys would be safe.

Listening to their voices echoing in the woods and motivated by an urge to check out the scenery, I caught up with Bat's well-trodden trail.

"Chief, smell this air. It's so… sweet."

"Yeah, it's a cool forest even in winter, with the pine trees mixed in with the hardwoods. What a great place for the boys to play."

What a pair: Small Ice with his Bedouin desert complexion and Thunder, gangly, with almost prince-like features. I imagined them hewing at Face's walls, building muscles and healthy bodies as my gang had. Their chests stretched their t-shirts, and more growth would come. I wondered what their stories were. In the mess of Iraq, I did not know if they were orphans or abandoned.

The boys ran from stump to tree picking up rocks, sticks, and throwing them for fun, hoping to flush out any wild critters. Bat and I kept far enough behind to let them think they were alone so they could burn off the extra energy.

"Whoa! Wait, my brother!" Thunder yelled. "Check this out."

Ahead was a thick vine that wrapped around a high branch of tree before hanging down almost to the ground. Ice ran ahead and climbed the rope-like plant like a young Tarzan. Thunder grabbed the bottom of the vine and hollered, "Hold on!" Taking a few backward steps, pulling the vine taut, then running forward, Thunder lifted his feet off the ground. The vine carried both boys back and forth.

"Swing it harder and faster," Ice said. "I see a drop-off from up here. Let's swing over it."

Thunder tied a knot at the bottom of the vine pulling it far back. He took off with more speed, lifting his feet at the last moment while standing on the knot. Like an acrobat, he controlled the pull and push of the vine until the swing became wide and high.

We enjoyed watching them for a few minutes, knowing we would have done the same thing at their ages. Bat and I were reminiscing about the night at Point Park when a horrible snap pierced the air. We looked up just in time to see what happened—the high branch cracked and broke off. Bat zigzagged like a linebacker, pushing hands outward to bag Ice as he plummeted to the ground. He threw a second bag as Thunder flew over the edge of a precipice, still holding on to a piece of the vine. Bat and I sprinted to the ledge where we saw Thunder floating face down in the rapids below.

"There's no bag!" Bat screamed. "Oh, man, I must have missed. Oh, no—not a kid!"

"Ears, Healer: Emergency!" I said, standing completely still. "Send Fly and *hurry*. Send Fly!"

Bat dissipated Ice's bag and held him as Ice cried in terror. "It's my fault. It's all my fault."

Fly landed next to me with Healer and Ears, their eyes searching mine.

"Thunder fell over the cliff into the rapids," I said. "Find him, Fly."

He dove over the ledge before I finished my

sentence. We watched him flying a foot above the water but lost him as he rounded a bend.

Healer stared at the water, shaking her head at the height of the drop. Ice fell to his knees when he saw the depth of the ravine. Healer pulled him away and bear-hugged him.

"It will be alright, Ice," she said. "It will be alright."

"Healer, take Ice back to the car. Tell the others what happened. We're going after Thunder."

She nodded, holding Ice close as they hurried to exit the painful scene. Bat, Ears, and I followed the river's flow from above when Bat began apologizing.

"I missed him. I tried to bag him, but I missed." His words came out in a rush. "I'm sorry, Chief. Healer asked me to watch over the kids. I failed, man. I failed."

"Bat, we aren't human anymore, but we're not Face, either. We are in between and still new at this. Do not blame yourself, no matter what Fly finds—because I sure don't."

Bat plowed down the brown foliage and vines on top of the ridge like a bush hog, making it easier for us to follow. We paced ourselves, jogging as fast as the terrain would allow and stopping only seconds to peer over the cliff for Fly and Thunder. Once past the second bend, we stopped to catch our breath.

"Guys, I hear someone around the next curve, I think," Ears said. "The noise of the water makes hearing more difficult."

We took off, renewed. Following the ridge around, we hoped for good news.

Instead, we stood gaping in horror at the riverbank below us.

Chapter 13

Two campers performed CPR on Thunder, who had not responded. One of the campers pulled out a flip phone. Ears relayed the conversation:

"… on the trail by station thirty-four. We can't climb back up because it's too steep. He's a youngun' but tall, and my son and I ain't spring chickens. Yeah, we can set him on a gurney for ya. My son's still working on him, but he ain't come to yet. The kid's beaten up pretty bad. Yes, of course, we'll keep tryin' with the CPR."

Fly appeared next to us. "Chief, I'll carry him up to the rescue vehicle, but Babe isn't here to influence them to forget."

"Thunder's welfare comes first, Fly. Carry him up with the man who's trying to resuscitate him.

In shock over the whole situation, I was utterly dumbfounded as to what to do next. We inched closer to the conversation. As the two men concentrated on their CPR attempts, Fly appeared behind them on the trail.

"What in tarnation?" the old man asked. "Where'd you come from?"

"Don't stop working on him—he's my friend. He fell from a ridge into the water. I've been trying to find him."

"Yer lucky we was here." The old man spat out tobacco. "Hospital is a scant five mile away. Rescue won't take more than minutes to get here, but it'll take forever to get him over this here ridge. Dang, I can't figure how we're gonna do it."

"I'll take him up there," Fly said.

"Well, son, that's something I'd like to see." The old man spit again. "It's a vertical climb, as you can see."

"Mister, you're going to see me do something you can't tell anybody about. Do you understand? Please don't tell anyone." Fly scooped Thunder into his arms. "Get on my back," he said to the man's son. "Continue CPR at the top."

The son, graying at the temples and soaked to the skin from the rescue, backed away, appalled at Bat's request. "Get on what?"

Fly demonstrated, lifting a few feet off the ground. The son turned white, and the old man looked faint.

"It's hard to believe, but you saw me," Fly said. "Hold on to my back, my shoulders. There is no time to waste. Let's save this boy's life."

The son listened. Fly took off on a quick ascent to the roadway above. He laid Thunder on the ground. "Now… please start CPR."

"Whatever you say." The graying man squinted, making sure Fly was on solid ground.

"There's no reason to be afraid."

"Yeah, right." He pumped Thunder's chest before giving mouth-to-mouth.

Fly returned to the old man, who still looked dazed. "Sir, I'm going to carry you up to the ridge, okay? Your son's waiting for you."

Before the elderly man could protest, Fly scooped him up as the old soul fainted in his arms. Fly set him down at the roadside where he came to, jumping up faster than a man his age should.

"Dang!" he exclaimed, almost fainting again.

"Thunder, breathe… breathe. Please breathe," Fly begged. "We need Healer," he said for Ears' benefit. We saw how damaged Thunder's Face was—his hair matted with blood from head wounds.

"You're my family, Thunder," Fly said plaintively. "Please stay with us, man… please."

All of us stood there, mannequins in hiding, tears escaping despite our bravado. The rescue siren sounded as it rounded the curve, giving us hope.

"Remember, Thunder, we'll come back for you," I said. "We will come and get you. Do you understand—we'll return."

Fly nodded and disappeared before rescue personnel parked and took over CPR.

"Okay, he's breathing," one of them said. "But barely."

As they slid Thunder into the rescue vehicle, their somber faces sent chills down my spine. One man continued bagging Thunder when they closed the door. I left the cover of my tree and ran up to the driver and his colleague.

"Miracles happen every day," I said, tears streaming down my face. "Please, treat him as if he was your little brother. Make him live."

"We'll do our best, we promise."

As they drove away, Fly retrieved me under the safety of invisibility.

"Did ya see that, son?" I heard the old man say below. "Two more disappeared."

A sheriff's jeep arrived as the paramedics sped away. We watched as the old man and son tried to explain the events. They pointed to Fly, but deputies saw no one. Fly stayed hidden, conflicted whether to follow the rescue squad or return to our vehicles.

"You good ol' boys ever take a breathalyzer?" I heard the deputy ask. "I reckon you saved a boy's life, but you got maybe a still down there or you're smokin' weed?"

It might have been funny if we weren't worried about Thunder. They prepared to administer a breathalyzer while the pair complained.

"You don't know what we just saw, what we experienced. Right, son?"

"Right, Pop."

I worried that if the general picked up this story, he would pinpoint our location.

"Is he going to live?" Bat asked with a shaky voice.

"I don't know—it doesn't look good. If we hurry Healer to him, maybe."

"The man said the hospital was about five miles that way," Fly said.

"Then let's get back to our cars. Fly, take Ears back. Tell Motor to map the way to the hospital."

Fly and Ears took off. Bat and I jogged out of the woods, where everyone waited for us in shock. Picker wiped his eyes, and Ice was still crying and blaming himself for wanting them to swing from the rope. T.D. pulled him tight against his chest, and Healer comforted him, too.

"It's no one's fault," she said. "Accidents happen. They are a part of living in this world. We will feel Thunder in our hearts to give him strength. We don't have time to take on blame that is not ours."

Healer turned her compassionate eyes to search

Bat's helpless face. He remained silent and stooped over, his head hung in shame.

"Fly, carry Healer and Babe ahead of us," I said. "Babe, same routine as before. We'll get there as fast as we can."

"Chief, I'm ready to go," Motor said, already at the wheel of the ambulance.

"Lookout, Ears, help us travel," I said, as we took off. Lookout rode shotgun, peering through the trees, past mountains, and pointing the way.

"Chief," Ears said, his fingertips to his temples. "The police are joking about a flying boy over the radio. The general may learn we're here. That means more trouble."

"Thanks, Ears. Keep me posted for repercussions."

The curves and hills made the trip longer than we hoped. Relieved at our arrival, Lookout and Ears jumped out of the van to find our friend.

"Bat, stay behind and make sure we don't get trapped. Motor, we were never here."

I squatted on my haunches to consult with Ice, who was wrapped in Top Dog's arms.

"If they know your brother is hospitalized here, snow will not do any good to cover our tracks. Have any ideas?"

"Cold is what I do. I am thinking ice... ice on the hospital parking lot will slow the bad guys down if they do come after us. If they fly in, maybe a blizzard over the hospital?"

"Good thinking. It is more tactical this time. Stay here, keep watch. If you see the general, make sure there is a patch of ice with his name on it... real slippery ice. Okay, buddy?"

"Yes, sir!" Ice saluted.

"Picker, you'll come with me." I hoped Picker's spirit would rebound inside the hospital. "But first—" I turned to T. D., "—take it easy. He's your boy, but we've got this covered."

T.D. nodded tensely. Although I saw his mind racing, I didn't have time to question his thoughts. I wanted to save Thunder.

He was my responsibility.

The first two medical centers dwarfed the mountain hospital before us. Walking inside without being spotted would be tricky. I peeked through the revolving door and saw the attendant on the phone. I sent Ears and Lookout ahead to search as I walked to the welcome desk.

"Yep, deputy brought them in to check him over. Feller claimed he saw a flying boy," the attendant was saying, an older, mustached man. "The strange thing is, his son saw one, too. They must have been sippin' on the same moonshine, hee, hee."

"Ahem."

The man glanced up at me. "Gotta go." He ended his call. "Can I help you, young man?"

"Yes, sir, rescue brought a boy in earlier this evening, maybe an hour ago. He almost drowned, beat up bad."

"Are you family?"

"Yes, he's my little brother." Those words rang true in my heart.

The man peered at a ledger. "Name?"

"Well, they couldn't know his name when they brought him in," I said, thinking fast, "because we weren't with him when the ambulance picked him up."

"Ah, John Doe. They're still working on him. He will be moved to intensive care when finished, but you can't go in there. It's after hours."

"Sir, if he were your brother or son, would you let someone turn you away?" I asked.

The attendant sat back in his chair and looked me square in the eyes. "That's a good question." He looked down at the floor before he spoke again. "This is a small facility, but busy at times. Since it's quiet right now, I can take a break. I suppose I'll walk back toward intensive care. I couldn't stop someone following me—that person would wait in the anteroom until the boy comes out of surgery."

My heart soared.

"That person might have a long delay, because the boy is banged up bad from what I hear. That person must be quiet. Nurses don't want anything loud around here."

"Thank you so much, sir," I said, grateful for the man's soft heart.

"My pleasure, son."

Picker and I followed as the attendant regaled us with the story of the flying boy, a lad who carried two grown men up to a fifty-foot ridge. He got quiet as we neared the ICU and put his finger to his lips as he peeked through the small window.

"This is it. Remember, it is a quiet place. You can pray for your family here." He patted me on the back and left. We found Ears and Lookout pacing the floor.

"Any news?" I asked.

"Healer's in the operating room working as a nurse," Lookout said. "Babe just moved outside the door, ready to influence the doctors and staff."

Ears shook his head. "Thunder might die, Chief. He

is screwed up from top to bottom. They're worried about brain swelling. He has a punctured lung, a lacerated liver, and a busted spleen. I don't remember how many of his bones are broken or which ones they are. This is really upsetting."

"Healer's sharing her light—she's the reason he's still alive," he added. "But he's coded twice."

I could only nod. My thoughts had dissipated into nothingness. Nervously, we sat and picked through worn and tattered magazines. We waited more than four hours before they wheeled Thunder from the operating room. Healer nodded to me as she stayed beside the gurney in her scrubs. Once she situated Thunder in ICU, she contacted Ears, saying it was all right for us to visit… and warned about Thunder's appearance.

We peered through the ICU window before opening the door. Tubes, wires, and an IV connected Thunder to life. A machine breathed for him. We moved to his bedside, staring at the gauze turban wrapped around his face, leaving openings only for his nose and mouth.

Thunder looked unrecognizable: a cast covered two arms. Splints braced both legs, one traveling up to his hip. Healer explained that pieces of his skull were removed to give his brain room to swell. My heart ached for the boy.

"Hang on, my young friend," I said, thinking back over our brief time together. Thunder had been all eyes and wonder. He didn't say much or step out of line. Remorse weighed heavily on me; I should have taken the time to get to know him better.

Silently, I asked Face for another chance.

Healer rested her hand on Thunder while speaking to me.

"He needs a long recovery, but not at this hospital—they've done all they can do," she said. "Injuries this severe require top people with special equipment. He needs expert care, Chief." Her eyes welled with tears. "My son needs trauma care, like a military hospital provides. They'll do everything to keep him alive. With evil intentions… but they'll sustain him, as will I."

"Wait, what are you saying?" I asked.

"To let the general capture us." She took a deep breath. "Tell Harry I love him. I will always love him, but Thunder needs me. His survival depends on my connection to Face, so I'm staying here. The rest of you need to be on your way. Even the doctors were joking about a flying boy."

A voice boomed toward us like the rumble of a ball in a bowling alley.

"No, Helen. You aren't going anywhere." T.D. stood behind us, straight and robust. "I'm well enough, Helen. Thunder needs Face's intervention. I'll take him there—it'll speed up both our healings."

"Take me, too," Healer insisted.

T.D. touched her chin tenderly, though his voice rang with an authority that inspired me. "Ice needs you. So does this mission. Believe me, Helen, I'll be back—I promise you."

"Of course, I believe you… I'll wait forever if I have to."

Babe hung on to every word before she leaned into me and whispered, "For a married couple, they are shy with the romance in front of us."

Ears frowned and touched his fingertips to his temples. "I'm getting a signal. No time to waste, Chief. The general's helicopter is almost here."

T.D. grasped my hand. "Leave now! Take care of my wife and Ice, Chief."

"I'll protect them with my life," I said, stunned by the turn of events. Healer took her hand from Thunder and turned to her husband. She gave him a brief embrace. He pulled her closer and kissed her, lingering longer than time allowed. Babe, looking sad because of Thunder but thrilled at witnessing Healer and T.D. 's love, clutched her hands together and sighed contentedly.

"That'll have to hold us over, Helen," T.D. whispered. He placed his hand on Thunder's forehead, pulling the essence of Thunder from his body. We saw an opaque, wispy Thunder float free. He waved, looking pleased to be free of his battered remains. T.D. wrapped his arm around his son, looking at the boy with a father's love, which the ghost—the soul, the spirit of Thunder—returned. Thunder blew a loving kiss to Healer as he took a step backward with his dad. Their appearance shimmered before the two faded like breath on a winter's day.

Chapter 14

"Ears you're right. It's time to go," Healer whispered urgently. "Let the military take his body and warehouse it the way they did for all of us. We were in no danger until we awoke. Hurry now. I have a feeling we aren't far ahead of the general."

We banded together, leaving the ICU behind. Babe bewitched the staff with the forgetfulness routine. Motor finished with the monitors, and Picker pulled up with the ambulance. We piled inside, leaving one piece of evidence that we were there.

Thunder's body.

"Just in time, Chief," Ears said. "The general's landing in a minute. We need to hustle."

Ice curled against his mother. His eyes rolled back, his face wet from tears. Healer sighed and stroked his hair. We all took our getaway positions: Bat at the back window for protection, Babe next to him, Picker driving, Lookout riding shotgun, the rest of us crammed in the middle.

"Where to, Chief?" Picker asked.

"South."

Everything had changed. First, Driller left us, then Top Dog and Thunder. We had to re-shift again.

"This is no one's fault," I said. "I hope each one of you understands that. We live in a dimension where chance is as crucial as fate and where good and evil work toward different goals. We can't understand Face and all that he is, even as Insiders. But he loves us. Face will make it work out for good whether we see it or not."

I wondered about Top Dog as we drove. Walking through dimensions was Face's highest gift. Without a thought to his well-being, T.D. had saved troops and civilians from a bomb's conflagration. Could I ever be that brave?

We drove in silence respecting Healer and Ice's loss, keeping our grief to ourselves. I could not imagine what else could happen to keep us from our quest.

Lookout pointed the way to the nearest state road going south.

Ears and Lookout gave reports of the general and his unappreciated lieutenant:

The general supervised the loading of Thunder into the special medevac'd helicopter, his spirit torn between the failure of not capturing more escapees and success for having caught one.

"One. We found *one* battered-up freak. I am sick of these kid-freaks outmaneuvering me, but Insiders will not abandon this one. Helen and T.D. will return one day if I don't catch them first."

"General, he doesn't look as though he's going to make it," the medic said.

"Keep him breathing, Soldier. I do not care how many damn hoses and machines it takes. That's an order."

"Yes, sir."

"And get some meds for my back—a damn patch of ice. I ought to sue that hospital. And Lieutenant?"

"Sir?"

"Notify the police that we lost a handful of convicts.

Fax them photos. They know these mountains better than we do. Meanwhile, establish a fifty-mile perimeter. We need choppers in the air with heat-reading sensors, now."

"But the Smokeys, at night, Sir, in this weather… ?"

"*Now*, Lieutenant," General warned as he climbed into the copter holding his back, each step paining him. "Argh—I'm going to sue somebody for the pain I'm in!"

"Yes, sir."

While the lieutenant passed on his orders by radio, the general's copter lifted into the air. When the officer finished, he realized the general had left him behind without warning or transportation.

"Berating me is not enough," the lieutenant scowled. "You added abandonment to your nasty deck of cards. Leave me nowhere, too, you…"

We guessed that he resolved to make the best of the situation by interrogating the doctors, nurses, and aides. None of them—not one—knew what he was talking about. Finally, he stopped the browbeating and concluded that they knew nothing. Maybe they had earlier, but the freaks had influenced their brains.

****

The closest military unit for a driver and car was Fort Bragg, North Carolina. The base was situated hours to the east—the lieutenant had a long wait ahead. He must have decided to make use of his time.

"Where would I go if I were an Insider?" he asked rhetorically. "The coast would not allow a good escape route. A city, however, offers lairs for hiding." The officer focused on his map. "Atlanta… of course," he muttered. "Atlanta will be their next stop."

"Chief, are we going to Atlanta?"

"I hope not, Ears. I prefer this countryside to hide in

until Face says otherwise."

"Oh, boy. He's going to be in big trouble. He radioed an order for a net around Atlanta, per General Mack, and warned that The Insiders were not to get out. Each car would require a stop and search."

"Ha. Atlanta can't be our destination." A round of chuckles filled the van. Even Ice managed a smile.

While we traveled south, Healer explained that Top Dog was capable of walking between dimensions with his physical body—he could visit Face when called upon. His brain differed from the rest of ours for that reason. And he was the only Insider with the gift.

"Face will heal any damage the surgeons created," she said. "But if he desires T.D. to stay, he will. Both Harry's and Thunder's fate belongs to Face."

"Yeah, but that's true for every living thing," Motor said.

Despite the separation from her husband and Thunder, Healer's peace came directly from Face. I wondered if the dove comforted both Ice and her. The boy had cheered up but sat closer to his mom than usual. They often smiled at each other, knowing that events were just as they should have been.

I pulled myself away from my thoughts and peered out the window. A giant billboard beckoned us that read WELCOME TO CHEROKEE COUNTY.

"There! Cherokee, North Carolina."

It made perfect sense. The American Indian had respected Earth as a living entity for centuries and still believed it. They had known the truth all along. We followed signs around mountain roads that led to a casino, legal on the Cherokee reservation.

"This is it. I know it." *We will be safe here,* I

thought.

"Are we stopping to win more money, Chief?" Motor asked.

"No, man. I feel it in my bones. This is where we stop for the night… or two."

The palatial casino seemed ironic to me. First, the white man stole Indian lands. Now, the Indians profited from them in the casino. Even though the Cherokee had agreed to adapt to the white man's ways, our government said it wasn't good enough. Tribes were rounded up and walked to an Oklahoma reservation with Indians dropping dead along the way—kids included. History called it The Trail of Tears. But some Cherokee defied the order and hid in the mountains.

We were about to meet their descendants.

An odd calm filled my spirit, a knowing that we belonged here. "Park in the back again," I said.

We pulled behind the building and found a corner to park our uncomfortable escape vehicle. Before we had a chance to stretch our legs, a geriatric wearing a beaded vest stepped out from behind a tree and startled me.

"You are late," he said authoritatively. In his native tongue, he talked to older teens who had been waiting with him. They came at us carefully, looking us over in awe. "The boys will hide your vehicle."

They pushed our ambulance further into the trees and threw a camouflaged tarp over it. The old man left them to their work and said, "Follow me. We picked up radio conversations from your irate general. Something stalled the landing of his helicopter." The old man chuckled. "It seems he slipped on a patch of ice and threw out his back."

I gave Ice a thumbs-up and ruffled his hair.

"I knew the great spirit would bring you to us," the man wearing the vest continued. "As a boy, Spirit told me to protect Insiders. I waited to meet you for a long time."

We followed the interesting man down a set of stairs into an old cellar full of roots and canned goods. It was chilly there, good cover for the heat we emitted. The ancient Cherokee pressed one of the stones that formed the far wall. It creaked open to the next room, which contained beautiful furnishings with modern amenities—an underground log cabin that smelled of natural cedar.

Our rescuer said, "Don't be concerned, my friends. There is plenty of room for all. Rest here until events calm down on the outside. Let the traffic of the casino cover your presence."

I thanked the man. "What is your name, sir?"

"I am Chief Sky Hawk. But the outside world calls me Daniel on their paperwork. It keeps the bureaucracy confused," he winked.

"It's good to feel kindness, Chief Sky Hawk. We awoke and ran. We haven't had time to enjoy our freedom."

"Son," the old chief said, "you have no freedom here, just as you had no freedom inside. When bound by code and certainty, the choice is made. The road appears in front of you to keep you safe within its continuum. I suggest you enjoy the bondage of your allegiance, knowing your choice is eternal."

I nodded.

"Eat now. Rest," Chief Sky Hawk added. "Do not under any circumstances venture outside. Your needs will be supplied. When you see me again, it will be to bring you above ground. Peace."

He left the room before we could ask questions.

But what could I say? His words were true. I was glad to be Face's follower, content at last. All eyes were on me. I knew my next words would set the mood. "Let's eat." We filled our bellies with sandwich fixings and juice. Only Bat had room for the grapes and apples provided.

Just as we put up our feet to relax into plush leather couches and chairs, Ears announced that a patrol car had pulled onto the reservation with lights on and siren blaring.

"Chief, we have company. Repeating."

"Are they here yet, Chief Sky Hawk?"

"Yes, sheriff, they arrived safe and sound."

"We'll keep it that way, Chief."

"The tribe is proud of its members who keep the old ways while performing tasks needed in the modern world."

"We bear this burden with honor."

"Come talk and eat, my friends. It will take hours for two men to search this reservation. Spend time inside and talk with me."

Relief wafted through me as two more Cherokee friends protected our location. Ears held up his hand.

"Police radio blaring. Repeating…"

"The general wants every nook and cranny searched, and every rock turned over."

"Roger that."

Continuing interference from law enforcement (those who were not tribal police) would be dangerous. Suddenly, an idea flashed in my head.

"Motor, how about we give the local and state police

force a decoy?"

Motor smelled something fun cooking. "I'm listening."

"The ambulance needs to travel to the west."

"Oh, a decoy. I can do that." Motor sat back in a recliner with his feet up. "Looking at maps. Yes, Chief, it should be through Tennessee, or further by sunup if we start soon."

"Here's the thing, Motor: we need to give that ambulance a big ending at dawn. But make sure the license plate is legible—after the car burns to a crisp."

"Do you think the general will buy it?" Healer asked.

"No, but the police will. Unless he wants to divulge a military secret, the general must agree with them. Meanwhile, local law enforcement stops searching."

Healer raised her hand. "One other thing: Motor can make the vehicle run with no fuel in it. But it won't burn without an accelerant, will it?"

"Jeez. Good thinking, Healer," Motor said. "I let that not-so-minor fact slip by me."

"Any suggestions?" I asked.

"I know a way to burn it," Healer said. She opened a supply bag and pulled out a canister which read DIETHYL ETHER with a FLAMMABLE 4 sticker on it. "I took the liberty of adding a few extra supplies while in the hospital."

"Yes, that will do the job," Motor said eagerly.

"Give it here. I'll put it inside," I said.

"No. Chief, I've handled this material before," Healer said. "I know how to open it a crack so it will work when needed."

"Healer, if you're sure," I said reluctantly. "It's

dark. Better get it done before the casino gets too busy."

Despite Chief Sky Hawk's directions to stay inside, Healer snuck outside unseen, avoiding the casino's patrons and employees.

"Lookout keep an eye on her, please."

"I already am, Chief. She made it to the car with one close call—a group of birthday celebrators. She's struggling with pulling the tarp off the ambulance."

"Holy Toledo! I should have sent Fly."

"He's already out there, Chief. He's invisible, but the tarp has just been lifted and thrown to the side."

I was grateful Fly acted before I gave him a directive. "So, what about Healer?"

"She's making certain all the windows and doors are sealed tight using duct tape. She's now securing the canister to the front seat. She just took a deep breath— she's opening the canister."

Ears cocked his head. "She *barely* opened it. I hear a minimal hiss escaping."

"She eased the door shut and... ooh, she just went invisible!" Lookout said excitedly.

I opened the door for Healer and Fly, impressed with her ability to get the job done fast and without any nerves.

"Thanks, Healer. You saved the day."

"My pleasure."

"Fly...?"

"Uh, a spontaneous reaction, Chief. I couldn't let Healer out there alone."

"I'm grateful. But in the future, say something before you disappear. Otherwise, I worry. Deal?"

"You worry about me? That's a deal, Chief... I'll try to remember." He grinned at me.

"Motor, are you ready?"

"No time like the present." Motor reclined his seat to the point that he was almost lying down. He placed his hands behind his head as he kept me abreast. "Ambulance engine is active, backing up. I have coordinated its movements with the map I see in my head. North to Route 40, then due west—no lights needed. We are on the road and traveling in the dark. You guys get some sleep while I drive."

****

Morning came too soon for me. The sun had barely peeked above the mountainside when I slipped out of bed to check on Motor.

"How'd it go?"

"I'm crossing the Arkansas state line now, Chief. Give me a couple more minutes." Motor's eyes moved left to right in hyper-speed. His skin became pale and sweaty. This job must require all his strengths, I thought.

"Boom!" Motor exclaimed while holding his finger in the air. "Wow, Healer knew what she was doing, all right. That van is burning to a crisp."

"And the license plate?"

"It's laying by the side of the road just like you requested."

"Motor, you rock!" I said.

He smiled. "Not bad for a motorhead, huh?"

"Not bad at all, my friend. Your dad would be proud."

Motor yawned. "Thanks. Yes, Dad sure would be."

"I can see the job drained you—get some rest. The rest of us will be sleeping in today, too, if for nothing else but regeneration."

"Thanks, Chief. I bonded with this chair. I'm going

to snooze right here, man."

We enjoyed safety in this underground haven. Our new lives would take off with a more precise direction from that point on. I tiptoed back to my room, careful not to awaken anyone who desperately needed rest. My sleepless night urged me to crawl under the still-warm covers. Relieved by Motor's success, I fell deep asleep, lulled by a false sense of security.

No one anticipated the danger that surrounded us while we dreamed.

Chapter 15

Earth continued to spin as she had for eons, but she tired of adjusting to humanity's greed. Factories that fouled her oxygen also poked holes in her protective ozone layer, letting dangerous ultraviolet rays into the atmosphere. Ice caps that had deflected the sun's rays back to space began to melt. Fewer ice caps to deflect the rays allowed them to warm Earth's temperatures; that warming caused massive melting at the polar caps. The melted water flowed into the ocean, flooding highly populated areas. Icecap water made the winters colder and summers hotter.

How much longer could she regulate her functions when oil wells depleted reserves of fossil fuels that ran through her veins like blood and too often spilled into pristine waters, killing wildlife and ocean plants? Nuclear blasts above and beneath her surface changed her natural movement and flows.

Aging nuclear power plants cracked like broken eggs, their waste contaminating everything.

Earth distressed for all the life upon her. Many would not adapt when she, Mother earth, Gaia, changed. If only humans followed the law like the wild creatures: take what is needed and no more. But humans took from her non-stop. They built on her fault lines and lowlands but cursed her when earthquakes rocked the overpopulated ground while tsunamis washed her shores clean. They did not understand her natural events. How would they survive the earth re-adjusting?

A chill pierced Earth's crust; she shivered. She continued her spin with the wobble in her rotation growing stronger each year. Only Face's love and support relieved the ache she sustained for far too long. She yawned and slumbered, dreaming of pure oceans, clean rivers, tropical forests, and clear, starry skies. She dreamed she was young again with the peaceful existence she enjoyed before man interfered.

Then she dreamed of how it would be before too long.

Chapter 16

PREFACE

Brazil's moonless midnight camouflaged handlers who herded children across railroad tracks, encouraging swiftness with a crack of the crop as though the little ones were cattle. The perfect night blended with their mocha skin and black hair. But it did not ease the traffickers' nerves. Their eyes shifted left to right, fearing discovery by *policia* as they forced one group of prisoners after another into the open boxcar.

"Oldest first... move back... all the way into the corners... make room."

The linebacker-sized supervisor looked and sounded frightening enough with his deep, threatening voice. The clandestine operation had become more dangerous after a five-car accident blocked their route, delaying their effort. Timing was crucial to success, as miscalculations earned jail time if caught. The possibility of returning to that hell stirred up animal-like fears.

"Next time not so late, eh?" the callous engineer spat. "I must adhere to a schedule."

The wrangler cringed because he understood the severity of the masked threat. The engineer would leave them behind next time.

"Si. No more mistakes," the handler said, thinking of how he could gain the upper hand with the crusty old engineer. "Quickly now. Quickly."

The handlers lifted smaller children and threw them into the car. Their terrified faces wore dirty masks, but they kept silent like muzzled dogs. The traffickers jumped in just as the train began to move. Once the boxcar doors slid shut, their stress level diminished.

"Now I sleep, dreaming of riches soon to be mine," the oldest handler mumbled as he sat on the floor in darkness. He wiped sweat from his brow but was happy for a successful day's work as the train lurched and chugged out of the station.

The rocking rhythm gently invited the youngest to fall asleep. Older victims, used to a life of slavery, sat staring into the darkness, accepting their fate whatever it would be. The oldest prisoners, who had become too mature for their original captors, sat like empty vessels void of content. They recycled without much thought—the journey was nothing more than a followed order in exchange for food and shelter.

For the youngest and newest prey, sleep brought dreams of faraway homes; maybe a mother's smile, a father's strong arms—a brief remembrance of happiness.

Waking is what brought them nightmares.

****

Human trafficking required steely greed and stupidity that was often mistaken for guts. Evil schemers calculated that the train would forgo the usual inspections when pulling two tankers filled with lethal gas. Past performance proved every inspector on a tanker's route passed a lethal train through quickly to the next vicinity, hoping to avoid any possible dangers or accidents in their territory.

The engine chugged along with little effort for over

an hour out of San Juan before the engineer noticed a problem.

"Come on, you piece of old metal," he barked. "You've taken this hill too many times to count." He pushed the lever forward to kick in more power, but the engine acted sluggishly. He pulled a second locomotive that needed repair, but he doubted the extra weight would affect his newly overhauled engine. "Don't give up on me, old girl, or I turn you to scrap. Come on... get over the top."

He prepared for the steep downward plunge that came next. He patted the control board, anticipating the speed to come as his old locomotive managed to clear the peak. For the next quarter of a mile, the old man smiled like a child on a rollercoaster ride. After forty years with the company, a downhill plunge still exhilarated him.

I can retire with the payout from this run.

His happiness turned to terror when the wheels caught a stretch of damaged track. The first engine tilted when its left wheels lifted off, throwing its master hard against the opposite wall. As it twisted to its side, the other engine lifted, the hind end disconnecting it from the cars behind. It flipped up and over the first engine sideways. Both locomotives continued a downhill slide pushed by colliding rail cars and tankers from behind. The train squealed, cracked, screamed, and banged, settling into positions like a game of Pick-up sticks.

The bloodied engineer moaned. He pulled himself up on unsteady legs, grateful to feel no other pain.

"Okay, no broken bones," he whispered while the rest of his body ached from being tossed around like insignificant trash. Escape from his mangled quarters required a climb up the side of the control dash and out the window that faced toward the sky.

He gathered his strength and concentrated on the blue patch above while reaching, contorting, and pulling until he stood on the side of the controls. He poked his head out the window, surveying the carnage around him.

"Forty years with no accidents, no trouble… and now this."

As the shock to his brain eased, he panicked, remembering the other lives on board that could tarnish his reputation. He took a deep breath, lost consciousness, and crumpled to the floor.

****

Dawn revealed the nighttime carnage. Field after field displayed dead cattle, legs up.

Hysterical farmers called *policia.* The police, in turn, called rescue. Knowing the severity of the situation, both rescue and police called the military. Emergency medical technicians, military, and scientists arrived wearing hazard suits and gas masks while *policia* contained the citizens, warning them not to leave their homes.

While a few scientists took samples from the dead bovine, most headed toward the train, knowing there would be at least one fatality—the engineer. After finding him dead, they searched the boxcars and gasped. In front of them lay children, piled in heaps.

An inspector glared at the dead perpetrators with disgust. "Damn devils," he muttered.

The scientist moved to examine a young girl closest to him. Focusing through his mask, he muttered, "Impossible. Dr. Mendoza, come quick. Come see."

Mendoza ran over to the gruesome scene. "She is

dead, is she not?"

"Si and no. Look at her eyes."

Mendoza, a chemical engineer, leaned in to observe the victim. "Impossible."

The child's eyes danced under heavy lids as though in a REM dream state. Yet, he detected no heartbeat, no breath. His team checked child after child but found the same results. Scientists knew the gas. It killed; it did its job well. But eyes that moved? No muscle movement should have been possible with this poison, as toxic fumes attacked the muscles first.

Mendoza radioed central control for help. Soon, every available ambulance, rescue helicopter, and emergency vehicle arrived. Hazard Control evacuated the children by twos, sending them to area hospitals under strict quarantine. Confounded doctors found no heartbeat, no breath, yet the children's brains produced plenty of activity. They were put on respirators, and while their lungs functioned and their hearts started beating, each child remained asleep.

"I don't understand if it is a miracle or a fluke, Presidente," Dr. Mendoza said. "Research produced no comparable scenario. Even the traffickers and the engineer died, but the children survived. The impossible has happened."

"Protocol dictates military be informed of every find, Doctor Mendoza. They must study the situation too and keep me informed. You will give them your full cooperation. Is this understood?"

"Si, El Presidente, but I assure you they will find our tests impeccable."

Mendoza stared at his phone.

"Hello? Presidente? Now, Presidente hangs up on

me… what next?"

To avoid panic, officials told citizens the train wreck carried a gas strong enough to kill only animals, secreting the deadly truth. Meanwhile, scientists worked to understand the gas that killed fields of animals but left the boxcar children in a strange state.

The event remained a mystery until each child woke up stronger and smarter four years later. But before authorities could question them, they all disappeared from their hospital beds at once.

"What do you mean, they vanished?" Mendoza demanded to know.

"They aren't in their rooms. We checked the other facilities too," he was told. "All the children, all of them are gone."

Dr. Mendoza sighed. "Find them now. Meanwhile, I'll call Presidente and hope he does not kill this messenger."

****

While earning their gifts from Face, the boxcar kids planned to assemble at the *favellos* in the Brazilian capital of Brasilia. No longer typical in the human sense of the word, they were children, teens, and young adults with a purpose. They would save lives with the transporting gift they shared. Their superhuman talents made anything disappear and reappear in other places. They would provide a vital service for rescue and survival.

Transporters, still in their hospital gowns, enjoyed a few minutes of familiar sites before their leader called out, "Insiders, get ready for our first job. As we practiced on the inside, line up. *Vamos fazê-lo. Até logo.* Let's get it done!"

Transporters, links in the chain of travelers capable of traversing inner space, held hands. They numbered over two hundred souls that formed a circle. As each of their energy vibrations increased, the line began to waver, bend, and create the haze of a large, spinning wheel that lifted off the ground, disappearing moments later.

They touched down within minutes. But mountain terrain and towering trees prevented a smooth landing around the Cherokee casino. Though bumps, bruises, and an occasional broken limb would plague the group, they healed in minutes from the painful distractions.

They stared in awe at the helicopter set before them. Its futuristic angles and black-as-night paint were impressive. The leader surveyed the situation.

"Big building… a palace. Nice copter. Well, we start with these big ones, good practice."

Chapter 17

Chief

After Motor destroyed the ambulance, relief washed over me, knowing that my family had found safe accommodations at the Cherokee casino. But my mind had stuck on Motor's mission all night, leaving me to toss and turn. I decided to take advantage of a chance to relax and enjoy the warmth of my oversized quilt.

I fell deep asleep—big mistake.

As I made like Rip Van Winkle, the hush of a high-tech helicopter failed to invade my dreams. By the time I sat up to inspect some unfamiliar noise, I was handcuffed, gagged, and unable to shout for help. I tried to send a telepathic message to Healer (telling her to wake up, grab Babe, and run) while the barrel of a gun pushed me toward the living room area. That's where I saw Motor, who had been tazed, bound, and gagged.

Shame overcame me. I let this happen.

As Healer and Babe shuffled out, both in shackles and with their eyes taped over, I hung my head. Apparently tazed in their sleep, Fly and Bat recovered to find themselves bound with their eyes and mouths taped shut. This was by order of the general who was not sure what part of the body Bat used to protect the others. He knew Fly wouldn't take off in a blind flight, I guessed.

Luckily, Ears, Lookout, and Picker were missing. I hoped they had escaped. My hopes soon dashed when soldiers paraded Ears and Lookout before me.

"Sorry, Chief, I slept so hard," Ears said. "I didn't recognize the sound. We tried—"

"Shut up," the general ordered.

"These last two tried to escape through the venting, General," a soldier reported.

The general counted his prisoners and studied our group again. "Men, you missed one: the redhead. Find him."

As soldiers searched other rooms, the general checked the tape on Healer's eyes. Ears leaned into me and whispered, "Picker found his way to the casino's kitchen. He jumped to the floor and says he is formulating a plan."

This lifted my spirits. Then huge claps sounded out of nowhere. Another one followed. I was horrified, afraid Picker had been shot. But the soldiers ran back into the room, followed by two more thunderous cracks.

"We thought you took gunfire, General," one of them said.

"What the hell was that?" the general asked, perplexed as the rest of us.

Another tremendous whack resounded before anyone said anything. Then the room began to spin like a whirling top. The general flew against a wall, pinned by an unseen force. His soldiers lost their balance, falling to the floor. They were pushed against a wall and anchored there. I watched my bound family rendered helpless by energy that sucked us to one wall or another. The general scowled at me. I tried to convey with my eyes that we were not responsible.

"What's happening?" Babe hollered over the whirring.

151

I shrugged my shoulders, forgetting she couldn't see me.

Healer smiled. "Ears, tell Chief the good guys came to our rescue."

Ears contained his happiness and clued me in.

Less worried, I wish I could tell the gang, especially Motor who said nothing about our capture. Even though he was bound, I knew that facial expression. Our genius was concentrating, feeling the energy around him, connecting. Suddenly, he vanished like a ghost leaving handcuffs and shackles behind.

What next? Will we all disappear?

As the whirring sound increased, soldiers covered their ears. We Insiders endured the deep resonating pulses until the racket decreased in long waves as though it had a dying battery. At the same time, the bumpy ride reduced itself to a few quivers, stopping with a hard thud at the end.

"Get up, men," the general barked. "The prisoners need attending."

"Yeah, they do, don't they, General?" Picker proudly announced his presence while holding an automatic weapon in each hand. "I suggest no one make a move." He continued barking orders: "Soldiers, slide your weapons to the middle of the room." He pointed to a muscle-bound giant standing closest to Babe. "You, get the tape off her eyes."

"Don't listen to him, men," the general commanded. "There are more of you than he can handle."

Without hesitation, Picker squeezed the trigger. Bullets danced around the soldier's feet. Everyone froze, and the general shut up. Picker pointed one of his weapons at the soldier closest to Babe.

"Again, cowboy," he said slowly, "take the tape off Babe's eyes first."

The soldier obeyed. He grabbed a corner of the tape and ripped it off... fast.

"Ouch," Babe said. "Really, Soldier, really? You couldn't have been gentler?" Her eyes seared into the soldier as she rubbed the irritated area.

"Sorry, ma'am." He cowered from Babe's glare.

The general shook his head and threw up his hands as Babe continued. "You aren't through, Soldier. Look at me... look at my eyes... you want to do as I say. Release everyone, starting with Chief."

"Yes, ma'am. My pleasure, ma'am," he replied, meek as a lamb.

"Thanks, Babe. And Picker, thanks for coming through, dude. Your timing was perfect." I rubbed my wrists to get the circulation moving. "Soldier, cuff the general and slap some tape across his mouth while you're at it."

The soldier checked with Babe first, who nodded her head in agreement.

"Soldier, do *not* come near me," the general warned. "That is an *order*. Son, you are hypnotized, but you are stronger than their suggestions. Refuse to do it... argh... you'll be court-martialed for handcuffing... mmm..."

Babe influenced the remaining men. They became obedient puppets, slaves to her every command.

"Chief, have you figured out what caused this colossal building to spin and how?"

"I'm about to figure that out right now, Picker."

A bitter chill infiltrated the room, spurring me on to solve the mystery.

"Okay. Let's see what we've got ourselves into this

time," I said. The once-hidden stone door had been ripped off, leaving a gaping hole. The chill turned into an icy cold that cut through me like a saber.

Through the aperture, sunshine reflected with a brightness we had never experienced outside the caves. In the distance, we saw nothing but white that blinded us. Everyone knew one thing: we were not in Cherokee County anymore.

"Lookout?"

Lookout shivered and began to jump up and down to keep warm. "There's some caribou a few miles ahead," he said glibly. "It's beautiful here, nothing but tundra."

"Tundra. You mean…?"

"Yep. Cold! North Pole cold," Lookout laughed.

"Bat, collect the soldiers' coats and hats so we don't freeze to death. Sunglasses, too."

As we explored the new surroundings, we saw that the building stood at least five hundred feet above a village on the seaside.

"There's a buzz about us down there, Chief," Ears said. "Repeating."

"Did you see that? A building… I saw a building land up on the ridge."

"You been drinkin' too much polar juice, man."

"No, he's right. I saw something huge land on top of the ridge, too. Look, see for yourself."

"I'll be a freakin' slippery seal. A UFO maybe? Come on, let's check it out. To the sleds."

"Company's coming, but nothing to worry about," Ears said.

"Don't ever stop worrying, Ears. That goes for all of you. This is my bad—I apologize for my complacency."

My friends were insisting on sharing the blame with me when a wavy image appeared. Suddenly, a long line of people in hospital gowns stood before us.

"Você está bem. Não se reocupe."

I eyeballed Ears.

"Repeating," he said.

"You're okay? No worries?"

Their leader called on his translator to step forward.

"Hello, I am Anna Marie. I shall interpret for Augusto, our leader. He says that everyone needs rescuing sooner or later. It is a pleasure to meet the famous Chief of Poop." The interpreter covered her mouth and giggled. "You are a legend to the children of Brazil, Chief."

"I suppose the YouTube video made it around the world when we were with Face?"

"Yes, around the world a few times, I think," she said.

Her boss belly-laughed. "Mucho Poop."

Transporters applauded, hollering *"Viva, Poop Chefe."*

Augusto rattled off a few sentences. Ears took the opportunity to show off in front of the stunning translator.

"He says they're transporters," Chief. "They did not have time to dress before getting the call to rescue us. They brought the casino along as a safe house for the villagers."

Again, the Brazilian leader spoke. Anna Marie stepped forward.

"Yes, it is a big building," she said, "capable of withstanding extreme winds. It will survive the sea levels rising. Cold up here, si?"

"Anna Marie, there could be some clothes inside," I said. "You must be freezing."

During our conversation, Motor appeared out of thin air. Nothing much about Motor surprised me anymore—I wondered if his growth would ever end.

"I'll answer that, Chief. They feel some chill, but they vibrate faster than normal—it keeps them warm." Motor faced the leader but did a double take when he saw Anna Marie. He stepped forward and reached out to shake her hand. "Ahh... everyone calls me... Motor."

I hid a smile, noticing a slight quiver in his voice as he held on to her hand.

"Hello, Motor. My name is Anna Marie."

"That's a beautiful name, Anna Marie."

It was a first: Motor took an interest in the opposite sex. Our genius turned to rubber, his speech becoming gobbledygook.

"What are you doing here, Anna Marie? I mean, I *know* what you are doing here. But how long are you staying?"

Anna Marie turned to her leader and repeated Motor's question in Portuguese. He replied to her, and she turned back to Motor.

"He says we go. We have much to do and little time to do it, Motor. I must go."

Ears stepped in front of Motor. "Anna Marie, I'd love for you to stop by—you know, if you are ever back this way..."

"You plan to stay here?" Anna Marie asked with a giggle.

"We'll help the villagers for a few days and be on our way, too, unless you plan to pick us up," I said, winking at Anna Marie while saving my love-struck amigos from each other.

Augusto stepped forward and shook my hand. *"Vejo vocês mais tarde meus amigos."*

I made sense of the short phrase. "I'll see you later, too, my friend. *Adios.*"

The line re-formed. Anna Maria waved a flirtatious goodbye before she joined hands. Their leader announced something which probably amounted to, "Let's do this!" We watched the process of transporters turn from a line to a wheel, becoming airborne before disappearing.

"Okay, lover boys, time to work," I said to Ears and Motor.

The gang burst out laughing. Picker, bending over to catch his breath, pointed at Ears.

"Excuse me, Anna Marie, do you come here often? May I buy you a drink… of snow?"

"Joke all you want, Picker," Ears said. "But she is a ten."

Motor sighed. "No, Ears, you're wrong. She is a *hundred* and ten percent perfection."

"Hey, where did all the snow come from? And the trees—where did the trees go?"

We turned at the familiar voice. Chief Sky Hawk walked out the front entrance yawning, stretching, and scratching his butt. He looked profoundly confused. "I must be dreaming."

"Chief Sky Hawk! Sorry, you aren't dreaming," I said. I was puzzled by his appearance but happy to see him. "Your casino is somewhere near the North Pole."

The Chief's eyes grew to the size of plates. With a slow understanding, he burst out laughing, caught his breath, stopped, and turned himself around.

"Don't worry, we'll get you back to North Carolina," I assured him. "Somehow."

"I'm in no hurry, Insider. Good thing I have hazard insurance, but how do I explain a missing building to the bureaucracy?"

"I don't know, Chief," I said to him, "but I think the Cherokee area in North Carolina will be part of a safety zone. You might get a significant influx of refugees. I suggest, sir, when you get home, build fast and build large."

I wondered how to get a message back to Chief Sky Hawk's people that he was alive, but their casino wouldn't be returned... ever.

Chapter 18

"Repeating, Chief: Bark, bark. Mush, mush."

"Funny, Ears."

"Ha. I couldn't resist, Chief. Villagers will be here in a few minutes."

I heard the dogs first. After all I experienced growing up, seeing dogs pull a sled and driver was still cool. When the sledges pulled up, drivers jumped off, astounded by the building in front of them. The dogs continued barking at the smells, strange and new. A man spoke in Inuit.

"Translating, Chief..."

"How'd you get that palace up here?"

"Tell him it's a long story, Ears, that we come in peace and to help them. Ask them to give us a ride down into the village where we can explain to everyone at one time."

Ears repeated my message. The startled drivers nodded. One pulled out a radio informing the elders that "exceptional" company was minutes away. With their eyes glued to the building, they shuffled backward to their sleds.

The dogs each pulled extra passengers on the way down to the village. Without a need for transport, Fly and Sky Hawk stayed behind to provide essentials for the handcuffed and shackled military. I didn't dare let them roam while we were all in town.

As a kid, I had never had a sled—never went sledding. The ride down the mountain exhilarated us as the clean frigid air invaded my nostrils and a spray of snow landed on my face. The whoosh of the sled's runners over the snow added to the ambiance.

Suddenly, Fly appeared over our heads, startling our drivers, and exciting the dogs. He carried Chief Sky Hawk, who was wrapped in a blanket and wearing a wool cap taken from one of the soldiers. I laughed when Chief Sky Hawk hollered, "Yahoo!"

As we came into view, the villagers had already gathered to greet us. Eyes wide, they encircled us as we disembarked from our sleds.

"Ears, tell them we need a meeting," I said. "We have news to share."

The Inuit led us to a little town hall made of stone that I assumed had been gathered from the ocean. They showed us their finery: sealskin coats, boots, and delicacies for us to eat like smoked fish and eel. Although some residents wore store-bought clothes, seals and caribou were still hunted for food and clothing. Though not a fan of so-called sport killing, I understood that this isolated tribe relied on their environment to eat and survive. I sensed they used every part of their prey like in the old days.

A girl appeared, ignoring us but shyly approaching Bat while holding out a tray.

"I make food… mmm take?" She looked Bat in the eye and giggled. Bat smiled, taken aback by the girl's kindness and charm. I doubted anyone had catered to him since his earliest years, if ever.

"Well, thanks," Bat said. "My momma told me I had a shark's appetite. Guess I still do." He popped a morsel in his mouth and nodded—it was good. Gesturing with his other hand, he said, "Please, eat with me." They found a corner where Bat ate while talking non-stop. The girl picked at the food, unable to take her eyes off him.

We had reached an age when attraction to the opposite sex was inevitable. I chuckled at the thought of Insiders in love—a sweet idea compared to the horrible news I had for our gracious hosts.

"Ears, be ready to translate, please." Then I cleared my throat and addressed the group. "You, the Inuit, are an ancient people. You learned the ways of Earth and respected her. You take what you need from nature to survive in this cold country, but you take no more than you need. Face, creator of all, sent us to help you."

I waited for Ears to translate and for their astonished reactions to subside.

"First, the bad news: Earth tires, her rotation wobbles more each day. Soon, her axis will flip its position, changing geography as you know it. Your buildings, your village, will be destroyed. You *must* move to higher ground. The mountain with the large building provides safety for you from rising waters and catastrophic winds that may last for many months. We will help you move your belongings up the mountain."

The Inuit leader approached Ears. They huddled for a second. Then Ears turned to me. "Chief, he's asking when all this happens."

"Tell him that we don't know for sure, but the village must prepare now to save lives later. You will require proper shelter and large stocks of food and water."

The village leader shook his head.

"Repeating," Ears said.

"We live from the sea. But I will hold a meeting to decide when to abandon it. I will oversee the transfer of supplies up the mountain for the children and their mothers who will relocate there. The men will continue to hunt and fish for food. But we will watch the position of the stars, for they seem to have moved already."

I was surprised that no one had panicked when they heard the news—maybe I'd failed to emphasize how bad things would be. Healer caught my eye.

"He understood you, Chief," she said. "The whole village did. They face all truth with grace and dignity. They are a brave and strong people."

"I hope everyone is this accepting. Ears, I hate having to ask, but ask the leader if there's any transportation that we can use to return up the mountain."

They immediately volunteered the one caterpillar in town. We boarded it and followed the sled tracks back to the casino.

"This thing is modern, but it's too slow for an emergency," I said. "Motor, can an elevator be built to carry the slower moving up the mountain when time becomes critical?"

"Sure. We need Driller for it, though. He can dig a tunnel straight up the middle of this mountain right into the building if you want. But if things are going to get as bad as I think, I suggest the villagers remain underground until things settle down on the surface. I can design that, too."

"Brilliant, man!" I said with a smile. "Draw it up. Healer, put out the word for Driller, please. I bet he's working overtime these days."

"Probably is Chief. I'll do my best." Healer stood still as the rest of us retreated to the remaining warmth of the building.

"Okay, gang," I said. "Let's fuel up."

We raided the amply stocked refrigerators before the food spoiled. Chief Sky Hawk recommended burying the cold stores under the permafrost, which we did quickly. The next day, villagers arrived carrying the few things they treasured to store inside the building. They understood danger, as they lived in it daily. Between polar bears and freezing temperatures, survival was a way of life.

I wished countries had taught necessary survival skills in schools. It would have connected children to the Earth, taught them conservation, and allowed them to survive calamities.

Everyone would need survival skills soon.

****

"Hello, Chief."

I wiped the splatter from my face, and shook Driller's muck-covered hands.

"Thanks for coming, Driller. How did you get here so fast?"

"A couple transporters took time out of their busy day. One girl was the most beautiful I have ever seen. Man, oh man, what a beauty."

I nodded. "Anna Marie. I met her."

"She's gone." Driller sighed like a sad puppy. Then he shivered. "Brr—it's colder here than a well-digger's butt."

Babe arrived then with blankets and a hat and asked Driller if he was hungry.

"I could eat always," he replied.

"Picker says he's a good cook. I'll ask him to whip up something filling that can be made without electricity," Babe said. She trotted off to the casino.

"So, why am I here? What do you need, Chief?" Driller asked.

I had Motor explain his drawings while I tried to make sense of his intentions: drilling, ropes, pulleys, weights, and the method to the madness that was Motor's brilliant mind. I trusted both men, excused myself, and checked on the prisoners.

General Mack's grumbling reached my ears first. My inclination was to tape his mouth shut again. But when I saw beads of perspiration dripping from his pale face, I understood his problem.

"Chief, my men and I want a few beers," he rasped. "Bars in this casino should be well stocked."

"Sorry, General. You're withdrawing from alcohol right now."

"Withdrawing? Bah. My head is clear, you—young man," he added hastily. "I did not demand whiskey or vodka. I asked for a beer, a harmless beer."

"Beer contains as much alcohol as a harder drink, General. You're fooling yourself if you think it's harmless. Truth is, General, you're a drunk. You've been hiding it a long time, but the country—the *world*, for that matter—is going to need you. You'll want a sober head on your shoulders, but it will take time to clear the alcohol out of your system."

"You don't need to lecture me about—"

"We don't have time for this, General. I'll explain what we're trying to accomplish when you sober up."

The general tried saving face in front of his soldiers, but the truth was undeniable. He threatened me, using foul language not becoming an officer of his rank. A few days later, the general asked to see me. I walked him to a room away from his men where we could talk.

"I want to thank you, son," he said. "I didn't understand the extent of my need for alcohol. I must continue this sobriety. Meanwhile, I have studied your kind—you Insiders. I thought you were a threat to this country, yet all I have seen are good intentions. Anyway, Chief, if you need them, my men will help the locals, too,"

"I appreciate all that, General. But I'm not ready to set you all free just yet."

The general wiped his sweaty forehead. "I don't blame you, son. I'd do the same thing in your shoes."

"What I will do is explain why Insiders exist, so you can understand our intentions and purpose."

I shared the little I knew about Earth's fate: she was going to change, and it would be disastrous. Insiders were vehicles to save as many people and animals as possible. He didn't need to know my special mission.

"Son, sometimes, I feel as if I'm in the middle of a dream. Flying boys, drilling men… it is a lot to digest. I understand why you were made this way by that Face the other Insiders divulged. I know it has nothing to do with accumulating power or threatening the red, white, and blue." The general shifted his feet. "If you could tell me more about that entity, I'd be grateful."

Nice try. I hadn't mentioned Face; he was probing. "Another time, General. You say you understand. I suppose when you are free, your actions will tell me if you do or not."

As I led him back to his prison, he said, "I'll talk to the President when I return and suggest all Insiders be released. Moreover, I will fly your entourage home to Philly, if that's what you want, no strings attached. Now, if you don't mind, I could use a cup of coffee."

I still didn't trust him, but the helicopter sat next to the building in perfect shape. Either Motor would pilot, which I had no doubt he could, or we would try a friendship with the General. Babe would control him during the trip, but would he stay true to his pledge?

As Driller continued executing the escape plans in the mountain's interior, we said goodbye to our Inuit friends. Bat hugged his new girlfriend and tried to turn away nonchalantly. But he took a deep breath and turned back, pulling Downu close and giving her a lengthy goodbye kiss.

I sighed happily. At that moment, I knew for sure that Bat and Babe did not exist as a couple.

I sprinted to the helicopter and nodded at Motor. He entered the grid as soon as he buckled up. Utilizing his powers and the copters' advanced technology, he created a viral email:

Leave the coastlines and find high ground. Once there, find an underground safe place. Stock it with six months' supply of food, water, medicine, batteries, books, pens, and paper.

We hoped to grab the attention of every age group. Motor aimed the messages to all school computers and included a skill set: HOW TO FIND FRESH WATER; WHAT PLANTS ARE EDIBLE. Everyone needed a chance at survival.

General Mack, on board with us, cleared his throat. "Alright, ladies and gentlemen, before we lift off, I want to share that this helicopter is a top-secret stealth machine called the TAPO Airwolf. You are among a select group of people that know of its existence. Flying in it is a privilege but keep this experience to yourselves.

We'll be flying to Thule, a base Norwest of Greenland. Next, we board a cargo plane to Philadelphia. Ladies and gentlemen, enjoy the TAPO."

We helped Chief Sky Hawk contact his worried sheriffs through the aircraft's secure radio.

"Don't worry about the casino," I told him. "Call the insurance company and get the paperwork started. I'll be home soon and explain what happened."

The general then told us that he required radio access. We granted it, though Babe monitored every word—we weren't at all sure we could trust him. But we were granted access to U.S. air space because of him.

We landed in Thule within the hour. Personnel loaded the TAPO into the biggest cargo aircraft I ever saw. We sat in benches that lined the walls behind the cabin.

"Ears, you're in the cockpit with the pilot and Motor," I said. Make sure there's no funny business even though Babe has convinced everyone to play nice."

Babe took a seat next to me. "We have the freezing seats back here, Chief? Would it be okay if I snuggle up to you for warmth?"

Would it be okay?

"Sure, we'll keep each other warm," I said as calmly as I could. Babe inflamed the hope in my heart that we would be a couple. Within minutes, we both fell sound asleep.

****

Nine hours later, Picker shook me. "Chief, we're landing in fifteen minutes."

I snapped awake. Babe was still curled against my shoulder. I'd never slept as comfortably before.

"That was the best sleep I ever had," Babe said,

yawning and stretching her arms.

"Me too, Babe," I said glad that her experience matched mine.

The pilot landed softly and carried us over the tarmac to a small building where the crew disembarked with paperwork in hand.

"General, this is where we split," I said. "The street kids here must hear the news. Please follow through and plead for our amnesty."

He assured us he would. We shook hands. Healer touched the general's arm.

"General, my Thunder—how is he?"

"Ma'am, well, he's being kept alive by machines. We hoped you would return with T.D. for a rescue—he won't live if we disconnect him, Mrs. Dogget. He's not thriving as you all did before."

"I want to see him, General."

Ice put his arm around his mom. "Me too."

"Wait." Caution morphed into anger. "General, why should I trust you with my family while they're in your labs from hell?"

Healer interrupted me. "It's okay, Chief—I feel he's telling the truth."

I shook my head, but the general held up a hand. "Chief, I'm a trained soldier. My job is to protect my country. I saw Insiders as a threat, but I know better now. After trying to steal their powers, I'm ashamed—but I did it for my country, not for personal gain."

I was about to tell him none of us were convinced. He held up his hand again.

"I give you my word none of you will be detained," he said firmly, looking at each of us in turn. "I will free the remaining Insiders in my possession. But I do have to warn you, others will think I have lost my mind. Make your visit with Thunder a short one. I'll release the remaining Insiders when you're ready for them."

"I want this chance," Healer said to me. "I'd be happier doing it with your blessing."

"Healer, you're free to come and go—Ice, too. I won't stop you, but please remember that rescuing Insiders eats up time we should use for saving innocents."

Healer whispered into my ear, suggesting we meet at the factory I'd mentioned in a few hours. I nodded reluctantly and wished her well—I wasn't going to change her mind. When the general escorted her and Ice to the awaiting hummer, I worried until I realized Fly was missing. Knowing Healer and Ice would be okay with our invisible flying friend, I relaxed.

"Chief," the general hollered. "The jeep is yours for as long as you need it." Before he drove away, he pointed to the parking space next to his. "I trust you don't need keys."

"Motor, Lookout, scan that jeep for explosives or tracking devices."

"Right, Chief," Lookout answered.

Motor seemed to be in deep thought as he scrutinized the jeep's engine, but he said it checked out fine. Chief Sky Hawk tapped on my shoulder.

"I'm sorry, I almost forgot about you," I said. "I bet you're ready to go home."

"It's okay. I am in no hurry. But I do prefer the cold country more than this place."

"Hey, this city is the birthplace of liberty."

"Yes, for you," Chief Sky Hawk said dryly. "Not for my people."

I remembered that the birth of our country began the destruction of his. "I see what you mean, Chief. Sorry about that."

Chapter 19

"Okay, gang, let's check out our past," I said after landing in Philly with our freedom assured.

We were all five years older and home seemed strange to me. The streets looked familiar, but I had no attachment to them. Everything looked smaller, too. I wondered if territories had changed for street kids. As we drove down Centre Street, I spotted them.

"Babe, would it be hurtful for you if we park by your old building?"

"Chief, no," she said, surprised. "Those wounds healed long ago. It's a good starting point."

"I know you want to warn the street kids, Chief," Lookout said, "but what are we going to do if we find kids held captive by traffickers or pedophiles right here?"

"We'll contain them until Healer, Ice, Fly, and Top Dog return. But I sense this is not our territory anymore. We won't be here long."

"Sounds good but what do we tell kids about the change to come?" Picker asked.

"We'll tell each one what's going to happen and where to go to be safe," I replied. "They decide what to do about it—the straight ones will know the truth when they hear it."

"Uh, Chief, we don't even know when—what do we tell them about that?" Bat asked.

"What we know and don't know. That's all." I shrugged. "Ears, check in with Healer."

"On it, Chief," he said. "Repeating…"

"It's just his body, Ice. He's no longer in it. He is not reacting like we did—our bodies got stronger and healthier on respirators. Thunder's body is not. That means he isn't planning to return to us."

"Did we do something wrong, Mom? Or did he?"

"No, Ice. Nobody did anything wrong. Face must need him for something special, important even."

"But I miss him. He was my best friend. We were like real brothers."

"You were real brothers—and are real brothers. Because we exist in different dimensions, it does not mean we stop loving each other. Try to remember that, Ice. Keep on loving him. You'll see him again."

"Okay, Mom. I'm ready now."

"I'm proud of you, son. This button will stop the breathing machine. When I push it, Thunder's empty carcass will die. Are you ready?"

"Wait, Mom—I need to do it. Thunder would have turned it off for me."

"Ice turned off the machine," Ears said quietly. "Thunder is gone… for good."

No one spoke—we were all wiping our eyes. Healer had said it all. Still, separation from someone you love hurts even if you understand the continuity of life.

"Is Healer okay, Ears?"

"Chief, you won't believe this. Repeating…"

"Mom, look. Look!"

"What, Ice?"

"The wall is wavering."

"Huh—oh my, it's your dad! It's Top Dog! He's

come back to us, Ice."

Ears said he heard a few kissing smacks, hug grunts, and a lot of laughing. "Repeating…"

"Dad, are you back? Are you back for good? Do you know about Thunder?"

"Yes, but don't worry, I just spoke to your brother before I returned. He was hoping you would turn off that machine since he is having a great time where he is. And you bet I am back. Face said it was time. We need to save the innocent."

"Yay!"

"And Ears, if you and Chief are listening, everything seems fine here. We're on a military base with no soldiers pointing guns at us. Never thought I would see this day. Good job, Chief. Oh, and I've taken the remaining Insiders back to the Face. They won't be able to function in this dimension anymore anyway. I'll see you soon."

"Okay, Ears, give them some private time," I said. We were emotionally exhausted after the last couple of minutes. "T.D. or Healer will call me if he needs us. Let's start warning kids."

"Chief, we need fuel, man," Bat said. "We're starving."

Babe agreed. Once again, we faced hunger without any money in our pockets. Picker approached Chief Sky Hawk humbly.

"Do you have any money on you, sir? Just enough to buy some chips and a soda?"

Sky Hawk pulled out a billfold secured with a silver and turquoise money clip. "I can afford something more nutritious for all of us."

"Maybe later, Chief Skyhawk," Picker replied. "I

only need some bait for the locals, but I'll take you up on your offer for good food after we're through."

We found a quick store in a couple of blocks. As soon as I stepped outside, a long-haired boy grabbed the goods, taking off before I could talk to him. Much to my surprise and concern, Bat bagged him.

"Harsh, Bat," I muttered. "And in broad daylight, too."

"He wouldn't listen, Chief. What better evidence for the truth than our powers?"

"Listen, we aren't going to hurt you," I said to the bagged boy. "We aren't cops or pervs, either. But we need to tell you something that will save your life. You ready to hear it?"

The boy, still in the bubble, settled down.

"Things with the weather are going down," I continued. "Any day, any week or month, we aren't sure when, but you need to move to the high ground west of Philly—mountain high. Catch a train, a bus; however, you get there, go soon. When you arrive in a place where you feel comfortable, find something underground that will protect you from the winds. Fill it with six months' worth of food and water. Do you understand me?"

"Yeah. Move to the mountains and squirrel underground," the boy said. "So, how do you know this weather thing is going to happen for sure?"

"Man, you're caught in an invisible bag. Do you want to question the people who can do that?" Bat gestured with his arm. "Or this?"

Fly landed on cue with Healer, Ice, and Top Dog. Our prisoner's eyes bugged out.

"Okay, I believe. Head west, mountaintops, store food, water underground. Got it."

"Tell other kids before you go," I said. "Make them believe it more than you do. Tell them, uh, tell them you got the information from Chief Poop. Will you do that?"

"You're Chief Poop? No way—Chief Poop is my age!"

"For real," I said. "Just a little older."

"Okay then, Chief Poop," the boy said. "I'll tell everybody—I'll save all I can."

He'd used the word *save*. My heart loosened up — my first connection was a natural-born leader. Bat released the boy from the bubble. He immediately went to Ice.

"Are you one of these guys?" he asked.

Ice smiled. "Yeah, I'm an Insider, and this stuff is all true. Make sure they know to leave here soon, even if they have to walk."

"Yo, man, I hear you." The boy turned to me. "Okay, am I free to go?"

"Here, kid, let me give you a lift." Fly swept him up in his arms and took off.

"Holy crap… not too high… this is cool!" the boy said, his voice fading as they climbed.

Fly set him down a couple blocks away. I sensed that our warning would spread and gave Ice a punch on the arm and a confident nod.

After the street kid took off to warn others, I welcomed my returned family.

"Top Dog, a pleasure to see you looking healthy."

"Chief, thank you for looking after my wife and son."

"Yeah, well about that…"

T.D. didn't let me apologize for our capture. "Face sent word. It's time we begin the specific job assigned to us. We'll work together—that okay with you, Chief?"

"Of course it's okay with me. Tell me more."

"Let's talk over pizza. I've been dreaming of pizza," T.D. said.

"Man, I'm famished too," Bat patted his stomach. "There used to be a great place around the corner. They make good cheesesteaks."

"Cheese on a steak?" Sky Hawk shook his head. "Hmph. I'll stick with spaghetti and meatballs."

The small restaurant had grown old and shabby. Although the tables and booths needed refurbishment, they were spotless. Aromas filled our nostrils and teased our guts. Quickly, we pushed smaller tables together and grabbed extra chairs. After we sat, we all reached for the menus at the same time.

After we ate, T.D. talked about Face and Thunder. We were glad to sit back and listen while the cheesesteaks, hoagies, and spaghetti digested. Then we got down to business as T.D. explained our mission.

"We've all seen the dark side of life," he said. "We know how it feels to be ignored, unloved. But there is an even darker side that exists on Earth. Face wants to right the wrongs done to these children and their parents. It's the kids he told us about, the innocents."

"You saying we have to get specific, T.D.?" I asked.

"Yes. Face will take care of the remaining street kids. We are going after the human trafficking victims. Babies, toddlers stolen right out from under their parents' eyes, never seen or heard from again. Some children were murdered, but more became slaves so early in life that they don't remember where they came from or the life that was supposed to be theirs." T.D. paused to look at all of us in turn. "Sometimes they turn into abusers because it's all they remember. Face wants to fix the entire mess, and we'll save all we can before the change. This is serious business."

"We were lucky, weren't we, T.D.? We lived on the street, but at least the predators missed us," I caught Babe's eye and realized my mistake. "I am so sorry… that didn't come out right."

"No worries, Chief. That was long ago. This is a job I'm going to love."

"Good for you," Healer said.

My mind fired off a plan. "Motor, you'll do the setup. Hack into predator websites and note where the biggest clusters of traffickers are. We'll go there, rescue the victims—" I turned to T.D. "—but what are we to do with them?"

"I'll take them from you to the Face. They'll need special healing for their minds, spirit, and bodies. After they're renewed, I'll bring them back to safe zones where they will meet their parents or guardians."

"Motor?" I wondered what he had found.

"Working on it—I'm in Oklahoma right now."

"Oklahoma?" Picker scratched his head. "I mean, isn't Oklahoma a waste of time?"

"Do you think Oklahoma is immune to human trafficking?" Babe asked.

"I never thought about it. It seems remote, like Kansas or something," Picker said.

"Human trafficking is worldwide," Motor said. "I'm beginning my search in the U.S., but pedophiles live anywhere and everywhere, Picker. Remember, Philadelphia may seem remote to someone in Oklahoma."

"I get it, Motor," I said, "but how can the birthplace

of freedom admit to allowing pedophiles and trafficking? Democracy's roots are here right under our feet."

Picker turned on his stage presence. "Four score and seven years ago, our fathers brought forth on this continent a new nation…"

"Ah, Picker." Lookout was shaking his head. "That was Abraham Lincoln. He came along a lot later and was from Nebraska."

"Okay. 'The Red Coats are coming. The Red Coats are coming.'"

"Sorry, Picker," Babe said. "Paul Revere."

He scratched his head. "It is now the time for all good men to come to the aid of their country."

"Sorry, Picker," we all said at once.

"Wrong century, man." Exasperated, Ears shook his head. "Think of Ben Franklin, Thomas Jefferson, George Washington, and all the founding fathers who signed the Declaration of Independence."

"Gosh, all are legends, but I can't remember one thing they said," Babe admitted.

"Motor, find some quotes on the grid. It'll be a good reminder for all of us since we were, uh, *distracted* when this stuff was presented in school."

"I don't have to search, Chief. American History was a hobby for my dad and me. Our founding fathers signed the Declaration of Independence while knowing if they were caught, they would be hanged. In fact, Ben Franklin said, 'We must all hang together, or, assuredly, we shall all hang separately.'"

"That goes along with Patrick Henry's quote: 'Give me liberty or give me death,'" T.D. said.

"My dad and I used to visit the Independence Hall, Christ Church, and the Liberty Bell," Motor said. "He was more than a motorhead. He taught me to appreciate the cost of liberty like ours. Our founding fathers paid a lot for it."

Motor wiped his eyes. I hadn't realized he was crying a little. "They didn't live 'happily ever after,' you know. Many were hunted down and hung. Others lost everything they ever owned and watched their children hunted as well. They all sacrificed to create a democratic country. The United States of America was a huge experiment that *succeeded*. It isn't perfect, but nothing is."

"John Adams said, 'Our constitution was made *only* for a moral and religious people. It is wholly inadequate to the government of any other,'" T.D. said. "People have forgotten a higher power, a creator, and a source of all things. If they can't see, hear, or touch it, they don't believe it. With no standards to aspire to, a populace loses integrity. Democracy requires honesty, but above all, integrity first on an individual level—and *then* on an elected level."

"True that, T.D. And Spiderman's uncle said, 'With great power comes great responsibility,' Picker said. "Hey, it's true."

"What do you think will happen after the earth changes, T.D.? Healer asked her husband. "I mean, what will happen to people as a whole?"

"Free will continues," he replied. "It allows everyone to choose their own path. I want to think people will turn to hope. Hope is unseen; it requires faith. Faith is the first footstep toward the hidden, the Face. Yet, it could go the other way with tyranny taking on the bewildered masses. Sorry, I don't see the future."

"Let's not think about that," I said. "We have a job

to do right here, right now."

Motor rapped the table with his knuckles. "Human traffickers get away with stealing a human being on one side of the world and transporting him or her to the other side. Why don't people see what's going on around them? Where is the suspicion? Why aren't perpetrators captured right away? People not wanting to talk about it is like turning their backs on thousands of kids. It isn't right!"

A familiar voice from long ago interrupted our discussion.

"Yo, Chief Crap."

Chapter 20

After an awesome meal, my stomach flipped when I realized Bus stood next to me. He looked older, more ragged, and still hung with the same two boyz—they towered over our table. Bus kept his right hand inside his coat. I glanced at Lookout, who nodded. Bus packed a gun, and he wouldn't be afraid to use it.

"*Ahwoo*. Well, if it isn't the hound," Picker laughed.

"I've been biding my time for years," Bus said menacingly. "Waiting for you guys to come back into my expanded territory."

Good grief. Bus managed to remain free during the years we spent inside with Face?

"Paybacks are hell, Chief," he said to me, as if reading my mind. "Now, I'm not worried about all these people, but you and the redhead need to say goodbye. Catch my drift?"

"Still wearing a whitey tightie," Lookout said. "That video should have told you something, Bus."

"You can't know that—hey, *you* was the one who threw dat shit on us. Now *you're* invited to our private party."

We had no time for Bus or his antics. "I'm sorry, Bus," I said. "We were kids, you know?" I extended my hand to him. He ignored it.

"You're sorry, huh? Well, you're gon' be sorrier." Bus moved closer to our table. "Get up."

"Chief is not going to stand until he wants to, you lump of stupid," Picker chuckled.

I gave him one more chance. "Bus, please—turn around and walk away."

"Maybe I ought to shoot you right here?" The dealer pulled out his gun, waving it around. The less we responded, the angrier he got.

Bat stood. "Listen, Bro, listen: I got you in a bubble, okay? If you shoot, the bullet will ricochet. You'll end up shooting yourself instead, and I don't want that on my conscience."

"Do what? I'm in a *bubble*?" Bus laughed.

Picker laughed harder. "Yeah, it's a big bubble for a big hound dog."

Chief Sky Hawk stood and spoke in broken English like the Indians were portrayed in an old-time western movie. "Mr. Hound-Bus, my friends don't care for scalps, but I take yours for my collection." I gasped when Sky Hawk raised a butter knife.

"Take a look at dem feathers on that one, boyz," Bus replied, chuckling. "You couldn't cut diddly-squat with that thing, old man."

"No? Maybe this will do." With speed and agility no one would expect from a man his age, Chief Sky Hawk reached up his sleeve and whipped out a knife with a twelve-inch blade. Our entourage began to hoot. That made Bus angrier.

"Don't bring a knife to a gunfight, fool. Maybe I'll play cowboy and put a hole right through that pretty costume. Sit down while the little chief stands up… boyz, get him to his feet."

"Boss? Yo, boss… we can't move. What the—?"

Chief Sky Hawk slapped the table and laughed

while slipping the knife back inside his sleeve just as fast as he'd pulled it out. Bus tried to turn toward his boyz, but he was stuck in position. Sky Hawk and Picker laughed hardest.

"The problem with you guys is that you don't listen," Picker said. "Your wrapping is getting tight, isn't it?"

Bus's nose began to smoosh.

"Check it out, bro!" Bat picked up a saltshaker and threw it. We watched it bounce off Bus's bag as expected. His eyes grew large as saucers. "Imagine a bullet doing the same thing on the inside of the bubble, Dawg. Get the picture?"

"We've wasted enough time with you, Bus," I said. "We're leaving. Bat will take the bag off you when we're out the door."

"Oh, and Bus, tell the waitress you'll pick up the tab—for all of us," Picker said as Bat made the bubble tighter.

"Yeah, yeah, sure—" Bus poked the bag with his finger. When he gave it a swift kick, he bounced across the room, knocking his boyz over, and landed on top of the pizza counter. He teeter-tottered but didn't fall off.

"I'll get y'all yet," he said through clenched teeth.

We were three blocks away when Bat released Bus and the boyz.

Within seconds, we heard a gunshot. People hit the ground, hiding behind shop doors, We ducked, too, until we saw Bat holding the bullet in his hand. Chief Sky Hawk laughed so hard, he couldn't even slap his leg or talk. But he managed to give our happy Picker a high-five.

"I about peed myself!" Picker exclaimed.

"I got this one," Fly announced, then disappeared. Suddenly, the gun flew from Bus's hand. Each time he tried to retrieve it, an invisible force kicked it down the street.

Then the gun disappeared while Bus lifted off the ground.

****

As Fly flew overhead, he shouted excitedly, "There's a dog park a few blocks that way."

Most of my crew took off, running in that direction. I turned to T.D., Healer, Ice, and Sky Hawk. "It's a long story, guys, but you'll want to see this." After all, we had given Bus fair warning.

"Come on, Sky Hawk," Picker said. "If you need help…"

Chief Sky Hawk smiled and broke into a slow jog impressive for a geriatric. Healer, T.D, and Ice ran behind him. We found the chain link fence that enclosed an acre of dog crap mixed with snow that had begun to melt into slush.

Fly carried his terrified and screaming gangster over the busiest area, flying in circles far above until we were all present. Then he dove, dragging Bus stomach down through the plentiful and mushy turds before releasing Bus's belt.

"Ugh." Chief Sky Hawk looked repulsed. "Much worse than fresh bear dung. Ugh."

Bus attracted dogs in the park as he tried to stand. "Get off me! Get off me!" He managed to rise to his knees until a bullmastiff started humping him, pulling him back down.

Picker was in rare form. "You got to pay to play, Hound. We warned you, but you wouldn't listen. Eww…

I smell a stinker!"

Passerby's and dog owners had pulled out cell phones when they saw two huge men flying above. A few captured the event: Insiders caught in the act, and their dog in the video, too. One enterprising teen caught the whole thing on his mini-cam—Bus soon to be humiliated around the world again, this time by Fly.

"The poop story was real," T.D. laughed as he watched Bus try to escape the mastiff and other dogs that lifted their legs on his head.

"Afraid so," I said.

"That took a lot of planning and calculating. You were how old?"

"About twelve. No big deal, T.D."

"Wrong, Chief. No wonder Face chose you—I bet he loved it. You guys are naturals for developing and implementing plans to save the children."

Fly flew overhead again. "Sorry, Chief, I missed a couple." Bus's two stooges belly-flopped in the stink next. "Now, let us alone," he shouted, "and we'll let you alone!"

"Chief, we need to move," Motor said. "The southern-hemisphere countries are in the most danger when the earth flips and have the highest congestion of traffickers from a cyberspace perspective. I suggest we start in Brazil—São Paulo and Rio, too. We need to leave. There's a lot of work ahead of us."

Motor shook his head no, answering the question I was going to ask. "This is about the kids, Chief," he said. "Not my favorite translator."

"Good work, Motor," T.D. said.

"Well, Chief, we have our starting point. But what about transport?"

"Oh, you don't know about transporters yet, T.D.?" I replied. "They move us fast."

"Yes, I know. I watched as they saved you in North Carolina."

"You watched it?" Babe asked.

"I saw you in trouble, so I called transporters to help. I witnessed many cool things inside. Insiders from all over the world went through the same things you and I experienced—like running from the military, using their powers to escape."

"You wouldn't believe the myriad of powers Face handed out, but we'll talk about that later," I said. "Face wants his directives followed first and right away."

On cue, transporters arrived. There were fewer than before, but no buildings needed relocating this time. Ears and Motor looked perplexed and forlorn when they realized Anna Marie was not with them. Augusto, the transporters' leader, and I shook hands.

"Chief, where to?" Augusto caught a glimpse of the dog park and heard Bus's obscenities. "Or… I call you Chief *Poop*!"

Augusto's crew broke into cheers. Mine laughed, and even I smiled. "Señor, the credit goes to Fly this time. His name is Peter. Peter Poop."

"Viva, Peter Poop! Viva, Peter Poop!" Augusto's crew chanted.

"Uh, thanks, everyone," Fly said. He did not look pleased with his new title.

"Augusto, we're heading to São Paulo, Brazil, with a brief stop in Cherokee, North Carolina. This is Chief Sky Hawk's first ride with transporters, at least while he is awake."

Chief crossed his arms over his chest. "Can't be

harder than riding a buffalo bareback."

"It easy peasy, *si*? You sit down, Chief Sky Hawk."

"Here, on a city sidewalk?" I asked.

"They no see much too long," Augusto said. "Change brings quick forgetting. Best you cross legs and arms."

We sat inside their small circle. "*Vamos fazê-lo. Até logo.*" The whirr began, but not like the first time's intensity. We started a gentle float, spin, and take off. We entered the vortex, enjoying the beauty inside the fabric of Earth, space, and time. Flashes of bright lights in the alternate reality landed us in Cherokee in a matter of minutes.

"Well, Chief Sky Hawk, how about that ride?" I asked.

"These old eyes now see a prophecy fulfilled: you will call Insiders your own; your eyes will see the unseen as you fly like a hawk."

"That's beautiful, sir."

"This was the best day of my life, Chief. Now I can die in peace."

We shook hands as the sheriffs pulled up to collect him. "I'm glad you enjoyed it, Chief Sky Hawk, but stick around awhile. I want to see you again, my friend."

I stepped back into the circle, anticipating a long journey. As we enjoyed kaleidoscope views, time seemed to disappear. When we landed in Sau Paulo, I asked the transporter leader to stand by for the children we would save. We all managed a thank you in Portuguese: *obrigado*.

"T.D., I've been thinking about ways to rescue the innocent without wasting time," I said. "If the president of Brazil grants amnesty for all pedophiles and traffickers, many children might be returned—older ones and maybe some little ones. What do you think?"

"It wouldn't hurt to try, Chief. Trust your gut—Face chose you for this job. I have faith he knew what he was doing. So… what part do I play in this scheme?"

"Your military demeanor will impress El Presidente. Plus, you're a natural-born negotiator."

"Okay, how do I gain access to the President?"

"Motor, find El Presidente. Fly will sneak you to him. Make sure he understands that amnesty must be issued immediately. Take Babe along in case you meet any resistance."

"Take me, too, T.D.—I mean Dad. I'll freeze them if they try to hurt us. Please?"

"Fly, can you handle three of us?"

"No problem, T.D.," Fly said. "My pleasure."

"Chief, that okay with you?"

"Sounds like Ice could be an asset. Go for it."

"Heads up," Motor said. "El Presidente is doing business from his beach house nearby heading southwest. His family is there celebrating something or other. That might work for you."

"Fly, find the largest house on the beach surrounded by guards."

I patted T.D. on the shoulder. "Good luck T.D. Fly, take care—you're carrying precious cargo," I added, shooting Ice a wink. As Fly took off, I turned to the group. "Ears and Lookout, stay sharp. Brazil is loaded with victims."

Although Lookout was able to peer behind walls, São Paulo's tall buildings made for a complicated mosaic that proved difficult to navigate. We landed in an alley with a brick road at one end that intersected with little traffic. At the other, major highways crossed at five points.

"This is one progressive country, modern in every way," Lookout said. "Where to begin?"

I suddenly saw a vision of an older part of town, underprivileged but adjacent to the new city. "Go that way," I said, pointing toward the quiet end. We took the intersecting street, walking at a good clip, and within half an hour the buildings were lower, older, and dingy. Across the street, a red awning stretched over an entrance to a small store or bar of some kind. It looked dark and seedy inside, but some force pulled me toward it.

Lookout's face suddenly went red with emotion.

"About ten kids and some toddlers are in there, Chief. Perverts want babies—this is awful."

"Yeah, but we have no time to judge or punish. Healer, call the transporters and tell them to find a haven in the mountains. Somewhere safe, maybe a church, until T.D. gets them to Face."

"Sure, Chief. I'll tell them we need their ongoing services."

"Good thinking. One of us must stay with the rescued kids... how about you, Healer?"

"I'd love to, Chief."

"Then it's settled. Time to save our first batch of victims."

Chapter 21

Our first job filled us with excitement mixed with intense focus. We crossed the empty thoroughfare, inching our way into the entrance—which stunk of stale cigarettes. Our eyes adapted to the gloom quickly. The place appeared empty except for a rough-looking barkeep concentrating on paperwork until we heard a young voice hush a whining toddler.

The barkeep shouted, "*Silencio*."

Lookout pointed toward the back corner. I nodded.

"Chief," Ears whispered. "Bat and I can distract the bartender."

Ears spoke fluent Portuguese as he presented himself. "*Cervaja, por favor. Cervaja. Andamos muito tempo no calor.*"

"*Estamos fechados, señor. Sair agora, por favor, señor.*" The bartender's words seemed kind, but I didn't trust him for an instant. As Ears and Bat kept him busy, Picker, Lookout, and I sneaked aisle to aisle to the back corner.

"Picker," I whispered, "you keep them quiet, okay? Let them know we want to help."

Picker didn't take more than a second to think. He got on all fours and made like a puppy, peeking around the corner. The youngest started to giggle. The oldest girl, no more than eight or nine, placed her finger to her lips, fearfully shaking her head. Lookout and I followed

Picker on all fours. Panting as puppies do, we put our paws to our lips.

"Well, well, the pressure got too much for you guys," Ears said. He and Bat split their guts laughing. Then Bat tried to get serious: "The bartender is taken care of, Chief."

Ears spoke calmly to the oldest. She was a beautiful little girl but grave, possessing amazing self-control despite her terror. She stretched her arms out to protect the youngest children. Ears took our lead and got on his knees to her eye level, speaking in Portuguese.

"Señorita, we come to help you. We don't want to hurt you. We want to take you home to your parents who have looked all over the world for you."

"Our parents died," the child, speaking English, said matter-of-factly.

Ears shook his head. "That was a lie, sweetheart. Your momma and daddy never stopped looking for you."

Her face did not change expression. Did she believe what Ears told her?

"We'll take you to a safe place," Ears continued. "Will you let us help you?"

Panic crept in. "No, no! My uncle—they will kill me. If I help you, they will kill me. Save the babies, Señor. It is too late for me."

As Ears interpreted, I was shocked. I never remembered feeling it was too late for me as a kid at seven or eight.

Healer stepped forward and bent down. "Ears, tell her no one will be hurt or be allowed to touch them again. Tell her we come from a magic place. This is what we do to bad people. Bat?"

As Ears translated, Bat hurried to the front of the

building, bouncing the now-bagged barkeep over to us.

"You see?" Ears asked gently. "He is stuck inside a big invisible ball until Bat lets him out. Bat will do the same to anyone who tries to hurt you, okay? It's his magic gift."

Ears translated Healer's words as the girl stared at the entrapped barkeep.

"Since you are the oldest child," Healer continued, "will you tell the others to hold hands and sit on the floor here with me?"

The children were happy to sit down—two of the youngest climbed onto Healer's lap. The oldest girl gathered the others in her arms, bunching them together while a boy, about the same age as her, sat close.

"Ears, tell them they're going for a magic ride to a beautiful mountaintop full of happiness."

He did. The oldest girl glared at our prisoner in the bubble—Ears and Healer had sparked some glimmer of hope inside her. She smiled at the youngest child, but her happiness turned to shock when transporters appeared out of thin air. Ears assured her it was okay as Healer stood by to help ease their fear.

"They are all yours. Enjoy," I said. "See you tonight."

"Stay safe, everyone." Healer glowed surrounded by children. She was in her element. We stepped back when we heard, "Get it done."

"Chief, Healer has a way with kids, doesn't she?" Bat asked.

"She sure does. I don't know how we're going to pull the next rescue off without her."

"Chief, our guys are at the palace," Ears said. "Repeating:"

"El Presidente."

"How did you get in here? Who are you?"

"We need your help, El Presidente. Look into my eyes; see, we are not here to harm you. You want to help us, don't you?"

The president immediately calmed down. "Si, Señorita."

"I heard you speak English, El Presidente?" T.D. asked.

"Si. Enough."

"El, Presidente, we want to solve the problem of pedophiles and human trafficking. You agree it is a big problem in the world today?"

"Si. Si. Big problem. What do you suggest?"

"An amnesty, sir. Stolen children end up on the streets or killed, thrown away like trash. But you can stop it. Tell the traffickers to hand in their children in places of your choosing. Grant them immunity. Assure the pedophiles they will not be punished ever in their lives. They could walk up to a police station, return the children, and no one will ask their name. They can live their lives without secrets or fear.

"Hmm…"

"In fact, I suggest you give bountiful rewards. If the boss says no, his or her workers may still turn in a child for the money. Whatever way you decide to do it, El Presidente, it must be done today."

El Presidente placed his hands on his hips. "You think these child thieves should succeed with their perversions?"

"No, Sir. I guarantee, there will be repercussions, but you will not be the one with blood on your hands. You could track their every move and prevent more kidnappings in the future."

"He's telling the President about the earth now, Chief. Fly did a number on him—he's a believer!" Ears laughed. "He agrees to it."

"I don't know how he couldn't agree with Babe there, but we don't know how effective this plan will be," I said. "Doesn't hurt to try though."

"There are plenty in this area, Chief," Ears said. "I hear them, their perpetrators. I'm unnerved by their gall. Look around; this is a modern country, yet they get away with it here as they do in Europe, the Far East, and the States."

I nodded. "What's the latest on El Presidente?"

"He's saying goodbye to our guys... now he's calling someone on an intercom, I think... ah, he wants an immediate press conference at his beach house with TV cameras!" Ears exclaimed. "He's asked for his family to join him—he's telling his secretary to send faxes to all police stations, churches, and fire departments."

"Let me know when he's on the air. Motor, can you get in touch with Fly somehow and let him know where we are?"

Motor found a running billboard in the same block where we landed and inserted a cryptic message. "Fly a half hour west," he said. "Look for the tattered red awning."

We pulled a table and chairs outside, enjoying bottled water and snacks in the fresh air. The few pedestrians that dared walk the area peeked at us before quickening their steps. The sight of gringos relaxing was too unusual. Soon Fly landed with his passengers intact.

"Good job, guys," I said. "I hope you didn't mind us

listening in."

"No problem, Chief. What happened after we left?" T.D. asked.

"El Presidente called for a press conference."

T.D. looked around and became alarmed. "Where's Healer?"

"We did some rescuing of our own, T.D., right from this den of puke. Transporters took Healer and the kids up to a mountaintop. They're waiting for you to take them to the Face."

"Guess the pervs won't hunt for them there." T.D. sighed. "I hope to travel with even more children if I can separate them from Healer. She must be having a good time. She's a natural-born mother."

"What do we do next?" Lookout was disgusted and down.

"Let's save more kids," I said, "but keep an eye on perverts who will react the opposite way to the amnesty and go into deep hiding. There will be a bunch, I'm sure."

"Chief, turn on the TV quick," Ears said. Motor turned the set on behind the bar as the barkeep begged for his freedom.

"Señor, *silencio!*" I snapped. I had no idea if I'd just spoken Portuguese, Spanish, or pig Latin, but the dirtbag shut up.

The news popped on. Ears went to work: "Repeating…"

"Attention. Emergency! The President of Brazil wishes to talk to his people."

"Good afternoon, citizens of Brazil. I want you to join members of my family on this, my birthday. My wife, Serena. My two daughters, Juanita and Joanna, and my son, Eduardo. Serena and I are proud parents. We love our children with all our hearts, and we tell them so every day. Without fail, they say to us, 'I love you too.' I hope every Brazilian child hears those words from their parents or family members: 'I love you.'

"Here, as in the rest of the world, many children do not hear 'I love you.' Worse, some children hear a similar phrase, but the words are spoken by perpetrators, thieves of innocence, violators. Those evil ones pay any sum to have a child for a few minutes, for an hour, or a day, and even years until the child becomes too old for their tastes.

"I cannot tell the citizens of Brazil why this perversion exists. I can tell you that they satisfy their hunger by stealing children from parents who then live in agony forever, not knowing if their child is dead or alive. These emboldened thieves lift boys and girls from their beds, from the beach, from other countries, and they bring them here to Brazil.

"Others steal our Brazilian babies and whisk them away to unknown places in the world. It is a perverted madness. I use the word perversion, but I do not judge them. Perpetrators who hear this broadcast; let me say again, I do not condemn you for your lusts. I am angry you steal babies from their mommas and poppas, yes. I feel anger when you throw them out like trash once finished with them.

"But I have good news for you: my heart has burst open. I see you cannot help yourselves, so, let me help you. From this day forth, I declare an amnesty for all human traffickers and kidnappers on one condition: take your child to the open arms of Brazil. You will not be detained; you will not be questioned; you will not be followed.

"A police officer, hospital attendant, priest, nun, minister, or firefighter will say, 'Thank you.' They will take the children from you and return them to their mommas and poppas and families. If you know the child's birth name or location of birth, perhaps you would put it in his or her pocket, si?

"I have opened my heart to you, pledging in full view of the public eye: from this moment forth I declare an amnesty for all child traffickers, and Brazil offers one hundred twenty-five thousand reals for each child dropped off. Will you do this now? Will you open your hearts?

"Chief," Ears said quickly, "in round numbers, that's a little less than twenty-five grand in U.S. dollars. Repeating…

"Brazilians open your eyes to this growing insult to the world's children. Step up and save a child, but please understand: if you turn in your neighbor's child for cash, severe punishment will be your reward. We want kidnapped, stolen, abducted children—and no one else."

"I encourage fellow leaders in South America to declare the same amnesty in their countries… indeed, the whole world. My personal contribution is the television time I bought to play this Declaration of Amnesty for forty-eight hours continuously.

"We are all children of the Creator, are we not? Each of us has the right to hear, 'I love you' from our real mommas and poppas. Let the amnesty begin."

The broadcast ended but repeated immediately.

"Check it out!" T. D. was overjoyed. "Cokes on the house everyone. That's alright with you, isn't it, Barkeep?"

"Si, Señor. You take—is yours."

"Lookout, I have a feeling someone will turn up soon for the kids. Keep watch. Bat, you better bag us." I turned to the barkeep. "Señor, what do you think about the news you heard?"

The barkeep shrugged.

"Repeating," Ears said.

"It will be good for older children. But most will keep the young ones, no matter how much money is offered."

"Señor, you seem to be sure of that."

Again, the barkeep shrugged.

"He doesn't want to share much, does he, Chief?" Motor asked.

"No, but he knows more. Ears, translate for him what I'm about to say." I turned to the man in the bubble. "You know a lot more about human trafficking than you do tending bar. Tell me who the baby molesters are—give me the names of every single person. I promise you, Señor, we are here to save these children. We'll do whatever it takes to get to them… you think the bag is unpleasant? Bat, show him how uncomfortable it gets."

The bag suddenly smooshed his nose.

"Señor, my other friend will fly to the top of a building and drop you off."

Fly lifted off the ground on cue. The thug's eyes bulged.

"Chief, something stinks!" Picker pointed to the barkeep's wet pants.

"I help. I help," he said in broken English.

Bat deflated the bag, but the man stood frozen, stiff, afraid to move. I tapped on the bar. "Write the names and addresses here."

"No addresses. They come here. I no go there."

"Fine, Señor. Write the names down *now* with phone numbers."

The man began to scribble in a fury. We found it hard to believe how many predators lived in the same area.

"Motor?"

"I'm researching the telephone numbers and coming up with addresses. They all show up in or near São Paulo—also Rio. How do we get there since we have no clue in this country? I wouldn't trust the GPS here."

"We need a comfortable ride for the children," Babe said. "How about a limo, Chief? It's big, comfy, and nobody is going to run from a limo. Also, it comes with a driver familiar with the country's addresses."

"Señor, call for a stretch limousine," I said.

"Si, Señor."

The barkeep picked up his cell phone. Ears kept a close tab on him and nodded that he was following instructions. When he was through, I explained we no longer needed his services. Between Ears and Motor, the limo driver would know where to go.

"Bat, set him in the corner where the kids were. Motor, notify authorities, but not yet. Bag him for forty-eight hours, then let *policia* know where he is."

"Señor, no bag, por favor, no bag."

Bat waved his hand. The bartender slumped, defeated.

I gave him an icy look. *You deserve worse than bagging.*

Chapter 22

Waiting for the limo outside, we watched as the driver approached us hesitantly—maybe he was nervous about navigating through the seedy side of town. We waved and smiled, then introduced ourselves with the help of Ears after we piled inside. He finally smiled when Motor handed him a written address. We guessed he was relieved to head toward a classier direction.

Surprisingly, the first address brought us back to the transporters' drop-off point. The driver explained in broken English that it was the European section of San Paolo—home of the elites.

"Chief, there are two addresses in the building right in front of us."

"That's interesting—and convenient," I said. "Driver, park here and wait for us, please. You'll be well compensated."

"Si, Señor, I wait forever here. *Obrigado*."

Wanting to get into the building before Picker, Motor determined the entry code, but Picker beat him to it.

"I saw that, bro. I saw what you tried to do there," Picker said, walking through the closed door and then punching Motor's arm.

"Yeah, yeah. You won… this time."

We scoped out the lobby and piled into the elevator. The building appeared to be an ordinary high rise from outside, but the interior reeked of the rich—*stinking rich*—with its art-adorned marble walls. Landing on the tenth floor, we matched the apartment number to the first address on our list. Picker tried the door handle and found it locked. He disappeared, opening it from inside.

We entered a foyer, ready for anything. The living room contained opulent furniture and more framed artwork on walls of white. Lookout pointed to the hallway on the right. As we crept that way, we heard a little girl singing the Sesame Street theme in English.

Her door had an outside lock.

"Pigs," T.D. whispered angrily, out of character for his easy-going demeanor.

Picker opened the lock. Babe followed him inside. The singing stopped.

"It's okay, sweetheart," Babe said. "I am a friend. I'm not going to hurt you. Do I have eyes that look as if they would hurt you?"

The little girl smiled and shook her head.

"My friends won't hurt you, either, and we brought happy news: we're here to take you home to your mommy and daddy, sweetheart."

"Mommy and Daddy don't want me anymore," the little girl said in a heartbreaking voice.

"Sweetheart, somebody bad told you that, but it isn't true. Your parents love you. They sent us to find you. Do you want to go home?"

The girl nodded her head, then fell into Babe's arms in a daze.

"This is my new friend, everyone," she said. "We're going to take her home."

I pointed to the next door. Babe nodded.

"Shall we open the other door first, sweetheart?"

The child perked up and smiled. "My friend."

Picker and Babe walked through first. Another preschool girl lay sleeping, curled up in the fetal position. Her little face bore tear stains. Her puffy eyes showed drug use.

"Uncle says she's new like me," the first girl said.

This hit me in a very soft place. I blinked back tears and watched T.D. tenderly cover the little girl and lift her, still sleeping. Picker, I noticed, was fidgeting.

"Maybe we should bring her doll?" he asked.

"She likes that one," the first girl said. "Mine too?"

"Of course, sweetheart. Your dollies want to go home, too, right?" Babe said. The second girl's eyelids opened long enough to point to her doll. Babe placed it in her hands, and she hugged it tight and closed her eyes again.

"Back down to the ninth floor, Chief."

"Thanks, Lookout," I said, knowing I needed to lead. "Picker, are you okay?"

"I don't get it, Chief."

"Yeah. Nobody gets it except them."

"To the left, Chief, at the end of the hallway," Lookout said. "It's a long way back to the elevator, but stairs are accessible if we need them."

Ears spoke up as we approached the second apartment. "Dog inside this one—a big dog."

"You hear a dog, but I don't see one," Lookout said. "Kids are inside, though."

Picker walked Bat through with him. We stood cautiously by the door; guard dogs still made us jumpy.

"Never mind, Chief," Ears said. "It's a CD. The dog growls for a while then he barks. This thing is noise-activated and will play all day."

"Yep. The speaker's hidden inside this bouquet of silk flowers," Lookout added.

"Is it to scare people away? Or to keep someone from leaving their room?" Babe asked.

"Probably both," I said. "Let's go, Babe."

The layout duplicated the first apartment. The prisoner, a five-year-old boy, looked fearful. He scooted away from us, but Babe's influence calmed him. He told us about his friend that also lived there.

Picker held out his arms for the little boy. A second little boy slept in the next room. Babe, picking him up, cradled him as if he were her own. As we closed the apartment door, we heard hurried, excited voices. We changed directions, turning toward the stairwell.

"Chief!" Ears hissed. "Repeating…"

"My two are gone… disappeared. If your two are gone, we will be in big trouble. All four are expected for delivery tomorrow."

"Let's round up the perpetrators while we're at it, Bat."

"I'll bag them extra tight, so they can't reach their cell phones to warn their amigos. I'll be down in a minute, Chief."

"Thanks, but don't take too long," I replied, noting the dark look in Bat's eye. I had no doubt he wanted to bounce them around and scare them to death. "Remember, other victims are waiting for us."

"Yeah—okay, Chief."

We took the stairs to the ninth floor, hoping to outflank them, then boarded the elevator. Our four drugged souls slept while the oldest boy smiled, enjoying the ride. The driver saw us coming and opened the doors. He looked worried when he saw the children.

"You turn them in for money?"

Figuring he could understand me if he spoke broken but coherent English, I explained that we were the good guys—and would be on a quest that would last most of the day.

"You *heróis*," he said, a smile spreading across his face. "You make me *heróis*, too! Where next to go?"

Motor handed our chauffeur the list of names and addresses. "Let's map this out first," he said. "We might re-trace our steps and waste time if we don't"

"Si. I help."

The driver diagrammed a geographic list. Meanwhile, Motor identified our first captured traffickers to the local police department—they would *not* receive amnesty. Bat joined us as we headed to our third location.

"I like to help *heróis*," the driver announced. He pronounced the word hero in Portuguese until we showed him that we could say it, too.

The next building was a true high rise with our suspect apartment on the thirty-fourth floor. As we entered the building, Ears signaled us to be quiet.

"Chief, they're on the elevator coming down. I hear kids crying, a couple of women, and a man arguing. Oh yeah… Bat get ready. These scumbags are talking about a new hideout."

"Wait till they step out of the elevator. We'll get them from the side," I said. "If you must, bag them all. Picker will pull the children out one by one."

"Right, Chief."

The elevator doors opened. Two women and one man stepped out, each saying *Silencio* to the other. The children looked pale with swollen red eyes, obviously drugged. Bat promptly bagged the perpetrators the way a vacuum bagged dirt.

"Who are you? Get out of our way," the blonde demanded. She tried to push her stroller forward and was shocked when it didn't move.

Picker reached inside and removed the double stroller, revealing three small children—I guessed between three and five years old. Babe and Ears spoke to them in gentle whispers. The bagged women began to scream.

"Shut up," I snapped. "We heard you trying to escape. There is no amnesty for you heartless witches." Top Dog placed his hand on me, trying to calm me down. I took a deep breath. "If you have a pencil and paper, write down the *real* names of these children, and the countries they were stolen from. Then, write down the names of anyone you know with more stolen children. That's the only way I can promise that Fly here won't drop you off the top of this building."

As Ears translated, Fly lifted their bag to the ceiling. Terror replaced their outrage. In broken English, the oldest woman spoke.

"Okay, yes, we tell you everything, but you promise to set us free."

"Fair enough," I said. "It takes a few hours for the bag to disappear, but sure, I promise."

"Chief…?" Bat sounded shocked.

"Bat, I mean it—a deal is a deal. I'm the chief, remember?"

Convinced I was resolute, the older of the females opened her purse and found a pen and scrap paper. The man protested but eventually turned his back to her so she could use it as a writing surface to list the information. The driver watched our operation while standing next to the stretch limo. Picker and Bat gave him a thumb-up. He'd lost some color seeing Fly lift off, but he opened the doors for the new children.

I stuck my head out the door. "Driver, Babe will stay with the children, but please help keep a close eye on them and the street."

"Si. I help too."

Picker reached inside the bag and took the list. "While I'm at it, I'll take your phones too." When the women hesitated, Fly began to lift the bag. They changed their minds quickly.

"Fly, set them down on the bench away from the elevators," I said.

The younger woman collapsed on the floor of her jail, screaming.

"She is claustrophobic. Let her out, please," the male perpetrator said, seemingly aware that we had no intention of setting them free. I imagined the terror that enveloped stolen children who lost their loved ones, then woke up to evil every day. I gave no mercy to their captors—none whatsoever.

"Wait, you say you let us go," the older female said. "We cooperate, now you let us go!"

"You are free to go… but the bag doesn't melt for another, what, forty-eight hours, Bat?"

"Yeah, Chief. Sometimes even longer."

We strolled out of the building to screams of obscenities, though Ears—as he translated for us—said he could hear the man blaming the women for delaying when they should have escaped earlier with the children. The kindest word he used was *fools*.

"Motor, do your thing, please," I said.

He sent another address to the police station for pickup and included the names the women had given; names we'd also check. As I explained to our crew, I hadn't lied—although I promised to set the captives free, I meant free from the *bag*, which would dissipate after they were behind bars. Once we filled the limo, T.D. signaled the transporters.

The human vehicle began to whirr. I reassured the driver of his safety as we lifted off the ground. He grabbed the steering wheel as if it were a shield.

"We drive to outer space?"

"No, sir. We drive through inner space. Enjoy, it's a short ride."

Our driver paled as his limo began to spin.

We experienced a gentle landing. It was amusing to watch the limo driver; his expression of pleasure, surprise, and wonder conflicted with his inability to take his white-knuckled hands off the wheel. Transporters set the car in a small clearing surrounded by a rainforest.

Healer and an order of nuns were waiting for us. The sisters made the sign of the cross when the limo appeared but contained their shock when we opened our doors—each sister reverently picked up a child. We followed a stone path under a tree canopy to what appeared to be a centuries-old church with adjacent adobe buildings.

Once we were inside one of the buildings, Healer gathered the information we had. Then she photographed the children's faces to send to Interpol for identity confirmation. After time with the Face, the children would be matched to grieving parents or a family whose child had died.

Mother Superior introduced herself. "You must be tired and hungry, Señor Chief," she said. "Come, we prepared food for you and accommodations."

We sure needed a break, but spending the night? Not me, I thought—more children required rescue. But for that moment, our stomachs ruled. We scarfed down fresh-baked bread, chicken, and salad like the starved kids we used to be. The nuns insisted we eat dessert, which they served with steaming rich coffee. T.D. sat next to me, punched my shoulder, and smiled.

"Chief, we aren't a solitary group of Insiders in the world, you know."

"Of course I know that," I replied.

"The children that we missed today will be saved by other Insiders with the same project as ours. Face is thorough; although he gave us superhuman powers, he also understands we are flesh and blood needing food and rest."

"Look—"

"I want to share what I saw inside," T.D. continued. "It's vital you understand what is happening in the rest of the world."

I juggled a piece of sweet between my teeth. "Okay, I'm all ears."

"No, *I'm* all ears," Ears joked. "Hey, that's the first time I got to say that."

"There are hundreds of Insider teams, Chief," T.D. said after the chuckles died down. "I watched a few of them wake up back on Earth, captured. Russia held a team from Iran, as Iran didn't have the laboratories to study them. Russia did, though. Impressive powers, too."

"Go on."

"Their prisoners consisted of three members: Hafez, meaning 'protector,' Javeed, or 'living forever,' and Dori, which means 'sparkling star.' They were hooked up to respirators. When they awoke, the first thing they did was kiss the ground beneath their feet and praise Face for choosing them above all the street children in Iran." T.D. paused, letting the tension build. "They tried to enlighten their captors. They explained how Earth suffered and what would happen, but no one listened. They didn't expose their powers until Dori was attacked by some lowlife guard."

"What did she do, Dad?"

"She let him have it! At first, I didn't understand, because she didn't say anything or wave her hands. She let instinct take over and glared at him." T.D. gave us a knowing look. "He screamed as the change began. When it finished, nothing remained but a high-pitched whimper from a ten-inch soldier doll. I admired her for controlling her middle eastern temper, but for a second I thought she'd kill him—the assault caught her by surprise. Still, she held it together. She learned to choose peaceful methods during her time with the Face. Of course, when she told Javeed and Hafez what happened, they agreed to run."

****

T.D. inspected his cake, took a small bite, and drank a good swig of coffee, drawing out the moment. "The Iranians' escape proved more difficult than ours," he finally continued. I enjoyed watching Healer as T.D. held court; she was smiling proudly as he shared his experience. "No one flew, no one bagged. None of them had our gifts."

"Tell us their powers," Picker said.

"Dori's gift is re-arranging the elements. She shrinks, enlarges, liquefies, solidifies, or turns anything into a gas. Javeed manifested the food they needed to stay alive on their journey, but his gift encompassed much more than food. Javeed called anything into existence like plants, animals, or earthly."

"What do you mean by 'earthly,' Dad?"

"When soldiers were almost on top of them, Javeed called upon Earth for a quake that occurred under the soldiers' feet. It was strong enough to throw them to the ground. Later, the Earth gave him a mini volcano, spitting out enough molten lava to block the pass that would have allowed their capture."

"That's pretty cool!"

"Sure is, Ice. But Hafez was the coolest because he bore the weight of his name. I don't know how he did what he did because of all the gifts, but this one paid honor to the Face."

Again T.D. paused, letting the anticipation build.

"Hafez became a sword and led an army of swords if needed," he continued. "He used his gift to protect their purpose: bringing peace to the Middle East. To accomplish that task, they required transportation to take them there. So, they stowed away on an ancient pickup that spewed smoke as it headed to Turkey—the first stop before their Iranian homeland. It moved at slug speed but made it to the border by nightfall. Before the truck stopped for inspection, the trio jumped into the darkness of a ditch, sliding under the electric wire past the guards.

"Alerted by the Russian military, border patrol searched every square inch of the vehicle. The impatient trucker had no choice but to put up with their thoroughness. When the guards waved him through, he started the truck, ground the gears, and punched out a huge plume of smoke as he crossed into Turkey." Top Dog laughed at the memory. "Well, the Iranians had crawled under the barbed wire while the guards were busy. They waited for the truck on the other side. Before he shifted into second gear, the trio repositioned themselves in the back."

"Didn't the guards see them, Dad?"

"No, they were still coughing from the smoke bomb and trying to maintain their footing from the mini earthquake beneath their feet. But once in Istanbul, our heroes met up with the Turk Insiders. The two groups set off together to meet other middle eastern Insiders. From Turkey, they traveled to Iran, Iraq, Saudi, Egypt, and met—get this—the Israelis in Jordan."

"Muslims getting along with Jews. It's about time," Ice said.

"You're right, son. Since they knew each other from their time with Face, they greeted each other as family. Face showed them how childish their animosities were toward those with beliefs different from their own. Anyway, each middle east Insider had learned the importance of truth. None of them wanted to deceive each other. They embraced honesty and integrity, attributes required to build the foundations of love and peace."

"That's great," I said.

"Before their time with Face, they were afraid to speak about peace. Dictators, both military and religious, squelched any talks about an armistice. Instead, they generated hatred, fear, anger, and intimidation all for their own need for power and greed. But once the masses experience their leaders' belittlement, which is happening right now, the peaceful will become braver and will step forward. They and their like-minded families will be moved to the safe zones. The countries will merge under an umbrella of peace after the earth changes."

T.D. faced me. "You see, Chief, it isn't up to us to save the entire world. We do as much as we can. There are many more peacekeeping Insiders, just like there are more of us with our mission. The kids we missed today will be covered by other Insiders. In turn, we will save those lost elsewhere. However, our success requires that we take care of ourselves—eating and resting. Everything is going according to plan, so don't worry so much, Chief. Have faith."

It was hard for me to let go of the burden. "Okay, the Face is in control. That doesn't mean we shouldn't work our butts off. At daybreak, be ready to return to the city."

Everyone smiled. They knew me and had not expected me to loosen up too much.

"Dad, did you see more Insiders?" Ice asked.

"Sure, lots more."

"Will you tell us about them?"

"Tomorrow, after dinner. Same time, same place. Time to say goodnight, son."

"Goodnight, everyone."

"Goodnight, Ice."

Picker banged the table, startling all of us. "I don't know about you guys, but I'm here tomorrow night for the story. We may never meet all the Insiders, but it's sure good to hear about them. Good night, everyone."

Chapter 23

My city ears experienced new sounds in the Brazilian mountains—birds, monkeys, frogs, and more. Babe held the crook of my arm while star gazing.

"It's beautiful Chief. So beautiful."

"Yes, it is." Babe was even prettier in the moonlight.

"Why didn't we notice the stars in Philly?"

"Cities put out too much light. Pollution hides the stars. They never caught our attention."

"I guess. The stars fill the sky here. They look close enough to touch. Look. A shooting star."

"Make a wish, Babe." She turned to face me.

"I wish for…"

A piercing howl rent the air.

Sisters laughed at Bat who jumped from behind a tree ready to defend us.

"Señor, it is the wolf." Another sound followed. "That is a howler monkey.

"You will be safe in your cabins, but the night will not be quiet in the rainforest. Please follow us, young lady. You sleep in our quarters tonight."

"Oh." Babe glanced at them and then, at me.

"Go on now, bitty-sis. Those nuns will keep you safe from the wild things around here," Bat stared me down.

"Goodnight, Chief." Babe walked hesitantly toward the nuns.

"Night, Babe." My heart still pounded from the

moment we almost shared.

Bat stood with his arms folded over his chest. "We bunk in that direction, Chief. Let's talk."

"Sure…" Before I could edge in a word Bat spoke forcefully and got right to the point. "I'm gonna say this once. She is fourteen. When Babe's eighteen, she can make her own choices but not now."

"I thought about that. You are right. But remember when we thought Baby was seven, then we found out she was nine? Who knows, maybe she is even older? All I know is I don't want to hide my feelings for her anymore."

"I'm not saying you can't be boyfriend, girlfriend, Chief. I'm telling you that you won't be more until she turns eighteen. I'm okay with you holding hands and a few kisses; but if I suspect you touching her in a way she shouldn't be touched, I'll put a permanent bag where you don't want one. Do we understand each other?"

"I suppose we do. Bat?"

"Yeah."

"Thanks for caring enough to be honest with me."

"That's what it's all about. Keeping it real."

We crawled into our bunks and listened to the wondrous sounds of the rainforest that lulled us into a much-needed sleep.

****

In the morning, we ate a quick breakfast but reassured the nuns we would return in the evening with more children.

"Heroes ready for a new day?" The jovial Ricardo asked. Everyone smiled at his enthusiasm while boarding the limo.

The transporters did not bother to materialize that

morning; we just began to spin. Within seconds, we entered the wormhole and landed in San Jose.

"Ricardo, do you know your way around San Jose?"

"Você está bem, herois…ahh, I raised here. I know all streets." Ricardo continued, "We save many children today. I watched the news last night, your plan work good. Many children returned safe now. Most are ten years and older, but the little ones—I think it is too hard a sickness for ahh, pedófilo, how American's call it… pedophile predators, to return them."

I took comfort knowing what we missed, others would find, but my whole being ached to save every victim. Forty-eight hours came and went fast. We kept the transporters busy with trips to the convent. When we cleared out one nest, we headed toward the next, stopping for food and short night-time rests.

City by city, country-by-country, South and Central American Leaders followed the Brazilian Presidente's example, especially once we told them of the safety zones available for them and their families if they cooperated.

Meanwhile, Interpol worked feverishly on all the data Insiders had been sending them. Thanks to age-progression computers, each child's photo helped match them to his or her original family. Parents, brothers, and sisters discovered that lost family members were found.

Insider counselors explained the curative powers of the Face. How the children would become new and return to their families fresh without emotional or physical scarring. Although they understood, families continued to agonize over the necessary delay of seeing their loved ones.

Other families were not so fortunate, learning their

child had died; but they found some solace in closure. Secret Safe Zone notifications had been sent to those families, too, along with an offer. Since losing their child left a hole, gaping and deep in their hearts, Face would match an abductee to them if they agreed. Children with deceased or unsuitable guardians would enjoy a life with good parents.

"It's hard for me to believe this evil stuff exists. All the perverts must band together online to create their sick network," Picker said.

"Evil doesn't have a hard job. Complacency is part of the problem. People, busy with their own lives, create their little worlds, too busy to see the darkness until it hits close to home. Who wants to see the crappy side of life or even hear about it?" I asked.

Picker shifted in his seat, exhausted. "Well, I'm glad to be a part of saving them, Chief. No matter how hard it is to see."

"No worries, Picker. The Earth will do her thing. That should rid kids of their enemies," Bat said while finishing his toast.

I shook my head. "It might not. All kinds of people could survive Earth's changes. What you describe is Heaven, a dimension that rejects all evil. Let's think about the present and our job. At least we whittle down their numbers. Finish your breakfasts; this should be our final day in South America."

By noon, we were through.

"Ears, Lookout?"

"Nothing," they both replied.

"Can't see anything," Lookout said.

"I don't hear a thing either," Ears chimed in.

"We're done here. Get ready to move on." I hoped

we had done our job well.

We arrived at the convent early with the last of the children. After dinner, Top Dog would escort them to Face. We enjoyed another meal, thankful for the nuns' hospitality.

"Dad, you promised us another Insider story tonight," Ice said.

"I did?"

"Yep." Top Dog looked weary. A journey through the dimensions was waiting. Still, he would not let his son down.

"Okay... tonight, I will tell you about Chinese Insiders. They are all transporters like the Brazilians. It's hard to tell this story because Chinese names are challenging to pronounce, but I will never forget three of them: Kali, Yung-qi, and Dawei. Let me start at the beginning.

"China is the most populated country in the world with many orphanages. Children in orphanages there eat breakfast around seven in the morning. But one morning—" Top Dog paused, as he often did, to let the anticipation build. "—none of the children showed up to eat. The workers found each one in their beds, unconscious. The diagnosis was carbon monoxide poisoning. You know the routine: eyes moving, brain activity, hearts restarted, and life support."

I nodded. I knew the routine all too well.

"The Chinese, a curious people, documented the children's growth on video while in the mysterious coma," T.D. continued. "Physicians met regularly to determine the cause. Of course, the Premier, paranoid of a potential threat, involved the military. Same ol' thing.

"Chinese Insiders had adopted the same plan as the

Brazilians when inside with Face. When these kids woke up, a few guards heard, "Let's get it done" in Chinese. Each one vanished and met at a predetermined haven. Of course, China thinks Transporters are the enemy, but they are difficult to pin down."

Top Dog sipped his coffee. "Then, son, buildings ended up on top of the Greater Khingan and Himalayan Mountain ranges. Child prostitution rings fell apart as designated Insiders helped. The rumor was that the premier became unstable, claiming that someone was whispering to him day and night: 'Move the peasants to the mountains. Move the population to the mountains.'"

"Was someone whispering to him, Dad?"

"Yes, Ice, and you'll be surprised who it was…"

"Come on, T.D., tell us," Picker urged.

He broke into a broad grin. "My son—and your brother, Ice—Thunder."

"No way, Dad!"

"Way, son. Thunder talks to heads of state in every country. He influences them in their dreams until the idea sticks. He's persuasive. He also manages a team of whisperers I trained."

"That's cool duty," Ice said. We all agreed.

"Anyway, that's my China story, Ice, and now it's bedtime."

He let his shoulders slump. "Aw, Dad."

"You need the rest, and I need to be on my way. Goodnight, everyone."

We all said goodnight, our spirits lifted by Top Dog's news. Babe and I sneaked out, happy for the story but hoping to be on our own. We held hands while meandering on grounds that were lit by oil lamps. We stopped to stargaze while inhaling the brisk, sweet air.

"Chief—"

I placed my finger on Babe's lush lips. I had to talk first.

"Babe, I've waited for you for years, and I'll find a way to wait some more. When you are eighteen, tell me how you feel. But don't do it now—those words would kill me because I want us to be… well… a couple."

"Chief—"

"Will you promise me that when you turn eighteen, you'll say if you still want me or not?"

"I won't say a *word* to you when I'm eighteen, because I don't want to wait," she said sweetly. "Who knows what condition the world will be in the future?"

"Uh, that's true, I guess…"

"We have now, Chief."

I looked into her eyes. "I promised Bat I'd wait until you were adult enough to make a rational decision."

"Rationality?" Still smiling, Babe rolled her eyes. "The kind of reasoning that made us Insiders, or makes the Earth need to flip? News flash, Chief: there's no reasoning about love."

I almost missed it. She said *love*.

My heart wanted to jump out of my chest.

"I made a promise, Babe, but… a kiss goodnight wouldn't hurt, would it?" I brought her gently to me. Our first kiss was soft and sweet.

"I've been waiting for this kiss forever," Babe whispered. She grabbed my shirt and pulled me close. We kissed again, longer and with passion. I began to quiver.

"Ahem."

It was Bat. I don't know how long he'd been standing there, but he pointed at the nuns' residence with a judgmental look on his face.

"Bat, you are *not* my daddy," Babe said. "And you aren't my brother or my keeper, either." She stormed into the nuns' cabin, slamming the door. I laughed, trying to mask my discomfort. Bat, I noticed, was looking past the nuns' cabin and into the distance.

"That girl has a temper," I said. "Might want to bag yourself tonight, dude."

"I hear you, Chief. And I hope you hear me—good things are worth waiting for."

I started to tell him to mind his own business but decided against it. I let his words hang in the air, figuring my silence would make my point.

"Let's get some sleep, Bat. We've got a long journey to Thailand tomorrow, and much work to be done there."

Chapter 24

A new set of transporters greeted us in the morning, bringing us one familiar face.

"Anna Marie," Motor said smoothly. "This beautiful day just turned even more beautiful."

"*Obrigado*, Motor. You say to drop by—how is your mission going?"

Ears ran out of the latrine. "It's great, Anna Marie. We've saved many children and turned in their predators."

"Ears, do you mind? We're having a conversation."

"No, I don't mind at all," Ears said, stepping dangerously close to Motor.

I stepped forward, getting between them as gracefully as I could.

"Anna Marie, it's nice to see you. Will you be taking us to Thailand today?"

"Si, Chief. We are best at long distance."

Babe said a quick hello to Anna Marie, then placed her hand firmly on my arm. "Chief, I think everyone is ready to go. Are we taking the limo?"

"Sure, Babe. I don't think it will raise eyebrows in Thailand—at least not in the wrong way. It sure comes in handy for the little ones."

"I already stocked it with milk and snacks," Babe replied.

"Oh good." Bat patted his stomach. "I'm hungry."

"They're not for you," Babe snapped.

I hid a smile—she still held on to her anger from last night.

"Señor Chief? I know not the streets of Thailand. I help you still?"

"Hmm... you better stay here, Ricardo, and warn family members," I said. "You know what to do now and where to go. Thank you for all your help, my friend."

"Wait." Ricardo held up his flip cell phone. "I take a picture with American heroes."

We obliged him with a group shot. "Will you be in trouble for losing the limo?" I asked.

"No worries. Mountain banditos must steal it, yes? Good insured."

I herded Ears and Motor away from Anna Marie and into the limo. She waved and gave the order: "Let's get it done."

****

The journey was longer than the one to the tundra but just as beautiful. We landed outside Bangkok on a dirt road.

"Chief, I've located the Premiere's residence," Motor said.

"Chief, since we wait for you and the children, we will learn the map and terrain," Anna Marie said. "We find a good place for the children. You call when you need us, okay?"

"Awesome. We'll take all the help we can get."

As the transporters disappeared, Motor and Ears glared at one another. I was losing patience and didn't try to sound nice.

"Guys, that's enough. We have more important things than your jealousies to worry about. After the earth changes, you can have your Anna Marie competition. For now, I need both of you at one hundred percent—nothing less will do. Got it?"

Both of my friends mumbled assurances that they were all in. That would have to do, I decided, and asked Motor how his Thailand research went.

"As you know, Chief, I didn't speak their language—but after a few hours I realized it could be downloaded."

Motor was minimizing Ears' gift, a passive-aggressive little dig. I pretended not to notice. "You mean it's downloaded in your brain?"

"Yep. There's a list of perpetrators for whatever driver you hire. Oh, and Chief?" Motor puffed out his chest. "As to Anna Marie—there *is* no competition."

Ears reddened, clearly angry. Motor gave him a smug grin and strutted away.

Focus. "Fly, time to see the Premiere."

"On it, Chief!" He took off holding Babe, T.D., and Ice, probably glad to get away from the rare tension between anyone in our group.

"Picker... Lookout... anybody, please point us toward the city."

"Honorable Chief, we go thataway," Picker pointed east, stifling a giggle. He got the biggest kick out of love's complications—while they did nothing but frustrate me.

****

Before long, T.D. approached the Thailand President with the experience and confidence gained from our South and Central American conquests. With Top Dog negotiating and Ears translating, I was encouraged about our chances, but the agreement—even with Babe's influence—was given grudgingly. This told me Thailand would give us trouble.

After Fly returned his passengers, he asked permission to go off and scout. While in South and Central America, Fly proved excellent at spotting unlikely villages with traffickers.

"Go on, Fly, but head due east," I said. "That'll take you to the boundary where we'll enter the city."

We listened to the amnesty announcement on the radio with Ears translating.

"It's a lame amnesty, Chief," he said. "Weak words, lacking sincerity."

Great. Trafficked children and child prostitution brought big money to Thailand. Did the head of state profit from it? Or was he scared for his political life or maybe his life in general?

"We'll do our best, Chief," T.D. said, reading my mind. "That's all we can do."

As we entered the city, an old man tapped on our window. Picker crossed the intersection and pulled over for him. The geriatric's toothless smile made him look harmless.

"I drive. I drive Bangkok," he said in barely passable English. "I know street. Yes?"

The old man yanked open the limo door shooing Picker over. Picker looked at me with a question in his eyes.

"It's okay, Picker. Give him a try."

"You sure, Chief?"

"Yes. Let's go.

I assumed Face had sent a driver to help us.

As we headed toward Bangkok, Ears relayed the citizens' reaction to the proclamation of amnesty.

"Chief, they aren't serious here. Repeating…"

"We turn them in, collect a bonus, and capture them again before they leave the country."

"No worries, Ears," I said. "T.D. will return them to Face before they can even try. Let's get ready to clean up."

The old driver took plenty of turns, confusing me as to direction. He slowed and pulled into a small parking lot with his window down. He smiled at the attendant, greeting him in Thai.

Ears elbowed me. "Chief—he didn't say hello to the attendant. He simply announced we were here." Then Ears raised his voice. "Something's not right!"

Bat woke up, but seconds too late.

The back door opened, and the butt of a gun hit him hard behind the head. He slumped over, out cold. We were exposed, unprotected like turtles without a shell. We stared into the muzzles of automatic revolvers. The smallest of three armed men with an AK47 slung over his shoulder ordered us out of the car with a growl.

"You come now."

We put up our hands as we slid out. An incredibly tall and large man with a singsong tenor voice began to speak, but it was no laughing matter with weapons pointed at us, especially without Bat for protection.

"You Insiders make powerful man angry," the huge man continued in better English than I would have imagined. "Most unfortunate day for you. People make many monies here with their children, but you try to stop them. Now we must dispose of you." The big man sighed. "Too bad you not a few years younger—you all good-looking. Go inside building. I don't want to make show outside. More private inside."

225

The man gave his companions an order. Two ran over to Bat, complaining in Thai as they struggled to pick him up. They dumped him on the floor indoors, where my eyes widened at the sight of blood leaking from a cut on his head. Knowing we were in serious trouble, I pushed Babe behind me while Healer moved forward, placing her foot under Bat's head.

"Oh, wait a minute—I see you little one. You a cutie," the huge man said. "Almost too old, but not. We keep her. Master be proud of me."

The men argued in Tai while I ground my teeth at the thought of any of them laying their hands on Babe. Ears leaned in.

"Repeating, Chief…"

"You have orders to kill them all right away. You take too long, and now you take a prize. You go against orders."

"I know my master's tastes. He would not want to lose this one."

To my surprise, he switched to English and looked around me at Babe. "Little angel, come here to me."

Babe whispered, "This is perfect." She moved forward, staring at our captor with innocent eyes. "Do you like me? Do you like my eyes? They are big. Tell your friends to look into my eyes to see how big they are."

The goliath rattled off some Thai. His men circled around to inspect her.

"Please, interpret for me to your men," she ordered sweetly. "I'm happy you love my eyes. I love your eyes, too. I know you love me… you won't hurt me. You do not want to hurt anyone. You do not want to hurt my friends, for sure."

The men, Goliath included, all stared at Babe.

"In fact, we will all be best friends," she continued. "I am happy you love us. We love you too. We heard how much you love your children—you want to keep them and protect them. Let us help you, my best friends. Take us to your children; we will love them together. Do you agree we will love them and protect them together?"

The obedient men nodded their heads, now sporting silly babbling grins. Babe had done it again! Amazed but not surprised, Ears leaned in, whispering, repeating, Chief :

"We help you. We happy to share love with you."

Babe waved us over. "My friends are your friends. They will carry the guns for you."

Picker took their weapons as Bat let out a moan. Healer encouraged him to wake up.

"Man, what happened… my head hurts."

"It will feel better soon." Healer placed her hands on him and explained why we were in the middle of a love fest. Babe winked at Bat, relieved he was alright. I had no problem with that; she and I were in love. My girl made it clear she wasn't interested in Bat that way.

"You know, Babe, we need the tall one as a guide," I said in a lilting voice I never used; I sure didn't want the pervs to snap out of her influence. "The other two require a nice long rest, don't you think?"

"What a wonderful idea our Chief has," Babe said to the large man. "Tell your workers they deserve a long rest. Curl up right here on the floor. We won't be long."

He rattled off instructions in Thai to his henchmen. They checked with Babe for approval. She smiled her melting smile, looked them straight in the eye while nodding her head. She pointed down—the two thugs fell to the floor, sound asleep.

"Let's get down to business, Babe, what do you say?" I said with extra politeness.

Babe nodded. "What a wonderful time we are having here in Thailand, my friend. Let us go visit the children. I bet they are gorgeous."

"Oh, yes. A most fortunate day for you, cutie," the big man said. "My master collects many children—all beautiful. You love them all. We go in through back door here."

"Wait, Chief." Motor rolled his eyes exaggeratedly. "Security! What a wonderful security system you have," he said, almost prancing with more than a hint of mockery. "What kind is it?"

Picker turned away and covered his mouth, stifling laughter.

"Oh, my master spares no expense for the children's safety, my friend. They use the same in the embassy, where he works for the ambassador. It is an impenetrable system—impenetrable," he said. "Give plenty of warning for master in case of trouble. But no trouble today."

"Oh, I see now." Motor sent a pulse of energy into the first detector, then pushed the gate open. "Let's go, Chief. The system is fried. They'll send security any time to figure out why."

"Motor, he would have opened it for us," I muttered. "Wait for my signal next time."

He looked at the floor. "Oh, yeah. Forgot about that. Sorry, Chief."

"Quick, show us the children, my dear friend," Babe urged the large man.

"Here, in the courtyard," he replied, apparently

unaware Motor had destroyed the security system. He opened another gate, revealing picnic tables with children.

They were eating their lunch with heads down. None were talking or smiling.

"Chief, look at all the nationalities," Ears said.

"Try English first," I said. Then Thai, Chinese… anything you think of after that, Ears. And Bat, bag the soprano and any other adult you see."

"With pleasure, Chief."

"What you do to me, big one?" the large man asked, initially amused before his eyes widened. "Oh, my. Oh, no. Oh, master be angry with you… please…" Bat bounced him in a corner behind some bushes as Babe talked to the few young Caucasians.

"Don't worry, children, we're your friends," she said gently. "We are here to help you. Does anyone speak or remember English?"

"A little," the smallest child said.

"We're going to take you home to your mommy and daddies."

She began to cry. "They don't want me anymore. They sent me away."

"Honey, bad people told you a lie," Babe said. "Your mommy and daddy never stopped loving you or looking for you, and now we've found you for them. We'll take you to a place where no one will ever again hurt you. See my eyes? I will tell you the truth, always." Babe held out her hand. "Come with me."

Ears rattled out words of comfort in many languages. The first child smiled, stood, and reached out to Babe. She held out her other hand to her friend. The rest of the children stood, linking elbows to the child next to them. I watched as they formed a long line while staying silent, like good little soldiers. They had been trained well—this time it would work for their benefit.

"Stop!" a loud voice roared as the last child went through the gate.

I turned, assuming the "master" the large man had referred to. He was angry but promptly began negotiating.

"If you return those children to me, I will allow you to live," he said. "We shall go on with our lives as though you were never here."

Six henchmen moved before us. All lined up in a Kung Fu stance.

"Are you kidding me?" Bat looked disgusted as he waved his arm. "Let's go, Chief."

He turned his back on our assailants and walked through the gate. Motor and I brought up the rear, smiling as Thai curses poured from each Kung Fu wannabe as they tried to karate chop their way out of the invisible bags.

"Slow learners, Chief?" Picker asked.

"Looks that way, man."

The courtyard quickly filled with terrified men that looked as if they were performing poorly with invisible pogo sticks. Finally, their master bounced over the balcony right into the midst of them. We thought it would be an easy escape until we heard a shot. The whiz of a bullet passed by my ear.

I wasn't bagged and spun around.

"That was *not* cool. Drop the gun, or I'll drop you." Fly shook the gunman and lifted him twenty feet off the ground. The saboteur obeyed, dropping the gun. He was surprised and disappointed when Fly planted him on a treetop anyway.

"Hurry, Chief, there's more on the way with automatics," Fly said to me. "I will try to hold them off."

"Better bag everyone, Bat," I said.

Bat waved his hands as we ran to the limo, packing the children inside. Healer sat in the middle on the floor. We squeezed more into the front seat when the whir began.

"Wait for Fly!" Ice shouted. "Wait for Fly!"

Fly landed on the roof with a thud. He would ride there on the way to our next stop, a Tibetan Mountain where monks awaited us. The religious order spoke many languages, and all the children understood their message of safety and protection.

"Many more in Thailand, Chief Poop," the monastery's top monk said. "*Many* more. You go. We protect."

"I guess we're going to be here awhile, my friends," I replied. We left Healer behind with the monks and kids; the children released their tension and were at ease with her in the same room. She made sure the identification processes began right away, which was a good thing. By nightfall, we had collected five hundred children.

Word spread—the perpetrators knew they were no match for us. Motor notified law enforcement of addresses for fleeing predators that we set outside under the trees like Christmas gifts. It made the job of finding them go a lot faster. My concern was T.D., who looked pale and drained after escorting so many children through dimensions.

"No worries, Chief," he said when I addressed the issue. "I'll have plenty of time to rest later." He was right to radiate urgency; influential people wanted us dead and the children they'd stolen returned to them.

One helicopter landed in the monk's compound. But Bat, thanks to a warning from Ears, bagged them as they came over the cliff. Afterward, T.D. took a defensive position and began two trips during the day to prevent children from recapture. We rested while he worked.

We trusted Face to keep T.D. going.

Chapter 25

When we finished our work in Thailand, the monks prepared a feast for us. We thanked them for their hospitality, hoping they would not reap punishment for their involvement in our rescue.

"You no worry. We monks, Insider," the leader said. "The magnificent Face calls us to serve. Our lives in danger always. We used to it."

Ice yawned loud and long. "Dad, I know you're tired, but would you tell us another Insider story?"

"Sure, son. How about a cowboy story?"

Ice nodded as we gathered 'round to hear.

"Every year in the United States, Argentina, and Australia, there's a summer program called Cowboys/Cowgirls elect. The program helps kids and teens who are lost in the shuffle of life; they are abused, neglected, and unwanted. Sound familiar?"

We all nodded.

"The program chooses kids who have changed the most, who developed a positive attitude despite their circumstances. They're sent to a summer cattle, sheep, or horse drive."

"You mean real drives, like in western movies?" Picker asked.

"Yes. Cattle drives still exist, though not as big as they were in the eighteen hundreds. Modern drives use all-terrain vehicles, motorcycles, trucks, even helicopters. Still, in the more remote areas, nothing works but a horse and its cowboy."

"Ahem," Healer interrupted.

"Oh, thanks Healer—cowboys and *cowgirls*. The program consists of horses and riders. Well, a truck or van replaces the chuck wagon, but that's it. The rest is rustic. They sleep under the stars. An adult keeps in touch by radio, but the whole operation is run by kids."

"Do they know how to ride before they get there?" Picker asked.

"No," T.D. said. "But they spend a month doing nothing but learning to ride and rope beforehand. They study maps and videos of cattle drives done by the pros. When ready, they go out into the field herding livestock more than one hundred fifty miles to a trucking depot that trucks the cattle the rest of the way.

"Once at the depot, they pick up supplies for the trip back to the ranch. They get a day off to regroup, talk about the drive, the problems they encountered, any personnel issues that cropped up, and how the kids fixed them. It's a great program that empowers kids for improved lives.

"Anyway," T.D. continued, "I'm watching and learning about the cowboys and girls, as we call them in the U.S. They are called *gauchos* in Argentina and Chile, drovers in Australia. The same basic program runs all over the world; the principles they learn are the same.

"I have to admit that it was fun watching the greenies learn how to ride. I felt sorry for the horses at first, but the riders got the hang of it as they practiced every day for hours. The youngest took the wrangler job, which is taking care of each rider's horses."

"You said that riders get more than one horse.

Why?" Picker asked.

"One horse needs to be a good runner in case there's a stampede. Another needs to have good nighttime vision. They need two for during the daytime drive, as it's easy to wear out a horse on a long trip. That adds up to a lot of horses needed.

"Remember now, they've been studying a map for a month. When a drive begins, they know where to go and what to do. Everything went according to plan with the Americans, and the livestock was delivered to their destination. While there, they bought supplies for their trip back to the ranch. That's when it happened…"

Top Dog drank down a full glass of water, making us wait.

"Dad, what happened?" Ice asked.

"Thunderstorms came in fast with lightning everywhere, son. The multiple strikes threw the riders off their horses, cold stone dead. Except they weren't dead—their eyes still moved."

"What about the horses, Dad. Were they killed too?"

"Yep, for a few seconds… but when the second bolt of lightning hit the ground next to them, the horses jolted to life, got up, and ran. The same thing happened to the herding dogs."

"Face let the animals live, Dad?"

"Yes and no. Face turned them into super-animals in a few seconds. Remember, they don't have egos to contend with; he gave them immediate powers. They returned to their barns, waiting for the day their riders— the Insiders would need them. A couple years went by before that happened."

"Wait a minute," Picker interrupted. "You're saying the riders spent only two years with Face before they were ready to return to Earth?"

"Yes, that's right, Picker. Is there a problem?"

"Yeah, there's a problem. Face kept us with him for *five* years."

"Okay," T.D. laughed. "What's the trouble?"

"Well, were we so awful that it took five years to get us to an Insider level?"

I smiled. "Yeah, we were wild, Picker. Remember, too, that we trained to save children, not animals. Our work requires more discipline and expertise."

"So?"

"We're doing the work nearest to the Face's heart," I replied. "We aren't in politics; we aren't saving animals and plants or moving buildings. We're helping children who were in a worse predicament than we were when Face called us." I paused, holding Picker's gaze. "Don't you understand that Face gave us responsibility for the neediest of all? That took *years* more training."

Picker turned bright red. "I feel stupid, Chief. Yes, I know that, but I'm still ticked."

"Man, you've been wound over this," T.D. said to Picker. "What's up?"

"It's this job, as usual. Why weren't Insiders assembled years ago to help these kids?"

"Picker, don't look at the past. Look at today. We are helping *now*. Face lives outside time. It is different for him; don't question his actions. Sure, it looks horrible to us, but his perspective is different from ours. We can't begin to understand it."

"You're right, I don't understand. I can't figure out why evil exists to begin with."

"It has to do with free will. How can we choose good if there is nothing but good? We'd be more like machines instead of humans," T.D. explained. "That's where faith comes in—it's a choice. I didn't wait for something miraculous to happen. I just started believing Face first.

"The benefits, Picker, began to accumulate after I chose that path. Faith lets the spirit rest. It gives peace. I'm the luckiest of all of you because I visit him when I drop off children, which I'm about to do now."

Healer appeared with an ample group of eager kids.

"Okay, everyone," T.D. said, getting to his feet. "I'm making an executive decision: we turn in early tonight and sleep late—we need a long rest. Tomorrow we'll start working our way back west through Afghanistan, Pakistan, and India, and we'll also see parts of Africa. It's a lot of travel and a lot of work. So, let's hit the hay, gang."

No one had to be convinced. I walked Babe to her door. She let a yawn slip out.

"You do need a deep sleep, Babe."

"Never too tired for you."

My girl took hold of my t-shirt, tugging me closer. I bent to kiss her.

"Hey, who's the chief here?"

"I am," Bat said from the dark of night.

We ignored him and kissed. Babe hugged me and whispered, "Tomorrow night, we ditch Bat." I tingled from the touch of her lips on my ear and would have agreed to anything at that point.

"Sure. Tomorrow night," I whispered back.

We never had a chance to ditch Bat as accomodations were rustic as we traveled through the remaining countries. Most times we slept on floors huddled together.

****

We woke up refreshed and ready for anything our last day in South Africa.

"T.D., did Face ever tell you when the calamity will happen?" I asked. "Because I get this feeling that we need to go home... now."

"Trust your instinct, Chief."

"Okay. We have more to prepare before Earth changes. We need a triage system for those who respond to the warnings and invitations. That's going to take time, and I don't feel much time is left." I looked at everyone in turn. "Is anyone else feeling the same thing?"

All the smiles answered my question.

"Then where is home for all of us?" I let them think on it for a moment. "I sure fell in love with the Smokies. It would be good to see Chief Sky Hawk again."

"North Carolina Smokey's were special," Babe said, a faraway look in her eyes.

"Chief, I'm sorry," Bat said, "but I'm going to the tundra. Downu and I, well, we took to each other. I want to protect her when Earth changes."

The possibility of my Insiders splitting up never occurred to me. We were family, after all. Babe reached over to squeeze my hand. I beheld her eyes, knowing without a doubt where I wanted to be—anywhere Babe was. I returned the squeeze, curling Babe's soft hand in mine, but the thought of Bat leaving upset me. I gave him a nod anyway while I tried to restrain my shock, my worry, my sadness. Ears and Lookout, meanwhile, nodded their agreement.

"We love the Smokies, too, Chief," Lookout said. "The views rock."

"And it's warmer than up north, so count me in,"

Ears added.

Their answer gave me some relief. I didn't need to question Picker—he would always stay with me.

"Healer, what about you, Top Dog, and Ice? You'll stay with us in the Smokies too, right?"

"We're Pennsylvanians, through and through, Chief," T.D. said promptly. "We'll head for the Poconos."

"I thought… I guess some of us just bonded… to the Smokies, that is," I stammered, then worked up the courage to face Motor. "What say you?"

"I need to sort things out, Chief," he said, looking away. "You know, with Anna Marie."

"Of course, Motor, but Anna Marie is always welcome."

"Yo, how come you haven't asked me?" Picker asked.

"You're kidding, right?" I faced him. "Like glue, you and me—we're brothers, Picker. No need to ask." That satisfied him; he sat with a silly smile.

I hid inside the wormhole of my mind, but my heart reacted to the confusion there. Why were Bat, Motor, and even the Doggets so willing to split up with… well, me? I thought we were a family.

Will I ever see them again?
****

"First stop, North Carolina," Picker said, his voice echoing in the limo as if spoken by a conductor on a train. "Yo, Chief, transporters are messing with us now."

The limo almost landed but started to go up and down like a yoyo. Finally, it touched down with a thud. "Very funny, you guys," Picker announced to the unseen.

"Let's enjoy the last evening together, everyone," I suggested. "Who knows when we'll meet again?"

"That's true," Helen said. "One more night together without work might be just what we need, Chief."

****

Sky Hawk greeted us. "Aha. You are late again. What do you think of the new casino?"

We and the transporters followed him inside the more spacious building. Anna Marie walked arm-in-arm with Motor, finding a secluded corner. Downu surprised Bat as he entered the room. He picked her up and twirled her around.

"What are you doing here? How did you know I missed you?"

"We both know here." Downu pointed to his heart. "Besides, too cold for you on Tundra—you stick out like black seal on snow… get eaten by bear. Driller call transporters. I hiccupped a ride, learn English for you."

They kissed and walked away with arms around each other. Babe sighed.

"Chief, when is it going to be us?"

"Babe, it *is* us. It was always us from the first day I saw you. But I thought you and Bat—"

She placed her finger on my lips, shushing me. "I meant, when are you going to twirl me around and kiss me in full view of everyone?"

"Right now, Babe."

I gathered her up in my arms, looked into her eyes, and pressed my lips to hers. It was Babe and me—nothing else mattered. We had become *us* after one short twirl. Helen interrupted our special moment with pleasant news when she blew an ear-piercing whistle.

"Everyone! Thunder is within earshot. He says

hello."

We sent back warm greetings into the air.

"He's taking a break today, too," Helen replied. "He wants you to be well rested because you will be busy soon. He says a lot of children will be delivered to the Smokey's. They are healed and renewed. So, we will situate them with their families." Healer laughed. "He says we need to build all the strength possible, as they are quite lively."

"Motor… where's Motor?" Healer asked.

"Yo, Motor, Healer has a message for you." T.D. hollered.

Motor turned, pulling Anna Marie close to his side. "Oh, sorry, Healer. What's up?"

"Thunder has a problem with gamers. The heads of state hear him, but gamers either don't hear or don't want to hear Whispers telling them to leave—they think it's an ad for a new game. He's wondering if you'd remedy that for him."

Motor and Anna Marie smiled. "Sure, Anna and I will fix them. Are you thinking what I'm thinking, my beauty?"

"If you're thinking about a cyberspace trip," she replied, "I would enjoy it much."

"Okay. We're going to eat first—saving geeks and nerds requires fuel."

"Great," I answered. "Anything else Thunder wants, Healer?"

"Yes, Chief. He tells Picker, 'Don't worry. Face is in control. He appreciates your love for justice, but do take it easy on him or else he will send the sword to remind you of his supremacy.'"

"No need," Picker hollered. "I get it, Thunder. Tell

Face no need for the sword here."

"Thunder says that he will see us all soon," Healer added.

"What does that mean?" I asked.

"I'm not sure what he meant, Chief, and he's gone. I'll ask him next time. For now, let's just enjoy this last evening together."

Healer's words shook me to my core.

Babe and I filled our plates and sat next to Sky Hawk at his invitation. It was an honor that he extended to all of us. We wondered about how different the earth would be after the change.

"Earth will be like, brand new," T.D. said firmly. "She will be refreshed and ease into a rhythm again. When the winds settle, people will go topside and find pollution washed away. Landmasses will appear that have not seen daylight for thousands of years. Others will have disappeared. And there's more: animals will evolve to adapt, while others won't ever be seen again—their time will be over. People who listened to us will survive to see it, to start over, and, hopefully, to live in peaceful harmony with Earth."

"Here's to Face and to Earth," Picker said respectfully.

We lifted our water glasses. "The Face. The Earth."

For the rest of the evening, the Cherokee treated us as dignitaries. We watched a presentation of their past to present that allowed us to realize the depth of their beings, and the anguish they as a nation had suffered. Our respect for all American Indian tribes had no boundaries. They most understood the planet long before anyone else.

As the evening slowed, Ice asked his Dad about the

cowboys and cowgirls. "You never finished the story, Dad."

"Okay, son. Where was I?"

"The thunderstorm. Lightening zapped the horses and cattle dogs. They jumped up on the second lightning strike, becoming Insider animals."

T.D. laughed. "I call them Insiders because of their special powers."

"What happened?" Chief Sky Hawk asked.

"Let's see, the cowboys and cowgirls are dead… but maybe not. Store personnel saw what happened and called in as many ambulances as possible. The ambulances picked them up, hooked them up, restarted their hearts, and they spent three years with the Face. You know where their bodies ended up."

"Secret Military Lab," several of us said at once.

"Yeah. But they learned about animals inside. Face charged them to save everything from frogs to prairie dogs to wild boars, bears, cougars, buffalos—everything you can think of."

I hoped flies were left off the list, but T.D. added that Face had trained Insiders for the survival of insects including flies.

"Chief, anything the Face wanted saved, Insiders had the skills to accomplish," T.D. said. "They also knew how to construct corrals to protect the animals. More species were to be saved in caves and underground."

"That's more complicated than what we do. Are there enough cowboys and cowgirls to do it all?"

"No." T.D. opened a new bottle of water, teasing Ice again. "You forgot about their help."

We all looked perplexed.

"The horses… the dogs."

"No way, Dad," Ice said.

"Way again, son, but first the Insider horses picked up their riders."

"What? How did they know where they were?"

"At the moment the lightning struck, Insiders melded to their horses, and the horses to the riders and dogs. They knew each other's minds, Ice. When those Insiders woke up in military hospitals, the first thing they did was whistle."

"Whistle," Picker said, winking at T.D. "Whistle a happy tune whistle?"

"I even got that one, Picker," Ice said, rolling his eyes. "They whistled for their dogs and horses, didn't they, Dad?"

"You got that right, Ice. Even though they were hundreds of miles away, their horses heard the sound that allowed them to fly to their riders. The dogs began herding the wildlife toward the safe areas."

"I had called drillers to complete their underground protection." T.D. took another break pouring another cup of coffee. I smiled at how he strung Ice along, making him wait at times for his stories to continue.

"Wait—what, Dad?"

"Well, son, the horses flew over their stall gates, corrals—what have you—and flew off toward their riders."

"Flying horses?"

"Yep. I saw them myself," T.D. replied.

"What about the dogs?"

"They went right to work with their gift of super-speed. They herded black bears, buffalo, and wolves, setting the stage for the horses and riders who joined in. That's what they're doing as we speak."

"Dad, you're lucky. Wish I'd seen that."

"Ice, they'll save critters all over the world until the last possible moment. Can you imagine trying to drive a herd of kangaroos? I don't envy that job; I bet a lot of drover hats and boots will be flying through the air."

"Wish I had a cowboy hat," Picker said.

"I wanted to be a super hero with a cape growing up," Bat said. "Now, I'd be happy wearing a Stetson."

"Me, too, Bat," I said. "I'd be a coogirl."

"Many Indians wear Stetsons out west. You would make a beautiful Indian," Sky Hawk wistfully said to Downu.

"Careful, Chief Sky Hawk," Bat said in mock seriousness. "Don't be coming on to my woman, now."

"Okay. I adopt you both as Cherokee, but your woman is prettier than you." The old Chief was smitten. "Downu reminds me of my first wife."

"You remind me of my... how you say... grandpop?"

Chief Sky Hawk laughed. "You take good care of her, Bat, or I will steal her away from you. The Cherokee will keep you plenty safe during the change, which my ancestors say is soon."

"Your ancestors are right, Chief Sky Hawk. That's why we're meeting—we need to work out the planning."

"You all stay in Cherokee country?"

"Not us, Chief." T. D. sighed. "As much as we love your hospitality, we'll be going home to Pennsylvania. Each state has Insiders doing the same as us."

"The rest of us accept your offer, Chief Sky Hawk, except for two who are undecided," I said. Again, my stomach sank. I glanced at Motor and Anna Marie. They were still goo-goo-eyed at each other while they ate."

Ears sighed. "Maybe she has a sister."

I winked at Ears while Ice was oblivious to the sweethearts.

"Dad, I've been wondering why Face doesn't save everybody," he said gravely. "Why do people have to die?"

"They don't. If citizens communicate with the Face, pay attention to the news and the visible signs, they will choose to react to it or not. Again, son, free will."

"Okay, I understand," Ice said.

"By now, Ice, you must know that those who lose their lives will continue on. That is the gift to every living being on Earth: we go on. No matter our circumstances on Earth, we will continue if we ask Face to let us. Free will exists right up to our last breath, Ice. Understand?"

"Sure, Dad. Thunder wasn't needed on Earth anymore; he dropped his body and went on."

"Exactly! That's the way it is for every living thing. That's why no one should be afraid of death *if* they're in line with Face. Death is nothing more than another beginning. Life is precious and it's everyone's duty to live it—overcoming adversity and becoming stronger for it. Now let's get some sleep, son. Healer, are you coming?"

"You better believe it." After Healer heard from Thunder, her glow intensified. She looked contented, and her quiet joy became contagious.

"Now that's a story to mull over in my dreams," she said.

"Good night, everyone. I'm taking my flying horse off to bed," Picker announced as he galloped away on the invisible horse in his mind.

"Me, too," Ears said.

"Me," Lookout added with a yawn.

"Hey, Picker, don't forget your herding dog," Bat said with a laugh. Picker was a good sport and howled at the moon. He knew Bat would rib him forever about his Brazilian puppy routine.

Chapter 26

Bat, Downu, Babe, and I strolled outside to stargaze, spreading blankets on a grassy knoll. Downu pointed out the constellations until a meteor shower supplied more visual entertainment. Motor and Anna Marie joined us for a few minutes before they entered cyberspace to rescue the geeks. In a quiet moment, I remembered a question.

"Motor, I forgot to ask: how did you disappear and reappear when the general captured us?"

"It involves a lot of physics, Chief. Simply put, with the energy the transporters put out, I was able to change my vibration to theirs instead of from the standard—you know, from the vibration we all share right now at this moment."

"Go on."

"When the transporters stopped, I became visible again to you. I couldn't keep up that vibration on my own, although I tried and succeeded for a few moments."

"I get what you're saying, Motor, but you didn't reappear with the transporters when they did. Where were you?"

"I transported to a new place, Chief. It's beautiful and unlimited."

"A new *planet*, Motor?"

"No, a new dimension."

"Hmm… who lives there?"

"We do, Chief. We all do or will."

"Oh? Is there something I… we… should know?"

"We need to concentrate on triage and safety for the incoming. There is a ton of work to do, including the cyberspace deal." He turned to Anna Marie. "No time like the present."

I understood that he didn't want to talk about it with the others present and figured I would determine the truth eventually. Everyone got up except Babe and me; she had fallen asleep in the crook of my arm. I looked at her beautiful face in the moonlight, forgetting everything else until Bat touched my shoulder and whispered.

"How about we all play cowboys and cowgirls tonight?" he whispered. "Downu and I will lay out some more blankets. We'll spend the night under the stars together."

Babe and I had long given up fighting Bat's wishes. Besides, the idea sounded perfect.

****

In the morning, I awoke to Babe's eyes staring down at mine. At that moment, I knew we would be together forever. I asked how long she'd been watching me. She placed her finger to her lips and pointed as Downu snuggled up to Bat.

"She looks like a pound puppy compared to him," I said. "A very contented puppy."

"She's the first woman he's loved since his mom."

"No, Babe, he loves *you*."

"Yes, but as a little sister. He protected me like he wanted to protect his mom; it gave him healing. Now, he has someone who loves him, who decided to put Bat first. Downu left her family home because she knew Bat didn't enjoy the cold. They're soulmates, Chief—they

249

have healed each other. I hope they aren't separated by the change."

Her last comment made me jump and manifested a sense of foreboding. I ignored it as Babe kissed my cheek, and chin before she landed her lush lips on mine. We locked lips until we heard the familiar "Ahem."

"Argh! You were sound asleep, Bat," Babe muttered, moving to her hands and knees.

"You'll always be my little sister whether you want to be or not, Babe."

"Yeah? Well, I don't want to be, not for one second more." She stomped away and left me on the blanket alone.

"Yeah, I know, Chief, I need to bag myself again," Bat said with a laugh I didn't share.

"I'll wait like I promised you," I said.

"No!" Downu exclaimed. "No wait—you marry now."

"Hey, hey, now, my lady, don't be trashing my rules," Bat said to Downu. "Babe only turned fifteen last month."

"Bat, in my village, many marry when *sixteen*. Our lives bring grow-up quick. We survive first; happiness come second. At sixteen, we more mature than girls here. Some ready to marry. It okay, Bat."

"We aren't in your village, Downu. We're here in the regular world," Bat replied.

"Not regular world for long. You say change come soon. Many people die. Maybe we live underground for a long time—could be *we* die. We help others but not wrong to help ourselves, give love to each other if real love… like ours."

"You know, Bat," I said, "she has a point."

"There's no point, Chief. You forget what Downu doesn't know about Babe." He towered over Downu and me as he spoke. "Downu, you don't know how young she was when we rescued her. We spent a year rescuing kids like Babe whose own mother didn't protect her."

I interrupted his rant. "Yes, but that's in the past. Face healed us of everything we went through growing up."

"Okay, it doesn't hurt her anymore, Chief. But she doesn't know any better than to offer herself to please you? Do you not see that?"

I stood, trying to hold my temper. "Face healed Babe," I said slowly. "We fell in love, but our culture says to wait till she's eighteen. I see the immaturity in her and will stand by my promise." I held his eyes. "Now it's time for you to let go of her—time for you to have faith in her and me. I mean it, Bat."

He stared back without a word.

"No more stalking us, man. You have Downu, and that's all you get. Maybe one day you'll have a family—maybe one day we'll both have kids. I hope visiting each other is in our future, but as it stands now, you are pushing Babe away. And you're pushing me away, too."

"How do you know, Chief?" Bat shouted. "How do you know if this is real love and not her eyes influencing you? At least tell me that."

"Because I loved her from the first time that I saw her, man—dirty, wounded, lost. From that moment on, I wanted to be the one to protect her. But you jumped at the job first. She turned to you because you put yourself in that position."

"Now wait just a minute, Chief—"

"That time is over, Bat. And this discussion is over."

I turned toward the dining room and left Bat and Downu in a heated discussion.

Babe was still angry as she studied the breakfast bar, waiting for it to open. I knew her well enough by now to pick that up loud and clear."

"Doesn't it all look delicious, Chief? I'll start with an omelet. How about you?"

"What?"

"What's going on, Chief? They filled the bacon pan and you aren't even salivating."

I sighed. "Bat and I had a major disagreement. That's probably the best way to put it."

"Over me, I suppose?"

"Yes, Babe, over you. You'll be glad to know Downu stood up for you—she thinks you're old enough to be in love, and that sent Bat over the edge. The short version is that he does care about your welfare, but I think seeing you with me makes him jealous."

"Why, when—"

"Yes, he's in love with Downu, but he's forced to let go of you," I said slowly. "A future that doesn't include protecting you doesn't compute just yet."

Babe's smile made my heart swell. Her face still shone with the peace she found in the cave.

"The Face made us imperfect," she said, "but he knew what Bat and Downu needed before they ever met. It is all the way it's supposed to be—now it's Downu's turn to help him. She's taken my place, and that's a good thing because you are my priority."

I had never been at such a loss for words in my life. My mouth fell open as I tried to express what was inside me. Babe stuck a piece of bacon in my mouth before I made a fool of myself and pointed at the buffet. She grabbed two trays, loaded them with an assortment of culinary goodies, and picked a table on the grand porch. When she winked at me and patted the chair next to her, everything in my life couldn't be any better.

****

After breakfast, dealing with the safe zone meeting seemed more plausible. I quieted everyone and began the session, telling T.D. to get us started.

"Alright everyone, we had a good rest with some fun, but there's not much time left," he said. "We need to be prepared. Over a year ago, I ordered diggers to safe zones all over the world. Teams are still drilling at each as I speak. Catacombs now exist through these mountains with many entrances and exits available for people coming in from all directions. Volunteer doctors and nurses should arrive any minute with supplies to treat most any wounds that may occur. Even in the interior of the mountains, the change won't be easy for anyone. Chief?"

"Motor and Anna Marie, any reports on the cyberspace rescues?"

"Chief, we don't want to disappoint you, but hardcore gamers are addicts. They'll die gaming before listening to some random dude who pops up in their computer warning them of impending disaster."

"Don't be random—be creative. You can make yourself irresistible to a gamer with your skills. Besides, who would ignore Anna Marie?" All the men in the room smiled, as I knew they would. "Give them a chance. Do the best you can do."

"No worries, Chief. We can do it," Anna Marie said. "Anything else we should know?"

"Yes. Hurry. Time isn't on our side. I don't want to

lose either one of you."

"On it, Chief." Motor held Anna's hand as she whispered, "Let's get it done." Then they disappeared.

"Now that's cool," Ice said.

"Wait a minute, Ice, I disappear, too," Fly said.

"Yeah, but you don't say anything cool before you go invisible."

"Well, what should I say?"

"Fly, Ice, we're in the middle of a meeting," I said impatiently. "Fly you're every bit as cool as Motor and Anna Marie." Fly placed his hands on his hips, content with my compliment. "Now listen up: Healer has information she wants to share with us."

"Thank you, Chief. At this point, our jobs have changed. Face is giving everyone in the world a fair chance through the Whispers—they are warning everyone everywhere. We will help the arrivals; each family being united with children has a private area and must be shown it.

"Chief, Face told me you're permitted to stay in Cherokee with any member of your family that wants to stay," T.D. said. "Today, Ice, Healer, and I will fly to Pennsylvania—probably the transporters' last trip too. We won't see you again until Face decides we do."

"But, Mom, what about Fly?" Ice asked.

"Fly needs to make a choice, son." T.D. turned to Fly. "Healer and I have grown to love you, and we see how close you and Ice have become. If you want, we'd love to have you as a part of our family."

"Wait, T.D." I managed, as shocked as everyone else at this. "You didn't tell me about this. Fly, I always presumed you were a part of *my* family."

"Chief, you never asked me to be a part of your

family," Fly replied. "You rescued me, and I am grateful. But Ice has become a brother to me. I'll go with him and the Doggets if it's okay with you."

Be a leader, I thought. "Man, Fly, go where you want. You were an integral part of every adventure and saved everyone. You'll always be one of us no matter where you choose to be."

Inside, I shook to my core. I'd taken Fly and the Doggets for granted, and now my close-knit team was about to break up. Picker blew his nose, wiping away the dead silence of the room.

I approached Fly and hugged him. "I'll miss you, man." I looked him in the eye for a moment but did not want him to see my weakness. As everyone lined up to say their goodbyes to Fly and the Doggets, I took the nearest exit.

I had to get away and think.

****

"Hey, Insider, what are you doing in the woods?"

"Chief Sky Hawk," I said. "I'm walking, thinking, feeling. I am feeling too much."

"Ha! I remember how emotions were at your age—always a frightening thing. I would rather face the Sasquatch with a full bladder before feeling the pain from love or sadness. But I learned that I cannot walk or run away from emotions. No matter how fast I moved, they followed as a hungry wolf ready to attack. They will follow forever if you do not face each one and question its source."

I nodded. He was right.

"Be brave. Ask the hard questions and let yourself feel the pain, but briefly," he said. "Each time I face my discomforts, my strength soars afterward. Eventually, it brings truth and understanding. It takes practice. Even Dr. Phil says it takes practice."

That made me smile. I knew who Dr. Phil was. "Thanks for the advice, Chief, but my problem is—well, I don't know why I'm feeling messed up. Isn't everything connected with love good?"

"Ha! Love is a sword that slays you, cuts you down, makes you your smallest, and turns you into nothing. That is when the wolf goes away, Chief, for you have disappeared from his sight. He can no longer smell the darkness in you because it died into truth."

I thought of Face's sword, remembering how it had slain us as kids. It was just as Sky Hawk said. "Thank you, sir. I needed to hear those words."

"Sometimes, I wish for someone older than me to whisper words of wisdom in my ear, but there is no one older than me—ha!" He slapped his knee and had a good laugh.

"Where are you going, Chief Sky Hawk?"

"Come, son, and share my favorite place."

I followed Chief Sky Hawk off the well-worn path. He turned to inspect my shoes. "No time to teach you to walk as a ghost. Let's remember to cover your tracks when we return. Come."

He led the way. His moccasins left no twig or leaf out of place. I tried to mimic the old man leaving the ground as I found it, but it wasn't easy. We came to a stop in the thick of the woods. Sky Hawk pushed aside the shrubs.

"Come."

We made our way through the tangled mess of vines. The narrow entrance to a small cave appeared. I ducked my head to enter, but the ceiling became higher a few feet inside. Chief Sky Hawk ran his fingers over the ledge, searching for a flashlight he kept stored there.

"It won't be long now," he assured me. Within minutes I saw a light ahead. But as I stepped out, shielding my eyes from the burst of sunlight, Chief Sky Hawk grabbed my arms.

"No further," he said. We stood on the edge of a cliff. I peered over the side. *Way* down the cliff were boulders and flowing water.

"Wow," I murmured. "That's a long drop. Shouldn't this be roped off?"

"No one knows of its existence but for me and now you."

We were surrounded by a misty beauty. A waterfall next to us cascaded and crashed into the depths. The river below sped to the southeast. I had a good view of a bear cub at the water's edge drinking alongside a fawn. Across from us stood a taller mountain shrouded in a blue haze. In my childhood, nature's beauty escaped me—the smell of sweet mountain air was unknown. The past year had exposed me to the darkest evil living within congested cities and in beautiful environments.

Something inside me gave way.

I sat next to Chief Sky Hawk and sobbed. I cried for the destruction to come; I cried for Bat and me arguing for the first time; I cried that Babe was young; I cried for the children with stolen lives. Our jobs had been dirty— we interacted with the worst of the worst. My team was successful because of each person in it.

How could I continue with my family torn apart?

There. I'd said it. It was true—my family. They weren't only people I loved. After all we had been through together, a part of my spirit was tearing away.

What would prevent more of them from leaving?

The truth hit hard. My family was falling apart. Wasn't I as important to them as they were to me? Betrayal, and abandonment pushed me into a black hole of despair. I turned to tell Sky Hawk of my epiphany, but he was gone.

There was only one person for me to talk to.

Face.

He would straighten me out. But I had been away from him so long that I began to tremble.

Chapter 27

"Face! Face, where are you?" I shouted. "Where are you... you... you..." My echoed voice mocked me, but I didn't care.

"Face, you ask for too much. I am tired, Face. I am yours to do with as you please. I am your prisoner, but I have nothing left to give... give... give..."

I let the echo die off before continuing.

"Face, tell me I'm through dealing with darkness every day, because I can't face it with my family torn apart. Face, help me... me... me..."

I sat for hours, missing lunch and dinner as I pleaded with Face to appear.

"I'm not leaving until you talk to me, Face, even if I have to stay all night, all of tomorrow, and all of the next night. Do you hear me... me... me..."

At sunset, the mist thickened except for one open patch that allowed the twinkle of a star. The temperature dropped quickly. I hugged myself, sliding back against the wall of the cave.

"I'm not going to sleep, either, Face, until you talk to me... me... me..."

Long after midnight, I saw a beam sparkling, wavering in the air. I kneeled, touching my head to the ground. I expected Face's full wrath.

"You call me from my work."

The sword hovered at my neck.

"My Face, I'm sorry, but I'm tired. I have seen too much evil," I whispered. "I have the weight of survival on my shoulders. If I fail—if I am wrong—death and destruction will visit the mountains, innocent people, and my family. I can't handle anymore."

The dove landed on my shoulder.

My muscles relaxed; a deep love permeated through me.

"What do you ask me, son? Say what you want."

My throbbing head was still on the ground. I was too weak to lift it.

"Humans and their emotions," Face said. "Feelings. You feel things other entities would not understand. It's sad that as a species, you fear yourselves more than you fear any danger. Yet you evolve as I intended."

I started to interrupt, but Face had at last responded to me—I heard him out.

"Chief, I chose you. I allowed your strength to surface. Fear drove you and bettered you. Will you always need a sword at your neck to compel your understanding? Look at what is right before you. Do what you must, but know I am always. You wait too long to commune with me."

My head was still on the ground. "I thought you wanted my family to do this on our own."

"You are mine, Chief—you are my children. I will never leave you. Why do you leave me? Healer speaks to me all day in her heart as you should, as should every Insider. Do you think I will ignore your needs? Talk to me—give me your burdens. You wait so long that you explode."

"I think of you during the day, Face, always."

"If you trusted me, you would accept your place in

the events to come." The sword pushed against my neck. "You fear the decisions I make are wrong?"

"No, Face, you are never wrong. If I get out of your way, all events will work out—I get that. But for my family, why doesn't it include the Doggets and Fly? Why can't we stay together? Why doesn't Fly want to stay with me—or the Doggets? Love shouldn't hurt this much, Face."

For the first time, I heard the dove speak.

"Creator, he fears love. He fears to have love. He fears *losing* love."

"Yes. That's it, Face. Why am I so afraid of losing my… my family?"

****

I heard a familiar voice as sunshine found my eyes.

"Ears, I found Chief! I found him! I'm bringing him home."

"Fly," I whispered. "I'm freezing."

Fly cradled me like a newborn baby as he lifted off the cliff. "Don't worry Chief. I'm taking you home, man. I'm taking you home."

I drifted in and out of consciousness the next two days as my fevered body battled with the remains of my fear, my fear of losing family. I was aware of Fly asking others if I would be okay. I remembered Babe's beautiful face filled with worry and sadness. I heard Chief Sky Hawk insist that the great spirit was strengthening me, and to show no fear.

Events blurred until a black bear approached me, stood, and roared. As weak as I was, I got up and slid my leg over the bear's haunches and climbed onto his back. The bear raced into the woods, veering toward the path of Sky Hawk's sacred place. He continued through the darkness of the cave, out into the sunlight, and leaped off the cliff, flying toward the river below. We glided over the wild waters where I saw creatures unafraid, drinking, resting.

"Do not be afraid," each creature said as we passed.

The dangerous woods could have kept these animals in a constant state of fear, but they seemed content. "Why are none of you afraid to die?" I shouted.

The wolf laughed. "The shadow of death comes to everyone. Why fear it? We realize Earth is time-framed. When I shed this coat of grey, I will run towards the light of the free range. Shall I show fear there, too? I think not. I shall enjoy experiencing this earthly life for as long as Face graces me with it."

"Aren't you afraid for your family, your children?" I asked.

The wolf shook her head. "Why should I fear for them? If they hunt the rabbit in a short life here, the light of the range awaits; the same result occurs if they grow old. It isn't a difficult concept. Enjoy the problems, enjoy the hardships for they will pass." The animal became agitated with me as a mother does when pestered too much. "Why do you fear your place at this time? Why do you fear it ending?"

The bear flew off before I assimilated the wolf's question. He made a sharp right, heading toward the wall of a mountain at full speed.

"What are you doing? You are going to kill us both!" I shrieked. I wanted to jump from his back, but I was dead either way.

"Ahh…"

At the last possible second, a hole appeared. The bear and I flew through. I tried to catch my breath as my heart pounded.

"Why do you believe I would kill you? Do you think I want to end my own existence and take you with me?"

"No—yes. You could leave me like my family's leaving me. I don't want you to go, ever."

"I am a part of you, son. Yet, you depend on others to feel good. Depend on me. Lean on me—give yourself to me. Forget the outside world."

"You have time for me?"

"Time exists for mortals to evolve his being. Humans need structure. I do not."

"Alright, my Face. I give to you my pain of... of loss. I fear to lose the people I love. I fear to carry all this love inside. It hurts too much. I give you control—total control."

****

"Chief Sky Hawk, are you sure he'll be alright?" I heard Babe cry somewhere close to me. "Please let Healer in. He's burning up."

"Your chief is on a necessary journey, little one. He learns to handle his deepest pain this way. It should not be much longer."

The tribe's shaman moved around me as I lay stretched out in the middle of the sweat lodge, my vision jumping between it and the black bear. Sky Hawk sat cross-legged by my side, enduring the heat with me. I heard myself moan.

"I want my family. Tell them not to leave me," I rasped. "Babe... tell them I love them. Tell them not to leave." I had no control of the words coming from my mouth even though I'd figured out I was atop of the bear.

I was aware of Babe sprinting from the tent to the rest of my family waiting outside. "He's burning up!

He's delirious and begging for his family to stay together. Please, Healer, fix him. I'm *begging* you! I'm terrified I'll lose him."

From a distance I saw Healer hold her close. She whispered, "I won't, Babe. Face says not to intervene. This is Chief's battle—he has important decisions to make. Have faith in Face. He knows what He is doing."

Frustrated, Babe pushed away from Healer as Bat and Downu approached her.

"This is your fault, Bat—*your* fault!" she cried. "You started the trouble. If Chief dies, it's on you, and I will never forgive you. *Never*." She pounded on his chest until she collapsed. I was aware of Bat picking her up like a father with a newborn and setting her on the shaded veranda while Downu comforted her.

****

The bear carried me to a new environment. I remembered Motor saying, "New place—we are here, Chief."

Had Motor talked about this location? If so, why did he come back to us? This ethereal place I found myself had floating hues that exuded peace. I asked where we were.

"A dimension for Insiders to live," the bear answered.

"Aren't we going to help out after Earth changes?"

"No. Your powers would hinder the survivors' connection to me. They would worship you instead, which would limit the full link and benefits from me. Your powers are needed preceding the change, but not after."

"You'll put us here, Bear?"

"Yes. All Insiders will live here, marry here, and

have children here. You will populate this world, a world made with great care, and it will suit your needs. It will provide some rest from the turmoil you experienced on Earth."

"Is it heaven?"

"No, it is not heaven as humans know it, Chief. No eternity exists here—it is a place of time. It will be up to you, up to all Insiders, to form it the way you wish. Time here is slower, giving Insiders a chance to adapt and enjoy long lives while experiencing hardships too."

"How do we get here?"

"To reach this place, you must sacrifice the bodies you have now. New bodies will clothe you at once. As I said, you will experience long lives. Then, as in all dimensions, you will die of old age and join those who live in eternity, or heaven as you call it."

"It is peaceful and beautiful," I replied. My body's tensions unwound and floated off the bear into ethereal bliss, yet I kept a glimpse in my mind of the goings-on of my friends. It was like being in two places at one time."

"Chief! Chief! T.D., he's not breathing!" Healer yelled. Sky Hawk questioned the shaman who lifted my eyelids and felt for a pulse on my wrist.

"The Great Spirit has need of him now," the shaman said. "We can do nothing."

Chief Sky Hawk stared at the shaman in disbelief. "No, no… not dead."

"Your friend stays with the Great Spirit."

"No!" T.D. said firmly. "He doesn't get to *quit*."

I floated peacefully above and watched T.D. carry my limp body outside and place it on the ground. "We're family, Chief. You don't get to quit us, you hear?"

He began pumping my chest as Healer performed mouth-to-mouth. While Ears dialed nine-one-one, Lookout, Ice, Bat, and Fly paced, all imploring me to come back.

"We love you, Chief! Don't leave us!"

T.D. and Helen made room when rescue arrived. Immediately, they bagged my airways and readied the electroshock paddles.

"Clear!" The current did nothing.

"Clear!"

"There's no heartbeat. How long has he been out?"

"Thirty minutes, but we started CPR right away," Healer said, trying to encourage them.

The paramedic tried a couple more times, then studied the graph for any signs of life. He shook his head, and his assistant shrugged his shoulders.

"Chief, don't leave me. Don't leave me!" Babe screamed. "Don't you quit on him," she said to the paramedic, grabbing his arm and turning him until they were face to face. "We're meant to be together. You shock him again, again, again!"

Babe fell to the ground sobbing, her tears reaching my face. The sight of her agony got to the paramedic and his assistant, who both tried in vain to get my heart beating again. T.D. finally stepped in and said for them to stop. Bat held Babe back when she tried to intervene.

"Get your hands off me," she growled. "I think it's okay if I'm with him now, Bat. Will you give me that much?" He let go of her. She knelt next to me, kissing my lips and caressing my hair. "There will never be anyone but you, Chief. I'll love you till the end of time."

I heard the rescuers telling T.D. that they had to take my body to the morgue.

"No. Insiders take care of other Insiders."

"Insiders?" the paramedic asked, stunned. "Are you the ones trying to get everyone ready for some mass destruction? I heard you guys were immortal."

"As you can see, you heard wrong."

Nothing "on the ground" bothered me other than Babe's tears. But why was she upset? I loved the new dimension, with its mountains and ocean before me. Where would Babe and I choose to live on it?

Suddenly, I heard Bat cry over me. But it was more than that—his *feelings* touched mine."

"Chief took me in," Bat sobbed. "He made me feel useful. Cared about. He gave me hope."

Picker kneeled. "How am I going to make it without my best friend? You gave me clothes and dignity, man. You taught me that to be *me* was alright. You brought us to the Face."

"Face, he saved me!" Babe cried. "You sent me to him, but now you take him away from me. Why?"

"That's a fair question, Face," Ears mumbled as he choked back a sob.

"Doesn't Chief know how much we love him? Lookout asked in a small voice before he, too, began to cry.

As I listened to the voices that were a part of my life, I let go of the new world. I ran toward the sound, toward the feelings.

"Face, show me the way back home," I said. "I understand now—I have work to do."

I ran toward my friends finally seeing them all around my body. Then, I heard a horrific growl. An enormous black bear wandered toward them and, in an unfriendly way, rose on its hind legs, releasing a terrible roar. When no one moved, it charged, causing everyone to scramble away from my corpse. Bat threw a bag, but it did nothing.

The creature stopped before my body.

He stood on his hind legs and roared, coming down full force with a paw on my chest. In an instant, my body sucked my spirit inside it. I opened my eyes and gasped for air.

"Thank you," I whispered.

The animal rose on its hind legs again, roaring as if to say: "Don't give up. Do not give up on anyone… do not give up on yourself… and never give up on Face."

It ambled away, leaving everyone frozen in place and speechless.

My body felt like a piece of pounded meat. "Oh, man. Anybody going to help me up?"

"Chief! You've come back. You're alive."

I smiled at the beautiful young woman who loved me. "Babe, I saw a great place for us to live."

She cried, laughed, and kissed me. Her salty tears filled my heart.

"Take it easy on him, Babe," Bat laughed. "Come on, Chief. Let's get you up off the ground."

"Easy, Bat, my chest hurts."

"Ya think? You've been shocked too many times to count. After that, that huge bear pounded on you." Bat carried me to a porch lounge chair.

"Picker, what's with the tears? I'm alive."

"You're my brother, Chief. It was hell to lose you. Come here, man." Picker leaned down to hug me and wouldn't let go until I reassured him that I wasn't leaving him. One by one, everyone expressed their joy at my return. Face gave me the rest I needed, plus the answers

I wanted. I was stronger and calm.

Healer knelt before me, soothing and healing the burn marks on my chest. "You know, Chief, when you went missing, we decided as a family that we didn't want to be far away from you. When you died, well, it was unbearable. You see, we've come to love you as our family."

A smile spread across my face.

"If it is okay with you, we want to stay here in the Smokies and cross over with you. Do not worry, Thunder says it is okay with Face. He's arranged for other Insiders to take care of the Poconos."

"I'm not worried, Healer. I am over being worried. How about we celebrate with some food… death creates a big appetite."

I saw Chief Sky Hawk slap his knee, but the tears on his face did not come from laughter.

Their affection swelled inside me, giving more love than I ever had in my life.

Chapter 28

The next day I directed my family to check the water and food supply that Cherokee volunteers had transported to the safe zones throughout the mountain range.

To encourage gamers, Motor and Anna Marie made numerous trips into cyberspace with unusual personas that caught the attention of World of Warcraft, Rune Scape, and Call of Duty players. Everyone was directed towards higher grounds, away from tectonic plates, and they were told to bring necessities. Anna Marie was the bait, of course, dressed in interesting and slightly provocative costumes. She stretched the truth by guaranteeing a gaming tournament during the change.

Some gamers listened, arrived, and claimed a cubicle by writing their names on it. Many, unfortunately, insisted there would be time to use the Wi-Fi at the local library in the valley and then return. We thought about restraining them, but they weren't criminals. Free will is something we were not to mess with, and they were entitled to it. We hoped they would have ample time to enter the mountain but doubted events would accommodate and told them so.

Within hours, we watched a caravan of cars arrive at the casino. Excited parents of stolen children arrived and asked if theirs would arrive today.

"Yes, I received word a few minutes ago," Healer

said. "The first group will be in your arms today. Some of you have suffered the death of your child but volunteered to help children who never had a real mother or father to care for them. They come from Face new again, with open hearts."

"People, you can't bring suitcases," Lookout said. "There's limited room. You are here to survive a disastrous event and harsh conditions for many months. So, please choose three sets of clothes that withstand cold and dampness. Bring seven sets of underwear and socks. Think warmth and comfortability when you pick these outfits—oh, and two pairs of shoes or boots and one heavy coat."

"Also, two blankets per person and one pillow for each," Ears added. "Bring as much food and water as possible, and keep your medications and toiletries on your person. The caves are dark. I hope you brought batteries as instructed."

No one objected to the rules but expressed their gratefulness instead. We passed out garbage bags for each family to store their items—if it didn't fit, it didn't go. People raided photo albums to place cherished pictures in their pockets and bras. Some placed all their jewelry around their necks and on their fingers, mumbling that they would barter with each other later.

"Please load up the buses for your ride to the catacombs," Ears said.

Picker sat behind the wheel of the last overcrowded bus.

"Wait just a minute, Picker," I said.

I found Chief Sky Hawk. "Chief, it is time, sir. The Cherokee must take their place in the catacombs."

"My thanks, Brave Bear. They are ready." He

271

nodded to the young man next to him who spoke through a handheld radio.

"Brave Bear?" I asked curiously.

"Not many own the desire and courage to ride the greatest bear, but you did."

"Hmm. I do prefer that name to Chief Poop."

The old Cherokee laughed. "Yes, that was a good time, wasn't it, Brave Bear?"

"It was a fantastic time, Chief Sky Hawk. I will miss you, sir."

"It was my honor, Brave Bear. Take these and wear them on your journey," he said, handing me a set of beads. I pulled them over my head and embraced my old friend, knowing I would never see him again. "Perhaps, our paths will cross again in another place, another time."

"Maybe so, Chief Sky Hawk. Maybe so."

"Chief, come on," Babe said. "The bus is waiting."

"I'm coming, Babe."

Picker did an excellent job navigating the mountain roads, though some of the passengers turned white with nausea, clearly not used to mountain terrain. Their moans died down when we arrived at the southern entrance of our mountain. Ice, Fly, Healer, and Top Dog acted as a welcoming committee. They would pair the children with their parents. Not surprisingly, T.D. stepped forward to greet everyone.

"Welcome parents," he said. "Each family receives a map of the catacombs pointing to latrines, a kitchen with Bunsen burners, and a laundry complete with a small waterfall. Posted on your cubicles are basic rules of courtesy, along with harsher expectations of what's to come. Preparation is key; cleanliness is an order."

Babe and I showed them to their cave homes, orienting them as fast as possible. Before noon, all the parents and families arrived and were situated within the mountain. I wondered if we had cut enough rooms for each when Healer called me over.

"Chief, the children are here. They are beautiful."

"People, the wait is over. Your children are outside. Best to meet them in the sunshine," I announced through the bullhorn. I handed the horn to T.D., who read each name as the children stepped out from behind our bus.

"Maddie McDougal."

I heard a mother's gasp. She bolted toward the girl, her husband right behind. "Maddie, Maddie, Maddie!"

"Mommy. Daddy." Maddie dropped Ice's hand and ran to her parents and brothers. "It's okay, Mommy, I'm okay now."

Each pairing brought happy tears. Even the orphans bonded right away with new parents.

"Are you going to be my mom and dad?" a girl asked.

"If you like us, yes, we'd love to be your parents."

"Okay, but if you want me, you'll have to take Bobby. He is my best friend. We always stay together. The Face says it's perfectly alright, but up to you." The girl crossed her arms over her body almost defiantly after motioning to her friend.

The friend peeked around the edge of a boulder. "Surprise," he said.

I recognized the boy from the first group of children we saved in São Paulo. He was a slight boy then, pale and nervous, but now smiling and self-assured—and healed by Face.

"A son, too!" the dad exclaimed. "Today's our lucky

273

day, isn't it Mom?"

The boy hugged his new mother and tried to shake his father's hand.

"A handshake? Not in this family." The dad bear-hugged the boy and tousled his hair. "I'm so thankful to have both of you. Are you hungry?"

Picnic tables held a supply of peanut butter and jelly sandwiches, cookies, small toys, and coloring books. Children's laughter echoed throughout the hills. Their time with the Face had reached fruition—they were healed.

"Children," I announced late that afternoon, "it's time you see your new quarters—where you and your parents will be protected."

The children understood the importance of this place and walked in awe as they entered the mountain. Face had prepared them well; close quarters would bond families. Fear experienced during the change would bind them even faster. Later, a steady stream of cars filled with families arrived, families in tune with the reality of Earth's need. We filled our mountain and sent the overflow to various catacombs still open.

Many teens showed up without their parents. "They won't believe the warnings, but I do," said one boy. "Maybe my leaving will get them to follow."

In my mind's eye, I saw that plenty of spaces remained in the Smokies. I sent Fly door to door throughout the valley and low hills with an invitation. Many souls laughed at his commitment to a calamity they refused to believe, slamming the door before he could convince them. A few were unsure, but Fly fixed that by lifting off the ground.

Cherokee volunteers took our place to welcome and

orient the stragglers. Somehow, I knew they would be leaders and teachers of conservation on the new Earth. My family was finished—there was no more we were needed to do.

We drove back to the casino, making sure directions we spraypainted on large boulders would be clear enough to latecomers. The massive structure stood like a tombstone in a graveyard caught between the past and future. It looked able to withstand the winds, making a good shelter for everyone who arrived late.

We raided the fridge, knowing it would be our last meal on Earth. Ears lifted a finger.

"Shh… hey, Chief? Isn't Sky Hawk supposed to be in one of the mountaintops by now?"

"Oh, man. Are you saying he isn't?"

Ears shook his head. I followed him out the back door. "He's over there somewhere."

Chief Sky Hawk's voice echoed between the mountains.

"I know where he is, Ears. Thanks."

"Do you want me to bring him back here, Chief?" Fly asked.

"No. I'll talk to him."

I made my way through the woods and into the cave. When I reached the end, I saw Sky Hawk standing over a small campfire that spit as he threw herbs into it. He sang an eerie chant, which echoed throughout the mountain.

"Chief Sky Hawk?"

The chief almost fell over the edge before I grabbed him. "Sorry. I didn't mean to startle you, but you're supposed to be in a mountain by now. Why are you here?"

"My people are safe, but I am old, Brave Bear, and ready to join my ancestors. I will see the end here. I will die as a chief of his people should die—with honor, and not with a whimper in a dark cave. Are you here to die with me?"

"No, sir," I said firmly. "I'm here to save you."

"No, Brave Bear. It is my right."

"Sky Hawk, please…?"

"No, son. Are you still afraid of death?"

I hung my head. "No, not for myself. There's continuity to my life as there is yours. You are right in this circumstance. I understand."

"Good. Call the others—we shall die together. This time I go where chiefs go after death; you go to a new existence. Die with me as we watch Mother Earth change."

Nothing should have shocked me by then, but how Skyhawk knew of Face's plans was beyond me. "I'd be honored to die by your side, sir," I replied. "I will talk with my family first, though. See you soon."

As I entered the casino, everyone asked about Sky Hawk. Before I answered, I wanted to know more about our transition. "Top Dog. I need to be clear; how do we shift to the next dimension?"

T.D. looked at Healer.

"I mean, I know we die," I said. "I wondered how."

Everyone's head turned to T.D. "I'm… well, I'm not sure, but it should be quick and painless, Chief."

"I don't know how it happens, everyone, but it does," I said. "You all know we'll be fine in the new home prepared for us."

My friends nodded, seeming to have understood this long before me; I had not seen the truth because of my problem with control and attachment.

"Chief Sky Hawk invited us to see the change as it happens. Any of you game?"

"Sheesh, if death is a part of our future again," Picker said, "I want to see what's going to take me out."

"That's the spirit, Picker. Let me show all of you a spectacular view—Babe?"

"Chief, I'm with you, of course."

"Then let's go watch the show!" Lookout exclaimed.

"Wait, Chief," Bat said. "Downu can't go. She can't alter for that new dimension. I've got to get her back to the mountain."

"No, Bat." A power within me swelled—one that I never experienced. "She can go with you if she is one with you through marriage."

Downu smiled at Bat.

"Face will allow me to officiate."

Babe squealed. "A wedding dress! Downu needs a wedding dress."

"Chief, give us a minute. Let's see what's in the casino." Healer said, taking charge and pulling Downu along.

"Downu, do you know what's happening right now?" Bat asked loudly.

"You rescue me, my Bat?" She shouted as Healer tugged her toward the casino.

"Yeah, I marry you, Downu. Will you be my wife?" He hollered

Downu laughed. "Silly Batboy, I *alweddy* you wife in here." She pointed to her heart. The girls sighed. Picker made funny, in-love, smooching signs behind Bat's back.

"It isn't legal, Downu," Bat argued from a distance. "We will make it legal, so everyone knows in every creation that where I go, you go too, because we belong to each other."

"We make legal, my Batboy," Downu said before Healer yanked her through the open door.

"I'll see you when you're ready, but don't take long," Bat replied, exclaiming to her even though the door had closed. "We need to get this done now. Hurry." He looked at us, a goofy grin on his face. "Guys, I'm getting married today. Right here… me and Downu… married before the change."

I hoped Healer understood our time restraints.

****

The casino doors opened ten minutes later. Downu appeared as an Indian princess. She wore a white deerskin dress from the stage show. Babe and Healer followed in their own costumes.

"Oh, Downu, you're beautiful," Bat said. He couldn't take his eyes off his bride.

"I beautiful for my Bat."

"Okay, lovebirds, I have a wonderful place for you to get married," I said. "We have a personal invitation from Chief Sky Hawk. Follow me."

I led the eager wedding party through the woods and into the hidden cave. "Chief Sky Hawk, I brought company. It includes a bride and groom."

The old chief slapped his knee. "It gets better every minute. This is gonna be the best day of my life. Be careful though, it's a long way down."

We formed a semicircle around the happy couple. "Bat, Downu, we better get right to it," I said. "Are you ready?"

They nodded and held hands.

"Today is a special day for all of us. We have spent a lot of years together as a family. Now we are privileged to add a new member, Downu, who wants to be one with Bat. They do this with all of you as witnesses. I officiate with the blessing of Face, who brought them together." I paused, trying to take in the moment. "Bat do you take this woman, Downu, as your lawfully wedded wife?"

Bat nodded.

"Say 'I do' if you do, Bat."

"Oh, yeah, I do," Bat replied enthusiastically. "I most certainly do take you for my wife, beautiful, beautiful Downu."

"Downu, do you take Bat as your husband?"

"I tell the Face, too," she whispered. Stretching her arms toward the sky, she projected her voice. "I take Bat as my *huss-band*."

"Uh… I don't suppose you have a ring?" I asked Bat.

"Here… use this," a voice said from above. Sky Hawk, flat on his belly atop the cave, reached down to hand over the turquoise ring he always wore on his pinky.

"It belonged to my wife," he said. "She was a good woman—like Downu."

"Repeat after me, Bat," I said. "With this ring, I thee wed."

"With this ring, I wed you, Downu."

"I wed you back, my *huss-band*."

The two began kissing too soon. I finished fast.

"By the power of Face, I pronounce you husband and wife. You can kiss now or keep on kissing… uh, congratulations!"

"You're my wife now, Downu," Bat said. "Where I go, you go."

Chief Sky Hawk interrupted their second kiss. "Congratulations, Bat. Now, move over. It's my turn to kiss the bride." He climbed down the side of the cave's mouth, using footholds either provided by nature or those he had fashioned. The old chief's physical prowess was mystifying. We, on the ledge, shuffled to make room, some of us nudged back into the shadows of the cave. Chief Sky Hawk placed his hands on Downu's shoulders and nodded his approval.

"Good, strong woman," he said, his tenderness surfacing as a tear rolled down his face. He planted a gentle kiss on Downu's cheek.

Everyone lined up to kiss the bride and welcome her into the family. Downu giggled as each of us kissed her in an orderly fashion, ever mindful of the cliff's edge. Ears and Lookout each took a cheek and kissed Downu at the same time. As they stepped back, they said at the same time, "*Herzlichen Glückwunsch!*"

"That means congratulations in German," Ears added.

"Say what?" T.D. asked. It was rare that he was at a loss for words.

"My mom was German," Lookout said.

"No, *my* mom was German," Ears said.

"You couldn't possibly have the same mom…" I said, although something had always tugged on my heart about those two. "Wait a second—Ears your mom was raised in the foster system, right?"

"Yeah…?"

"Lookout, what do you know about your mom?" I asked.

"She was adopted when she was young, a toddler. But…"

"But what?" Ears asked.

"Well, she told me she had a weird memory of an older sister that she couldn't explain," Lookout said. "Records were sealed, so she couldn't research it. Sometimes she would get this faraway look in her eye. I knew she was trying to remember about that sister."

I couldn't help a smile.

"Her adopted parents—my grandparents—told her of her ancestry and kept a congratulatory card they found in a bag with clothes at her adoption," Ears said. "Her birth parents had apparently bought it. It said *Herzlichen Glückwunsch*. It was the only German she knew. But she used it all the time when I was growing up. Then she'd wonder about the phantom sister that lived in her brain."

"My mom, too." Lookout said. "She'd get this sad look on her face and tell us she once had a baby sister, but she wouldn't talk about it. Sadness seemed to live in her heart, but I never knew why."

It hit me all at once. A smile spread across my face.

"That's it, guys. That's it!" I cried. "You two are cousins. That's why you are alike!"

Chief Sky Hawk laughed and hollered. "Cousins. Blood cousins, of course."

As Ears and Lookout man hugged, I announced that we had two reasons to celebrate.

"Today we're celebrating Downu becoming a new member of our family. Ears and Lookout are celebrating, finding each other as blood cousins. Nothing can beat this day!"

"Yes. Now we all die together," Chief Sky Hawk reminded us with an aura of peace.

"Not before we have cake," Fly said, landing with one he retrieved from the banquet hall refrigerator. He squeezed a jug of milk between his thighs. "The forks are in my pocket."

Not knowing how we would die caused some apprehension—nervous energy compelled us to reminisce and joke. We were in the middle of a laugh when an odd silence began. As the air grew calm, the trees stood like statues. Below, the river's flow stopped, undecided about its direction. I looked questioningly at Ears and Lookout.

"We didn't want to interrupt the wedding or miss out on the cake," Ears said.

Suddenly, flocks of screaming seagulls jetted past with other fowl species that hid the sky like thunder clouds chased by a fierce wind. They headed west far behind the mountain ranges. Next, a rumble shook us— accompanied by a bellow like the sound of gigantic locomotives running hard. The closer it came, the more the cliff quaked.

The foothills in the distance moved toward us. We stood our ground, holding onto each other and the face of the cave as rushing water, whitecaps, and waves overcame the hills.

"It's the ocean," Lookout shouted. "The ocean in the Smokies."

The tall mountain across the gorge barricaded the flow at first, but the water dispersed around it, sucking in the river below. Sky Hawk was speechless at first.

"This is the best day of my life," he finally said with his arms outstretched. As shocked as we were, the statement brought a smile to our startled faces.

I pulled Babe close to me and kissed her with

everything I had.

"This will have to hold us until we reach the next dimension."

I turned to my family. "It was a pleasure being your Chief on Mother Earth!" I shouted at the top of my lungs when it struck me that Motor and Anna Marie were missing. I was about to duck my head into the cave to see if they were there, but a horrific gust sucked us all off the cliff. I gripped Babe's hand tightly as we flew over the edge, but winds tore us apart, lifting little Babe high into the air before she headed downward like the rest of us. As we fell toward the rubble-filled waters below, I realized millions of human beings and animals might be under the surface. Soon our bodies would join them.

"Wahoo. Now I live my name… Sky Hawk!"

The chief flapped his arms as he passed me, grazing my legs. I laughed at his joy as I plummeted downward. Still, I had one final thought on Earth.

Where were Motor and Anna Marie?

EPILOGUE

Our time on Earth seems long ago, but the irony doesn't escape me. On Earth, I gathered a small family and was desperate not to lose them. Here, on Tranquility, I am surrounded by a vast number of Insider families. We even call each other brothers and sisters. I have more family than I can handle.

Insider leaders meet weekly to discuss the needs of our people. All citizens come to make sure we stay focused on Tranquility's well-being and to elect our first President. By the way, they call me President Poop now. I suppose Fly will bear that burden one day when he is old enough. For now, everyone celebrates by calling him Junior Poop.

My job is to appoint committees to tackle decisions about housing, food resourcing, and finding spring water. Bat leads the exploration team because he is fearless. Unknowns exist on Tranquility like the void, and the magnetic vortex. They require study and research. Insider heroes would-be explorers in this dimension.

Growth here would come as it did on Earth—from involvement and adversity. Evolution is a mandate for all life. Meanwhile, we once-homeless street urchins continued to mature, marry, and have babies born free of child predators, human traffickers, and dealers. There is nothing on the outside here to destroy a loving family. I speak for all Insiders when wishing you the peace and love we enjoy on Tranquility as you begin again on new Earth.

As I compact the pages of our history, a somber Healer ambles toward me.

"Chief, transporters decided to hold a memorial for Anna Marie," she said. "They believe enough Earth years have gone by to test your theory. They want to know if we would like to include Motor's service at the same time."

"You can meet on it. But you know I don't believe they're dead."

"You've been saying that since we got to Tranquility. It's time, Chief," Healer said gently. "You need closure. Let go of them and pay your respects."

"I can't do that in good conscience, but please do what feels right to you and the others."

"Then we'll go ahead and combine the two services," Healer said. "Motor and Anna Marie would want that."

She sounds defeated even though she won the argument.

****

After setting them underneath the two suns, I hold up my written account of our adventures on the parchment-like leaves. The suns tell me if the berry ink is dry enough. It is ready to place into the vase that our talented middle east potters made. It's made large enough to hold my chronicles—waterproof, too.

I roll the scrolls and gently fit them into the pot. Tapping the cork-like stopper into place, I appreciate that our new bodies still have five fingers on each hand. Adapting to our new look took some time, but we understood changes were necessary since we live in a different atmosphere with different terrain than Earth.

Although we are hairier, the basic anatomy is there, but covered by our hair. Hey, we don't need clothes or wash laundry anymore. The hooves took some getting used to, but we have come to love them once we began racing to test our new speed. Yes, the speed dogs still beat us.

Of course, my Babe is still the most beautiful woman I ever saw. Bat and Downu already have twins, one with silver hair and the other with gold. They were the first babies born on Tranquility. Here, it takes time to figure out whether they are boys or girls. But because they are babies, we love them—no matter which sex they become.

As for Lookout and Ears, they built a bachelor pad and formed a band with other artists making instruments. When there aren't enough to go around, the most talented vocalists sound as the instruments they represent.

And my best buddy, Picker? He created a spiritual group that works to blend earthly traditions, which is a big job. I don't know if it's a permanent thing because his metamorphosis has made him very attractive to eligible singles here. It's hard for him to focus on work with females gathering around him all the time.

As for the Doggett family: Healer still heals, and Thunder, the only dead person allowed to live in this dimension, remains close to Fly and Ice. Both guys had a growth spurt and are as tall and taller than Healer, which is more than we expected.

"Yo. Need some help with that?" T.D. asks about the clay container I'm holding.

"Thanks for clearing my project with Face, man."

"No problem, Chief. Face is okay with people on Earth knowing about us."

"T.D. while you're passing by Earth, listen for some Motor and Anna clues…"

He's already shaking his head. "No can do, Chief. Any information beyond Tranquility is off-limits. Even Helen stays in the dark about Earth and other dimensions. It's important. I am sworn to keep all my activities confidential and recuse myself from any decision-making on Tranquility."

"If you insist, T.D."

"But if Face wants you to know something, he will contact you directly."

"He will. It's just frustrating to speculate what happened to those two. But right you are about Face—can you carry this to Earth?"

"That I can do, Chief."

T.D. takes a few steps backward and disappears. I often wonder if Face will ever need us again. I sure hope so.

Who knows, maybe my chronicles would reach Anna Marie and Motor somehow, someway, someday.

And help them find their way to Tranquility.

A word about the author…

C. S. Poulsen discovered a passion for writing fiction in 2010 after dreaming of the sword of death and was compelled to write about it. Since then, she has written five novels and finds writing a natural extension to her eighteen-year career as an entertainer, writing award-winning music and lyrics.

Poulsen attended the University of North Florida, Jacksonville. For thirty-five years, she lived on beautiful Amelia Island, in Florida. She moved to St. Croix in the Virgin Islands where she snorkeled, wrestled a fixer upper into submission, and wrote her fifth novel, Dream of Me. (Seven Rodgers)

She has one grown son, Luke, four grandkids, and three stray dogs that adopted her. She recently moved to the Smokey's in Franklin, North Carolina.

www.7rodgers.com

Thank you for purchasing
this publication of The Wild Rose Press, Inc.

For questions or more information
contact us at
info@thewildrosepress.com.

The Wild Rose Press, Inc.
www.thewildrosepress.com

www.ingramcontent.com/pod-product-compliance
Lightning Source LLC
Chambersburg PA
CBHW052008020726
47501CB00004B/1062